STOWAWAY

REDLEG SPACE CHRONICLES
BOOK 1

G000087978

Z.D. DEAN

Published by Zulu Delta Publishing
www.zuludeltapublishing.com

Copyright © 2015 Z.D. Dean.

All rights reserved. This book or any portion thereof may not be reproduced or used in any manner whatsoever without the publisher's express written permission except for the use of brief quotations in a book review.
If you would like permission to use material from this book, please contact zdeanbooks@gmail.com

First printing, 2020.

Publisher's note: This is a work of fiction. Names, characters, places, and incidents are either the product of the author's imagination or used fictitiously.

Contents

PREFACE

Alex Zade joined the army, looking for excitement and danger. Still, since his graduation from West Point, it had been nothing but bureaucracy, boredom, and repeated disappointment. Zade had chosen West Point, hoping to become an infantry officer. Despite his intelligence, he couldn't maintain interest long enough to keep his grades high enough in the lower-level classwork. He found himself putting off classwork to immerse himself in Sci-Fi books and video games and researching the far more exciting principles and probabilities contained within. At graduation, he didn't have the class rank to get infantry. His second choice was armor, but again, too low of a class rank, and the branch closed before he got to make his choice. Zade got his third choice, field artillery, which wasn't as bad as he had thought.

After graduation, he was sent to Fort Sill, Oklahoma, where he was trained on the finer points of calling in indirect fires from over 15 kilometers away. The schoolhouse instructors recognized that Zade had a unique capacity for strategic planning and implementation. In his file, it was suggested that he be put in charge of a Fire Support team—a FiST. Just before graduation from Sill, Zade pulled orders to go to Fort Bliss, Texas, where he would be in charge of a company-level FiST for an armor battalion. Still bright-eyed and naive, Cherry Second Lieutenant Zade couldn't have been more excited. The rumors going around the schoolhouse were that Zade's future battalion was deployed to

Iraq. Zade was sure his time had finally come; he was going to get his excitement as soon as he got to Texas.

Upon arrival at Ft. Bliss, Zade was immediately in-processed and given his equipment. Within 36 hours, he was on a flight to Iraq, where he would meet up with his first unit. He didn't remember the flight or layovers on his way to theater. The anticipation almost drove him crazy, and he strategized about how to not make an ass of himself in front of his men.

Iraq wasn't what he had expected. As the final unit in the country, the operational tempo had slowed dramatically from what it had seemed to be in the news stories he had watched growing up. There was no need for a field artillery officer in-country, as any indirect fires had to be approved by the president. Zade's company commander assigned him as an infantry platoon leader to stand in for someone who had been injured.

Zade spent the deployment running patrols that the commander felt were too risky for his actual infantry platoon leaders. Captain Schmit was a stocky ranger that was well past his prime. He had loved being a ranger and reminded Zade daily that "he ain't shit, cause he ain't got a tab." Rangers stuck together. Because the current infantry platoon leaders were slotted to go to ranger school upon their return stateside, Schmit assigned Zade to any mission that had any risk. Schmit would not do anything to risk sending his infantrymen to ranger school because they had gotten hurt on some mission in Iraq. However, when he looked at Zade, he saw a subpar field artillery officer who would never amount to anything. That made Zade expendable.

A few months after returning from Iraq, Zade pulled orders to deploy to Afghanistan as part of an advise and assist team. It was not the ideal mission for an officer trained to call in artillery, but the orders required that Zade call in air support. Zade was sent back up to Ft. Sill before deployment to learn the fine art of controlling airstrikes. This schoolhouse time also meant that Zade didn't have to participate in any spin-up activities, such as cultural awareness classes or connex load planning. Win-win in his mind.

Afghanistan was more action-packed than Iraq but didn't seem as exciting. Maybe "the new" had finally worn off, and the deployment thing had become boring. Perhaps the lack of excitement came from the fact that he was once again subjected to toxic leadership. Zade's team leader was the battalion commander from the logistics battalion. He had an ax to grind with every combat arms officer he ran across. Lieutenant Colonel Goddman had started his career in a peacetime army where he had been continuously bullied by the combat arms officers he worked with; this giant of a man was going to get his vengeance on any combat arms officer unlucky enough to be under his command.

Zade spent the better part of the deployment rolling with the local infantry units, both American and Afghan, providing air support functions. As the only joint fires observer in the Paktia province, Zade stayed busy. Across the nine-month deployment, there were only a handful of days that Zade didn't leave the wire—exactly how he liked it. When award time came around at the end of the deployment, all Zade wanted was his Combat Action Badge. It had been denied by Schmit because, in his opinion, any officer who wasn't infantry didn't deserve to be recognized for being in combat. Zade wasn't an award seeker, but he did want his CAB. It would be a symbol that he had been tested in battle, and Zade hoped that it would add validity to his leadership. Goddman, however, had different plans. Even though Zade had been on over 250 missions, many of which ended in enemy contact and air support, Goddman refused to submit a CAB for him. When Zade had asked him about it, Goddman had replied, "I, a lieutenant colonel, don't even have one. What makes you think I'm going to give an artillery lieutenant one?"

Another slap in the face by the big green weenie. To add insult to injury, Lt. Col. Goodman refused to award Zade with a Bronze Star, while granting everyone else in leadership positions, deployed or in the rear, with the Bronze Star with V. The Bronze Star, in Zade's opinion, was really just a participation medal for any officer who had been deployed, so having one didn't really mean anything. But not having one after deployment was a black mark on an officer's record. The "V" denoted that the award was given due to valorous action, usually in combat. Somehow, no one ever questioned why every squad leader in the support battalion, deployed or not, had been awarded a valor medal.

After getting back from Afghanistan, Zade realized that bureaucracy and petty bullshit were never going to go away. Still, they were a little more tolerable if you were deployed. Zade petitioned every senior officer he knew for another deployment. Their initial resistance was based on the fact that three deployments in four years were unhealthy for most. Zade didn't have any family other than his parents. He enjoyed being a warrior, and the deployment money was really good. He had to be deployed again. Finally, after months of petitioning and after mental health evaluations, Zade pulled orders for his third and probably final deployment. He was going back to Paktia province Afghanistan.

△△△

Lieutenant Zade had just gotten back from his last mission in Afghanistan. It had been a simple presence patrol through the northern part of Paktia province. Uneventful and quick, just like he was hoping for. After a quick debrief and shower, he headed back to his combat housing unit, affectionately known by the guys as a CHU. Tomorrow would be the last day of the American field presence in Afghanistan. Zade's company, Demon team, would be the one to close the gates. He returned to his CHU and finished packing up his gear for the movement out, which would happen just before daybreak the following day.

As the last unit left in the field, Demon team would catch a Blackhawk flight to Bagram Airfield, where they would hitch a ride via C130 to Manas processing station. Although Demon was the last field unit in Afghanistan, the US would be keeping BAF open. Something to do with the size and amount of funding that went into the base. Zade didn't really care about the geo-political circumstances surrounding the exit. This was going to be his third and final deployment to combat, and it had not really the grand finale that he had been hoping for. Either way, Zade laid down to grab some sleep before the move.

CHAPTER 1

BAM! BAM! BAM!

The pounding on the door of his CHU woke Zade up from a dream about wasting all of his deployment money on new cars and at the local strip club.

"Lt. Zade, are you in there? The commander wants to see us at the Ops Center. Says he has a mission for us," said the voice of Sergeant Fern.

"What the fuck? Go away, Fern. I just got back from the mission, and I want at least four hours of sleep before we SP tomorrow."

"Sir, you know how the commander is. We have to get down there," Fern responded nervously.

"I don't care. Tell him I went AWOL. That I decided to join the Afghan army. Hell, I've spent enough time here to become a citizen," Zade said, rolling over in his bed.

Fern was one of Zade's non-commissioned officers and possibly the best fire support NCO Zade had ever had the pleasure of working with. This was his 11th deployment, and he was already working on getting another one after they returned. They had met when Zade started doing the spin-up for this deployment and immediately hit it off. Fern was a true professional warrior:

competent, driven, and had the fighter spirit. Like Zade, Fern loved the excitement of being in combat and took every chance he got to deploy. Fern, a first-generation Mexican-American, swore that only Inca warrior blood ran through his veins. Zade loved the sentiment and could never bring himself to tell Fern that the Inca had never been in Mexico. What was the point of ruining the guy's identity?

As Zade sat up, he popped open the door to his CHU. Fern was standing just outside in full kit with a fresh camel cigarette hanging out of his mouth. Fern tossed Zade a pack of smokes and two RipIts, the energy drink of choice for the modern warfighter. Fern always seemed to know precisely what could motivate soldiers, even disgruntled lieutenants.

"Thanks. Did you get any more information from the commander on this one? If it's about anything less than the first lady being raped by the Taliban, I may lose my mind," Zade said, cracking open one of the RipIts and then slamming it in one slug

After tossing the can out the door, Zade threw a smoke in and began rummaging around in his uniform pockets for a lighter. With no luck, Fern tossed a lighter to him and began discussing the known facts about the mission. As Zade dressed, Fern explained that the commander was informed about some suspicious activity on the ridgeline just north of the forward operating base.

"I don't like the way the commander was talking," Fern said tentatively.

After 15 months working with Major McElry, both men knew the man's idiosyncrasies. The Major regularly spoke in the third person using his call sign when he was in "glory hunter mode." The Major also began to use individuals' first names when he was about to ask them to undertake an inordinate amount of unnecessary risk. For this particular mission, McElry had sent the message that "Demon 6 wants to see Alex and Jose in the talk."

Doesn't this guy understand that awards have already been sub-mitted? Zade thought, pulling on his boots.

After one final weapon and radio functions check, Zade and Fern began the 400m trek to the company tactical operations center, both finishing a RipIt and a couple more smokes on the journey. The FOB had the uneasy stillness of a place forgotten to time. Zade remembered closing up Iraq. His team had been the last group of Americans in Iraq; for the two weeks before leaving the country, the FOB was deserted, and it looked like a scene from the rapture. People got their instructions to go and just stopped what they were doing to pack and catch a flight out of the country. Trucks were left on the sides of the road, doors open, and keys in the ignition. Unfinished meal trays had been left sitting on tables in the dining facility. For two days after everyone had left, a strange whining noise was coming from the living area next to Zade's. When he couldn't stand it anymore, Zade took one of his guys to investigate. Upon their arrival at the other living area, Zade realized that it must have been where the contractors lived. After exploring for about 20 minutes, Zade found the source of the noise—a table saw that had been left running after its operator got orders to leave.

As if the uneasy stillness in the FOB wasn't unnerving enough, what was happening outside the FOB was the polar opposite. The locals knew that the Americans were leaving, and they were getting ready to cannibalize the FOB. Zade remembered looking at the aerial feed, where he could see hundreds of flat-bed jingle trucks lined up waiting to start dismantling every-thing. So far, for this closing, neither Zade nor Fern had been given information on what was happening outside their home. Both could guess, based on experience, that there would be an army of locals with vehicles waiting for them when they left the wire for this last mission.

Just as the men rounded the corner of the TOC, a private ran square into the front of Zade, causing him to spill what was left of his drink on himself.

"What the hell is the rush, Private? Watch where you're going!" Zade chided.

"S-s-sorry, sir. I was just headed out to find you," the private stammered nervously.

What is the rush on this one? It has only been 10 minutes since Fern woke me up.

The men ascended the stairs to the TOC and, upon entering, were greeted by an obviously flustered Major. Courtesies were rendered. As Zade waited for the ass chewing and briefing to begin, he noticed that the TOC had been completely torn down and stored for the move later that day, except for one computer screen with lights moving across it. None of the graphics and support documents regular to mission briefs were present. There wasn't even any staff present, just the Major. An uneasy sense of focus washed over Zade. Any mission this late in the game was bound to run across difficulties. In Iraq, when Zade's unit was making their last movement out of the country, they had been harassed continuously by indirect fire and hasty ambushes. The enemy forces probably felt that if they could videotape their fires driving the Americans out of the country, it would be a huge propaganda win.

"Demon 6 has seen strange lights on the ridgeline around the FOB. Demon 6 thinks that the enemy might be setting up mortar positions to stop our movement later. Demon 6 doesn't like when people are on his mountains around his FOB," MAJ McElry announced.

Jesus. He's in third person, glory mode, Zade thought.

The major then proceeded to show Zade and Fern the video feed from the aerial. Sure enough, something was going on about two kilometers north of the FOB, but it didn't look like the standard mortar setup.

"The enemy had never given away their position by lighting up where they were working like this before," Zade stated.

"Shut your damn mouth, Alex. You're going to do your damn job without the excuses this time," the major replied coldly. "Demon 6 wants Alex and Jose to take the security platoon up to that spot and deal with the problem. I expect you to be rolling in 30. Dismissed"

And now with the first names. What the hell is going on here? Zade pondered.

The major abruptly walked out, slamming the door and leaving Zade and Fern to work through the details of how best to complete this mission. Prep wouldn't be too much of a problem. The platoon worked together for months and was running like a Swiss watch. What bothered the men was the utter lack of information on the mission, the ridiculous risk, and the timing issues. The men decided to meet by the trucks in fifteen minutes. Fern left to rally the men, and Zade stayed behind to try and raise FOB Salerno on his radio. FOB Salerno was the base with the helicopters that were going to airlift the unit out in a couple of hours. He hoped that they had left some Apache gunships active to support the movement. Zade's radio lacked the range required to reach Salerno without the TOC's stationary antenna. After a few minutes of trying with no luck, he headed to the motor pool to link up with his men.

Zade entered the motor pool just as the 15-minute mark had elapsed. Fern had done an excellent job getting the men ready to roll, and everyone was in their trucks doing final checks. Fern had just finished his walk-through and was headed back to his vehicle at the rear of the column. Zade headed to the passenger side of his truck, truck two, and pulled out a smoke. Waiting for the final checks to be completed, Zade stood there pulling on his smoke, trying to pin down what was making him feel so uneasy about this mission.

"Sir, all trucks have reported in. Everyone is REDCON 1," Zade's driver informed him.

"All right, men," Zade replied, taking one last drag and stomping out his smoke. "Let's do this. Let's be the last heroes in Afghanistan."

After settling into his seat, the trucks began to maneuver out of the too-tight motor pool, and Zade grabbed his radio to send his report to the TOC.

"Demon TOC, this is Demon 36. Over."

"Demon 36, this is Demon 6. You will be reporting to me directly for this one. Over."

"Demon 6, roger. SP time now. Three zero pax, nine VIC. Over."

"Demon 36, roger. Be advised this is time-sensitive. You must be back before the exfil movement. Don't make me change my timeline. Demon 6 out."

What a jackass. Why do I keep putting myself through this shit? Maybe after this one, I'll become a private contractor. Sure, they still have idiots like him, but the pay is good enough to make it worthwhile.

The FOB movement was uneventful, as expected, since Zade and his men were the last souls to occupy the base. The trucks crept through the main gate slowly. Zade was surprised to find that the local trucks had not started lining up to destroy the

FOB after the American forces departed. Standard procedures required that Zade make periodic situation reports to the TOC. Since Zade wasn't reporting to the TOC, and since 6 was such an ass, Zade decided to maintain radio silence until he had something to say. After leaving the gate and getting one final check from his other vehicles, Zade began the movement to the objective.

Driving through the third world at night was always an exciting experience, especially when the third world individuals were bent on killing you. The first time you did a night movement, it terrified you. The added adrenaline and being hyper-alert made everything look like a potential threat. On one of Zade's first night-missions in Iraq, one of the gunners was a new kid right out of basic training. During a short halt when everyone had gotten out of the trucks to take a leak, the kid started lighting up a patch of desert with the .50 cal gun he was on. After regaining control of the situation and calming the gunner down, Zade found out that the gunner had seen something moving toward the trucks, so he engaged. None of the other gunners or drivers could see anything at the spot. Zade took his dismounts to check it out. When they got there, all they found were dog pieces and a long shadow cast by some village lights. Although, if that dog had been carrying an RPG, he was no longer a threat.

Night movements got more comfortable as time went on and soldiers were exposed to them. Everyone on the movement eventually relaxed and began to process sensory information better, like his seasoned platoon tonight. This team was able to key in on abnormalities or essential facts. This mission was uneventful so far, like the one Zade had been on last night. *The one that was supposed to be his last in Afghanistan,* Zade thought bitterly.

Approximately one kilometer away from the objective, Zade

ordered all of his trucks into blackout drive. It wasn't the stand-ard operating procedure. It was strictly prohibited due to the risk of accidentally running over someone. But nothing about this mission was falling under the standard operating proced-ures. Zade then ordered the trucks to move into a herringbone formation off both sides of the road. The objective was inaccess-ible to vehicles, so the last 800 meters would have to be covered on foot. Leaving gunners, drivers, and one dismount with every vehicle, Zade began the movement up the ridgeline toward the objective.

Zade was just preparing to crest the ridgeline and get eyes on the objective. It had been about 100 meters and 10 minutes since he moved out of the radio range of his trucks. He could hear them due to their antennae and more extensive power sources, but they could not listen to him while using his much smaller pack. As he peaked over the edge, Zade saw precisely what he was expecting and what he suggested to the com-mander in the briefing. Sitting on a small, round plateau were four jingle trucks.

"Fern on me," Zade whispered.

"What's up, sir?"

"Take a look. Like I said, some trucks are just staging to get on the FOB. Looks like 6 isn't going to get his shot of glory as the last commander engaged in combat during the Afghan war," Zade snickered.

"That may be true, sir, but how the hell did they get up here?"

Both Zade and Fern had patrolled this ridge hundreds of times during the deployment, and they had never been able to bring trucks anywhere near it because of the terrain. The fact had slipped Zade's mind. Both men had been around the backside of this plateau. The other side was just a 400-foot drop. How could four poorly maintained jingle trucks have made it onto the center of a table that sits 400 feet above any accessible roads?

"Fern, set up a perimeter at the very edge of this plateau, as far from the vehicles as possible. I'm taking my operator back down to communicate with the trucks. Maybe 6 can give some guidance."

"Roger."

"We're coming back up this side. Make sure none of the boots are pulling security over here. I don't want to be gunned down on my last day here, especially by some cherry jackass."

Fern began giving orders to his squad leaders, who would then relay them to the squads. With any luck, they would just finish setting the perimeter as Zade got back to them to tell them that the mission was complete and to start heading back to the trucks. Zade headed back down to get in range of the trucks. After a quick descent, Zade could finally raise the trucks.

"Demon 36d, this is Demon 36. Over."

"This is 36d; what's going on up there? Over."

"I need you to relay back to 6 for me. You'll hear everything as I talk to him. Over."

"Demon 6, this is Demon 36. Over."

"Demon 36, this is Demon 6. Go ahead."

"6, we are at the objective. The strange lights are coming from four jingle trucks. Doesn't seem like there is anyone around. Over."

"Roger. Send one of your men to get hands on the trucks. If everything is clear, return to base. 6 out."

I shouldn't have expected any less from him. Hasn't he learned that you don't go investigating strange vehicles, possible VBIEDs with no support?

After instructing the trucks to have the dismounts switch with the gunner to keep them fresh, Zade headed back up the ridge. On the way up, Zade contemplated how he would handle the investigation. On the one hand, he was pretty sure that the vehicles were no threat. On the other, he wouldn't ask any of his guys to take a risk he wasn't willing to take himself, and he still had reservations about the whole situation. At the crest, Fern was waiting for instructions.

"I could hear the trucks from here. Who do you want to send, sir?"

"Come on, Fern. You have to know me better than that. I'm not sending anyone. I'll go myself."

"You sure that's a good idea, sir? There is something very fucking weird about these vehicles."

"I'm as sure as I'm gonna be," Zade replied. "I am tired, and I want this thing done fast and right. I'll look for any wires, see if they smell like HME, listen for ticking. You know, the usual bomb stuff. When I'm satisfied, we can get the hell out of here."

With that, Zade dropped his assault pack, no sense carrying it since the radio didn't work. If he did have to move, there was no sense in taking an extra 80 pounds on his back. Stripped of the excess weight, he began moving toward the trucks. As he closed within 100 meters of the vehicles, Zade noticed something strange. The wheels of the trucks didn't seem to be making contact with the ground. It wasn't much—maybe a half-inch or so—but Zade could tell that something was wrong. The headlights of the trucks were bright enough to wash out Zade's night observation device but not bright enough or pointed in the right direction to see the details of the vehicles. As Zade got within reach, he stretched out his hand to touch the vehicle, but to his surprise, he couldn't feel anything. His hand passed through the side of the truck.

Walking around the first truck, he could see space between the front of the truck and the side of the next truck. As he moved toward the truck diagonal from him, he looked toward his feet and back up. He looked back up in disbelief. He could see nothing but the mountainside in front of him. Stepping into the gap, Zade felt a hard thud. His NODs hit something, but there was nothing for them to hit. He tried to turn himself quickly and move back to men, but his legs were frozen in place.

"Fuck!" he screamed into the night. "Someone help me. I can't mo...AHHHH!"

Before Zade could finish, a severe pain shot through him, and he blacked out.

△△△

Fern was already on edge, and as soon as he heard Zade start to scream, he ran toward him. Something terrible had clearly happened when Zade's sentence turned into an agonizing scream. As Fern closed in on the trucks and the plateau, they disappeared. Fern watched in horror as a sleek, silver ship, now in place of the four trucks, began to lift off the ground. The seasoned combat veterans around him were so shocked that none even got a shot off as their platoon leader disappeared into the night sky.

The platoon sat in stunned silence for a few moments. Fern was brought back to reality by his radio.

"Demon 36, this is Demon 36d. Over."

"Demon 36d, this is Demon 37. Over."

"We heard a large blast from near your location. It seems to have riled up the locals. Looks like we have a group of foot mobiles heading your way. Over."

Fern was still trying to process what he had just seen. How would he report it? Even with a platoon of witnesses, no one was going to believe their story. What happened to Zade? Was he alive? How do we get him back? How was their communication working again? Was it the ship that had been causing the interference and communication failures? Fern cleared his head and ordered his men to begin the movement to the vehicles. Zade was nowhere to be found, and there was no sense being away from the security of the trucks when the angry group of locals descended on them.

"Demon 6, this is Demon 37. Over."

"37, this is 6. Go ahead."

"Sir, there has been an incident. Demon 36 is gone. Not injured or killed, just...gone."

"Gone? What the hell happened? Explain yourself!"

"Something took him. I can't explain any more than that because I don't know. I don't know what happened to him."

"How the hell does someone just disappear? You know what, I don't care. Your mission is over; you are to return to base immediately. I will not have my time as the last commander in Afghanistan tarnished because some glory-seeking lieutenant went AWOL," McElry fired back.

"Sir, he didn't go AWOL. Something took him. He was there, and then he wasn't," Fern responded.

The following radio silence signaled that there was no help coming. Third platoon Demon company loaded up their trucks and headed to their FOB before local interaction could lead to more loss. None of the men spoke during the drive back to base. None spoke on the flight to Salerno. It seems that everyone was still trying to understand what had happened earlier that night. Fern guessed that some were shocked at the events that took place. He was even more appalled that the commander would leave a man in the field without even attempting to mount a rescue.

When the platoon arrived at Salerno, they were greeted by armed guards and a very upset Brigadier General. After a staunch dressing down, Fern watched as Maj. McElry was led away by guards. A plain-clothed man claiming to be from the Criminal Investigation Division requested to speak to Fern and the squad leaders. The rest of the platoon was led to temporary billets. Every flight out of Salerno had been canceled.

"Sergeant Fern, I am Captain Mathews. We need to have a discussion about last night."

While talking with Mathews, Fern discovered that some interesting electromagnetic readings surrounding the objective area had been found by the Airforce. High-ranking Airforce officers had been sent to Salerno to investigate the findings before Demon 3 starting their patrol. Salerno was having problems with communications; they could receive transmissions but not send them. The Salerno TOC had heard Zade requesting air support before the mission but could not respond. In an attempt to regain communications, the radio operator dropped down to Demon's internal frequency. After hearing the location of the objective while listening to internal chatter, the radio operator realized it matched the aim that the Airforce guys were flown into Salerno for. The radio operator told the battle captain, who then informed the general and Airforce personnel, who all crowded into the TOC to monitor events. Everyone in that TOC heard Major McElry falsely charge Zade with desertion and refuse to send out a recovery mission.

"The general has put together a list of charges, and the court-martial will happen here. It appears that the major came into the country as an Army officer but will be leaving as a felon. The dereliction of duty charge is pretty bulletproof," said Cpt. Mathews.

"That's probably for the best, but what about Zade. I saw him get taken away," Fern replied curtly. "We have to go back and look for him."

"I'm not sure what you think you saw, Sergeant Fern, but it appears that Zade accidentally stepped off the cliff on the north side of that area. Ariel reconnaissance has confirmed a body at the bottom of the ravine. A team of PJ's has been dispatched to recover him."

"I don't know who the fuck you think you are, Captain, plain clothes, but I know what my platoon and I saw, and it wasn't a clumsy lieutenant falling off a cliff."

"Sergeant, I understand that this has been a stressful situation for you. In either case, there is nothing you can do for Lieutenant Zade; however, if you stick to this ludicrous story, I am sure you will find yourself on the dangerous end of a court-martial, as you would have been complicit in the major's actions. Now, I thank you for your input. It has been helpful. Go to the billets with your men, shower, eat, and grab some sleep. You deserve it."

After six weeks, the court-martial was finished. Major McElry got what he wanted. In Fern's opinion, what he deserved, he would be remembered long into the future. The difference was big in Fern's books. He wanted to be remembered as the last great commander in Afghanistan; in reality, he was going to be recognized as a pompous ass who intentionally left a wounded, possibly dying fellow officer in enemy territory just so his timeline didn't change. After returning from lunch on the day before the platoon was supposed to fly to Manas, Fern noticed that all of the men had official envelopes on their gear. Somehow, all of them had pulled special orders for different units. Some of the older guys like Fern got orders stating that they would be forcibly separated with a total retirement due to drawbacks.

After Manas, Fern never saw any of the men from Demon 3 again. It was claimed that Lieutenant Zade's body had been recovered, but no one Fern knew had seen it. Just before leaving Ft. Bliss for the last time, Sergeant Fern, now Mister Fern, grabbed one last *Stars and Stripes*. Flipping through it, he froze on a page, refusing to believe what he was seeing. His former boss was in the obituaries.

"First Lieutenant Alex Zade, KIA Afghanistan 2017. Because of his excellent service and courageous actions, Lieutenant Zade was posthumously awarded the Bronze Star with V and Combat Action Badge. Let his character and bravery be an example to us all."

CHAPTER 2

Zade slowly became aware of the constant buzzing in his head, bringing him back to consciousness. Without opening his eyes, Zade slowly started taking stock of his body. Ever so slightly tensing his muscles, starting with his neck, to see what hurt. Nothing seemed to be broken or wrong.

There is no way I survived whatever happened to me without an injury, which means I will be remembered as the idiot lieutenant who went and got himself killed by a god damned jingle truck. Great. What am I going to open my eyes to?

As an army officer who had utilized airstrikes, Zade knew they weren't always as discerning about their targets as necessary. As a regular hellion, Zade understood that there was a distinct possibility that playing dead was the only thing protecting Zade from an eternity of brimstone. On the other hand, Zade had never done anything terrible. He did die in combat, so he should be opening his eyes to see Valhalla and a massive mug of beer surrounded by history's greatest warriors reminiscing about their exploits. Although Zade wasn't a devoutly religious man, widespread beliefs are widespread for a reason. With his luck, they were probably right.

Fuck it, here goes.

Zade slowly opened his eyes, giving them time to adjust to the light around him. The scene unfolding around him was not at all what he had expected. Zade was in what appeared to be some type of medical facility. It was highly high-tech, much better technology than anything around Afghanistan. Straining to remember what happened before he blacked out, pieces of the incident started to come back. Zade remembered not being able to move, hitting his head. Before he went unconscious, he remembered seeing what looked to be some kind of UFO.

Impossible. I must have been hurt bad. Unconscious for weeks while I was transported back stateside to recover.

As Zade was thinking about what had happened, he realized that he was thoroughly parched. He summoned the strength to sit up and look around his bed. Nothing seemed to be out of place. Zade was in a small one-person hospital room. The medical bed was in the center of the wall behind him. The door was toward the foot of his bed. There was a small table on his right side. Nothing out of the ordinary, except there was no IV. The lack of an IV was the cause of his thirst, but it also indicated how long he had been out. Zade decided to lie back down and wait for a nurse to make her rounds. When she came in, Zade would ask for something to drink. Hours seemed to pass with no interaction with the medical staff. Zade decided to gather himself up and head out of his room to look for someone or at the very least a water fountain and bathroom. Zade pushed the blanket off of himself, made it to his feet, and began heading for the door. It was then that he realized that he was stark naked.

It is not the craziest thing that has happened in my time, but I'm not even in a hospital gown weirdly.

As Zade turned around, looking for something to throw on for his foray out of the room, he froze. The head of his bed had been butted up against a floor-to-ceiling viewing window. On the other side, he saw someone in a lab coat and another person in fatigues. They were both rapt by a computer screen and, based on their body language, having a heated discussion about something. Neither has noticed that Zade was mobile. Either Zade had taken a pretty bad knock on the head, or the glass window was thick enough to change the perception of things outside of it. Neither person on the other side of the glass seemed to be the right color. Standing and observing the two for a few minutes, Zade noticed that the doctor, wearing the lab coat, had green, almost scaly skin. It reminded Zade of the news stories about the new designer drug sweeping across China, Krokodil. But that was only supposed to turn the injection site green; he had never heard about it turning someone's whole body green and scaly. He seemed to be a stout, well-built individual.

The other one in the fatigues had distinctly feminine characteristics. Still, like the first, her skin didn't seem to be quite right. Unlike her green counterpart, her skin appeared to be the slightest bit blue, not enough to notice right away. She carried a sidearm; she was most likely part of the military police, meaning that Zade was in an army hospital. She also appeared to have a Mohawk. She was probably one of those super butch soldiers whose only dream is to be the first female ranger. Zade chuckled to himself and shook his head.

Having seen enough, Zade moved back into his room, trying to find some way out. He started with the door, which was obviously locked if an MP watched him on the floor. Scanning the room, Zade could see no other characteristics, no vents, closets, cupboards, nothing. Moving back to the window, Zade saw the two individuals still arguing over the computer screen.

Well, let's have some fun with these two.

While standing as close to the glass as possible, ensuring that his better parts were fully pressed on the window, Zade started pounding on the glass in hopes of scaring the two. Both almost jumped out of their skin. Despite himself, Zade laughed. As he tried to regain control of himself to see their amused faces, those faces stopped his laughing abruptly. Croc Doc had two bulbous eyes with vertical pupils, no nose or ears, and a substantial toothless mouth. Lady Ranger had typical features, but they seemed to be the wrong proportion, specifically her eyes. They were almost human-like in shape but about twice the size and bereft of irises.

As the two approached, Zade gasped. The blue one was wearing an almost human scowl, and the green one seemed frightened, a few shades lighter in color than Zade remembered. While the two walked toward the window, Zade moved back into his room, realizing that it was probably more of a cell given the conditions. The rattled green creature knocked on the glass and pointed to the small device on the table next to the bed. After looking at it and returning his gaze to the beast, it motioned for Zade to place the device in his ear. Zade crossed his arms and shook his head, both out of fear and stubbornness.

Zade heard the click of an intercom in his room, the creature began talking again. Zade could only hear incomprehensible words. After clicking the intercom off, the blue creature leaned over a computer, punched a few keys, and video of a UN conference began playing in the top right corner of the window. After a few seconds of watching the video, the green creature pointed to the device on the table again. Still, instead of motioning for Zade to put it in his ear, he pointed to the video where a circle appeared around the translator headsets that the delegates were wearing. The creature alternated between pointing to the device and to the video.

Realizing what it must be, Zade questioned, "It's a translator?"

Not expecting a response. To his surprise, both creatures nodded their heads in unison. After picking up the device, Zade slowly turned it over in his hand, examining it. This elicited some conversation between the two outside the room. The machine looked harmless enough, almost like an early model

Bluetooth headset. If the creatures wanted him dead or wanted to cut him up for science, they would have already done it, or at least he hoped. He found himself wondering if they had done any other experiments on him while he had been asleep. Pushing the thought from his mind, Zade shoved the earpiece in his left ear. To his surprise, nothing terrible happened. The intercom clicked on again.

"Mr. US Army, I am Jorloss. The medical doctor and head of biological research on this ship," the green one stated. "Are you comfortable?"

"Well, I could use a drink and a pair of pants," Zade responded sternly. "Especially if your blue friend is going to keep staring at me."

This brought the scowl back to the face of the blue thing almost immediately.

"This is the captain of this ship. Her name is Samix. Do not be worried, Mr. Army. We mean you no harm. She is simply trying to determine if you are a threat to us. What is it that you would like to drink?"

"Well, I'm assuming that bourbon and rum are out of the question, so some water would be nice. How are we coming along on clothes? I'm not a shy man, but I feel that mankind's first contact with aliens should be done clothed."

"Mr. Army, if you turn around, you will see a small compartment next to the door. There is a bottle of water and one of our ship's uniforms," Samix replied, her voice almost musical in Zade's ear.

Zade spun around toward a soft, hissing sound from the back of his cell. A small compartment about the size of a microwave had opened by the door to his cell. In it were two bottles of water and a neatly folded set of black fatigues and matching boots. Zade grabbed a bottle of water, opened it, and smelled it, ensuring that it didn't have anything strange in it. He wasn't sure if he would be able to smell anything, but given the circumstances, he figured it couldn't hurt. After taking a small sip to ensure it tasted ok, Zade drained the bottle. Zade took the uniform and boots to the bed, carefully unfolding each piece of clothing, checking it for anything strange before donning it. Just as Zade finished tying and blousing his last boot, he heard movement behind him. Grabbing the second bottle of water, Zade turned to find a chair had appeared, facing the window.

"If you are satisfied, can you sit down? We have some questions," Samix said over the intercom.

"Well, I have never been satisfied so far in my life, but I do have some questions myself. The most important of which is where am I? With a runner-up of, why do you keep calling me "Mr. US Army?" Rounding out the pack with, where is my equipment, and why didn't you give me my uniform?" Zade said as he took a seat.

"Our location will be covered in due time. Your equipment is in another lab being analyzed, and your uniform was recycled due to its unserviceable condition. Is "US Army" not your name? We have been collecting and analyzing data from your species and found that the warrior class in your society puts their name on their uniforms. "US Army" was what was written on your uniform," Samix said.

Although slightly disturbing, everything Samix had said was correct. The army only issued three uniforms per soldier for a deployment. By default, one has to remain unworn and saved for the flight back stateside, meaning that two uniforms have to survive for 12 months of patrolling. Since it had been a busy deployment and Zade had decided to become an astronaut on the last day, the uniform he was wearing was pretty much rags. Zade also lost a couple of nametapes during the deployment and had to take the one off his uniform and put it on the other kit every time he geared up. The only tape on his uniform when Samix and her crew captured him must have been his US Army tape.

"You're right about the names, but our uniforms have two different patches. One patch is for the organization we belong to. The other is our name. Mine must have fallen off when you captured me. My name is Alex Zade."

"Captured you?" Samix recoiled as if she had been slapped. "We wanted nothing to do with your class two species. You moved on our ship and hung up on the side when we tried to break contact. If you are now comfortable, it is time for you to explain why you touched my ship, Alex."

"I am an officer in the United States Army," said Zade, his tension easing and curiosity growing. "The US is the most technologically advanced and dominant society on the planet, and as such has become the main target for a religious extremist group who wish to destroy anything that disagrees with their God. This group has been trying to gain a foothold and influence the world through fear and egregious violence directed towards innocents. Although military action is only being conducted against the extremists, many heads of state realize that all who follow this religious mindset are potential threats to mankind. These extremists operated out of the area where you landed your ship. In an attempt to quarantine the extremists, the United States has been engaging the enemy in that area for 16 years. Our base noticed strange lights and activity coming from your landing site, so my men and I were sent out to investigate. Because the enemy regularly tries to blend in with the country's populace and use innocent civilians as a deterrent for the use of force, we felt the need to further investigate the projection your ship had created. Our forces call the vehicles you were using as camouflage "jingle trucks," and speaking from personal experience, they are used regularly by the extremists to cause chaos. They will often pack these vehicles with explosives than detonate them in front of non-combatant targets such as schools and hospitals in an attempt to erode the will of US fighters. Because of this, I chose to further investigate. Once I got close, I couldn't move and lost consciousness after sustaining a severe electric shock."

It took almost two hours of explaining all of the details, periodically digressing to elaborate on specific details that Samix was unclear on. By the end, the demeanors of the two outside the glass had visibly softened and seemed to be less suspicious. *Time*, Zade thought, *well spent.* Upon completing his rendition of events, Zade was given food, which he ate, occasionally glancing at Samix and Jorloss. They were discussing and trying to confirm the validity of Zade's story. After an hour of watching Samix and Jorloss working on their computer systems, Zade retired to his bed for some shut-eye.

There's nothing I can do stuck in here. I should stay fresh. I'm sure they will bother me if they need something.

△△△

After Zade finished his story, Samix turned off the intercom while Jorloss instructed the ship to provide Zade nutrition. Jorloss began sorting through all of the unencrypted data and news feeds that the ship captured while around Earth in an attempt to confirm the geopolitical situation that Zade had explained in his story. Meanwhile, at the computer station adjacent to Jorloss, Samix began digging through the records, public and encrypted, to find information on an Alex Zade, looking for anything that would suggest that Zade was a threat. The first system Samix infiltrated was the US Army personnel data system. There she found a military record file for Alex Zade.

Zade's personnel file confirmed precisely what he had said. He was an officer in the US Army who was currently on orders to Afghanistan. Samix didn't notice any anomalies in Zade's file when she compared it to his peers' files, except for some extensive mental health and personality screenings conducted just before Zade's most recent deployment. The last two entries in the file were the most intriguing to Samix. The first, dated at the time of mental evaluation completion, simply said, "Cleared for Deployment." The second, dated two days before his deployment, said, "Upon completion of mental health and physical capabilities analysis recommend admittance in Phoenix program. High probability of success." The text was followed by a stamp that simply read USSECDEF. After further digging, Samix found out that the Phoenix project was a classified program where the US consolidated its best warriors and trained them to take on extremely high-risk operations.

We have been having problems on this ship that the SSILF haven't been able to handle. With one crewmember bedridden and another lost to indigenous forces, having a capable warrior aboard might not be the worst idea. Zade might be helpful.

"Everything I have researched seems to confirm his story," Jorloss said, jarring Samix out of her train of thought.

"Mine too. But, Jorloss says he is one of the best warriors in a class two species. He could become a threat if we release him."

"I know we have safety protocols to deal with a situation like this. I think we give him the treatment and let him go. Plus, if we let him out of his isolation chamber, he won't be bothering me while I work up here. We are a science vessel, Samix. We are not equipped to maintain prisoners."

"He was given the treatment when I brought him on board; otherwise, his wounds would have killed him. I will tell him our side of the events, and I want you to monitor his vitals. If there are any spikes to indicate aggressive behavior, he stays isolated. If he does not react poorly, we will give him a batch of nanites programmed to disable him at the first sign of threatening behavior. We'll release him from iso and let him stay in one of the extra rooms in the crew quarters until we can drop him off back on his planet," Samix said authoritatively.

"How are you going to get him to agree to receive the nanites? I will not force them upon him. I am a doctor, not a deranged experimenter."

"To Zade, we are a group of technologically advanced aliens. He must know already that we have technologically far beyond the capacity of his species. I will just make up a description and purpose for the nanites that make them impossible to pass up."

"I don't like this, Samix. If he finds out we lied to him, he is going to be a problem."

"Jorloss, I am the captain of this ship. That was an order. One which you will obey."

ΔΔΔ

Zade had been trying to get to sleep for almost an hour. Zade's body would not relax enough to let him sleep. His mind was racing through the scenario in which he found himself. It was simply too strange to fall asleep. Zade sat up and moved to sit in the chair, his mind wandering back to the Sci-Fi novels he had left behind during his deployment. After just a few minutes, he heard the intercom click to life.

"Captain Zade, we have confirmed your story, and in return, we will tell you our side of the events," Samix's said, her voice ringing through the small cell from the intercom speaker.

"That would be appreciated, but I think your records must be wrong," Zade said, puzzled. I am only a first lieutenant."

"You may have been a first lieutenant when you came aboard this ship, but while searching through your personnel file, it was noted that you had 'made the list.' You were going to be promoted when you left Afghanistan, which according to records, would have happened three days ago on your world."

Samix began to unfold her tale to Zade, who sat quietly in his chair, listening intently, still reeling from the news Samix had just given him. Samix began by explaining where she and Jorloss were from. Samix's species was the founder of an intragalactic conglomeration known as the Unity. The Unity consists of approximately 50 different species who call Hoag's Object home. Samix's people, the Xi'Ga, mastered intragalactic travel hundreds of years ago but only recently developed the other technology necessary for intergalactic travel. The ship that Zade was on was called the XES01, or Experimental Exploration Ship 1. It was one of only three ships created with the capability of deep space travel. It was tasked with exploring and cataloging galaxies. The crew of the XES01 was tasked with testing the range capabilities of the ship and thus were assigned a galaxy that was 600 million light-years away from their home galaxy, which landed them in the Milky Way.

The XES01 was equipped with a material reclamation system. It would need to be self-sufficient during the long flights away from civilized space. This system broke waste objects down into their core elements, then used the supply of different elements to create items required for the crew and ship's survival. Upon entering the Earth's arm of the Milky Way, the vessel had wholly depleted its supply of iron, forcing the team to search for a planet or asteroid rich in iron, where they could land to resupply. The ship had been traveling within 100 light-years of Earth and began picking up radio transmissions by sheer luck. Assuming that any species capable of creating radio waves was also utilizing iron, Samix ordered the ship to go to the source of the transmissions. By following the radio waves as they got more substantial, the XES01 found Earth and began a high orbit.

While orbiting, one of the scientists onboard determined that there was a large iron deposit close to the surface in the mountainous area; that was where Zade found the ship. As the ship descended through Earth's thick nitrogen-rich atmosphere, a malfunction caused the loss of primary power. The ship could only run the cloaking device on emergency power, projecting an image, hiding the ship. In this case, it was the image of some vehicles that were native to the area. Sometime between landing and regaining main power, Zade and his men had stumbled upon the disabled craft. When the ship regained main power, sensors came back online. As the sensor image resolved on Samix's command screen, she saw that her ship had been surrounded by primitively armed indigenous people. She ordered the ship into evasive jump procedures.

The evasive protocol began by raising shields to full strength and then break for orbit. On the XES01, the projector nodes were three-feet-tall to provide a kinetic weapon's cushion. Zade had been standing close enough to the ship to become trapped in the buffer. His body had also acted as a short between the shields and the hull, causing a massive amount of energy to flow through his body, which rendered him unconscious. While breaking for orbit, Zade's body was exposed to extremely high temperatures causing extensive thermal damage.

The next step in the protocol was to make a short warp jump to the last known hospitable section of space. Back in high orbit, the ship could not jump due to a hull anomaly. Making the situation worse, a solar flare was forecasted to happen within 30 minutes of the vessel regaining orbital status. With the time crunch, Samix chose to investigate and try to dislodge the hull anomaly personally. Usually, a SSILF would have been sent, but due to their limited processing power, there was a distinct possibility that it wouldn't have been able to fix the problem, and Samix would have to go out anyway. Sending the SSILF was a waste of precious time. As Samix moved over the hull toward the site of the anomaly, she saw Zade pinned to the side of the ship. Running a quick scan Samix was informed that all of Zade's essential life-sustaining functions had stopped; however, there was still electrical activity in the brain.

Samix freed Zade from the shields and brought him inside the ship. As the airlock's outer door closed, the ship jumped, but not before it was hit by the oncoming solar flare. Samix began providing first aid in the airlock while the pressure cycled. When the lock equalized, Jorloss helped Samix get Zade to the isolation chamber, where he received medical attention. While the ship was in warp, an initial diagnostic was run. The solar flare had damaged the sub-light engines and some of the ship's other systems. Jorloss spent the time in warp gaining a complete understanding of human physiology. He had documented everything to send the information back to the Unity. The ship had dropped out of warp just before Zade awoke, and the ship was on a three-day flight to an uninhabited planet where the crew could repair the ship. As Samix finished her story, she looked at Jorloss, who gave her a thumbs up.

"How long before you can return me to Earth?" Zade asked Samix.

"We are unsure, but as soon as we complete repairs, we should be able to take you back. We have no need or desire to interact with class two species, such as humans," Samix responded.

"Why do you keep referring to mankind as a class two species?"

"A class one species is a species that, although sentient, has not yet begun to look toward the skies," Samix explained. "A class two species is any sentient species that has made some limited trips into space but remains divided into factions, thus limiting their progress. Like Jorloss's and mine, a class three species have united as a society and conquered space travel."

"Huh, makes sense, I guess," Zade said, lost in thought about everything Samix had told him. Regaining his focus, he looked at Samix. "Am I supposed to just hang out in this 10'X10' walk-in closet for an undetermined amount of time while you fix the ship and go back to Earth?"

"You have two options," Samix replied dryly. "Option one is to remain in isolation for the duration of the flight, for your own safety. The XES01 is a multispecies ship. There are pathogens aboard that you are not immune to that would kill you. Option two is that you can receive a limited nanite treatment to immunize yourself, at which point you would be assigned quarters and have limited access to the ship."

"Nanites?" Zade inquired.

"Jorloss's species, the Garnoo, has perfected nanotechnology and developed the nanite treatments," Samix explained. "Nanites can be programmed to do anything and can be injected into the bloodstream, where they complete whatever task they are assigned—in this case, to build your immunizations. The technology has virtually eradicated disease and prolongs the lifespan of Unity members, with some species reaching 10,000 years old. The treatment you would receive would be the necessary Unity treatment that all citizens are given.

"Once in the bloodstream, the nanites utilize components of the host's intake to make necessary changes. Small changes are almost unnoticeable, whereas larger changes would elicit a strong hunger, forcing the host to increase intake and thus provide the nanites with the material required to manipulate the host's physiology. If a required material was not in the host's diet, it could be administered via injection by any medical personnel."

Samix explained that the treatment being proposed to Zade would complete two tasks. First, the nanites would alter Zade's antibodies and immune system, immunizing him for all known diseases. Second, the nanites would remove and replace the speech section of Zade's brain with an ultra-dense piece of brain matter. After the new speech center was in place, the nanites would transfer all available language data to it, allowing Zade to communicate with anyone from the Unity and other discovered languages without the aid of the translation device he now wore. Jorloss assured Zade that the procedure was completely safe, noting that both he and Samix had had it done when they were children, which is why they didn't require a translator to talk to Zade. Furthermore, Jorloss guaranteed that all of the nanites would be passed within six to eight Earth months and no longer be in Zade's body. The nanites would leave behind the new speech center, which would allow Zade to speak any Earth language fluently, as all had been added to the Unity's lexicon based on information collected while orbiting Earth.

Zade couldn't pass up the opportunity to see an actual spaceship. Plus, if he played his cards right, Samix might let him off the ship while they were at their repair stop. The idea of being the first human to set foot in a distant world was just too enticing to turn down.

"Let's do it," Zade said with excitement. "I want to see space up close."

While preparing for the procedure, Jorloss explained that Zade was given a sedative for his recovery. An individual's first nanite infusion was a strange experience, with most patients often complaining of a slight tingle, similar to having ants crawling all over them. Secondly, as the nanites replace the speech center of Zade's brain, he would be unable to communicate, so the time would be better spent asleep. Since Zade was going to be sedated during his recovery, Jorloss instructed him to eat enough to supply the nanites for the modification duration. As he finished the instructions, he opened compartments in Zade's cell that contained enough food to last Zade a week. Still, Jorloss assured Zade that it was the exact amount based on metabolism to complete the modification.

As Zade finished the last of the food, surprised at how good it was and at how much we had been able to consume, Jorloss looked at him nervously.

"There's one more thing," he stammered. "I have to enter your room to administer the nanites while Samix watches from the outside. The door will be locked behind me, and if you try anything harmful, Samix will raise the temperature in the room to 250 degrees Fahrenheit. My species can handle those temperatures, and as you know, your species cannot. Do you understand?"

With a nod of recognition, Zade sat down in the chair and waited for Jorloss to enter the isolation cell. With the hiss of air pressure regulating, Jorloss entered the small room with two syringes: one full of clear liquid and one full of a metallic grey liquid. Jorloss administered the clear liquid first. Zade assumed that it must have been the sedative. After a brief moment of silence, Zade's head began to spin, and Jorloss administered the metallic grey liquid. Fully sedated and as threatening as a newborn puppy, Zade was helped out of the isolation chamber and into the most comfortable bed he has ever felt in his life. Just before Zade closed his eyes for some much-needed rest, he saw Samix and Jorloss kill the lights and walk out of his room. Zade had the most vivid, pleasant dreams he had experienced since he joined the army, and for the first time in his life, none of them were in English.

CHAPTER 3

Z ade awoke in a dark room resonating with the sound of machinery. As he stood up, the lights in his cabin raised, highlighting the spartan yet comfortable living quarters that Jorloss and Samix put him in after the sedative and nanites kicked in. Although the room was comfortably cool, Zade's clothes were stiff with sweat. Looking around the room for any other amenities, Zade noticed a horrible smell that seemed to be emanating from somewhere near him. Searching for the source of the foul odor, Zade checked the bed, dresser, and small adjoining bathroom. Nothing. After moving back to the center of the room, Zade stretched and wondered what could be making the smell and if it was normal. With hands clasped above his head, the source of the odor was revealed. Zade was the source of the scent. His last shower had been the night before the mission in Afghanistan. Judging by Samix's description of events, Zade guessed that must have been over a week ago.

Pulling off his uniform and boots, Zade headed to the bathroom to try and figure out how the space shower worked. Like the central area of his quarters, the lights in the small bathroom were motion-activated, and as soon as he entered, they matched the lights in his living space. Noticing a remote keypad and screen just inside the shower door, Zade read the keypad and turned the shower on. Zade enjoyed his first shower, not taken in a trailer, in over a year. Turning the shower off triggered a set of warm air blowers that dried Zade off as he exited the bathroom. While heading toward the dresser to look for an undershirt to put on under the utilities provided to him in the isolation chamber, Zade noticed that the old uniform he had kicked into the corner was nowhere to be found. The dresser contained standard compression undergarments and socks. After donning the items, Zade searched through the other drawers to find they were empty. Doing a lap around the small room, wondering where his uniform had gone, Zade watched as a small door open just ahead of him on the wall. Inside the small closet were four freshly pressed uniforms and four sets of boots. Grabbing one of the outfits and laying it on the bed, Zade dressed, noticing how these uniforms seem to fit his frame perfectly. Zade wasn't a huge guy, but he didn't have a twiggy runner's frame either. One of the biggest problems he had with his army uniforms was finding a set that could fit across his broad shoulders while remaining trim enough not to tent over the rest of his torso. These uniforms had to be custom-tailored; they fit precisely like Zade preferred.

After doing one final check to ensure that he was appropriately dressed, a habit bred and fostered at the military academy, Zade stepped out of his room. Zade's room opened directly into a common area with club seats and end tables. To the left of the common area was what appeared to be the galley. It had one long table in the middle and some vending machines on the back wall. Jorloss was sitting at the table staring blankly into the ground while sipping on some hot beverage. Hoping for a hot cup of joe, Zade began walking toward the alien doctor. Just as he grabbed a seat across from Jorloss, he noticed movement behind him. Standing and spinning around abruptly, Zade saw a humanoid, robotic skeleton standing directly at his six.

"Don't worry," Jorloss said from behind Zade. "It's just the SSILF tasked with escorting you around the ship. Captains orders."

Zade was pleasantly surprised that he had understood Jorloss without a translator and reached up to touch both ears just to be sure there wasn't one there. His hearing was so much clearer than it had been through the translator. In the med bay, with the earpiece, Zade could still hear Jorloss's native tongue in one of his ears, and there was a slight delay between when Jorloss's mouth started moving and when the translator started speaking. Like the shitty Afghan bootleg movies, Zade had amassed across three deployments.

They were honest about the nanites. I can understand everyone.

"Any chance that y'all have coffee on this ship? I could really use my morning cup," Zade asked as he sat down.

"You could try the food machine, but I would suggest grabbing a cup of the stuff on the hotplate. The machine never gets the recipe right for extremely unique things like coffee. The pot on the hotplate has a drink from my planet called sloop. It is like your coffee, with all of the same stimulant effects, and I'm pretty sure it's safe for you to drink."

The food machine, which Zade decided to call the gut truck since it seemed to be better quality food than the kitchens in Afghanistan, contained various food components. It included protein paste, carbohydrate paste, an amino acid-based fat paste, liquid vitamins, liquid minerals, and water. Profiles were created for every person on the ship based on their species and planet of origin. All Zade had to do was select a meal item out of his profile, and based on the selection, the machine would combine the substances together to match the nutritional breakdown of whatever food had been selected. Sometime while Zade was sleeping, a profile had been created for him. Thanking Jorloss for his advice, Zade headed for the food processor. Looking at the screen, only one name was comprehensible to Zade, which was his. The others must have been written in their native languages. After selecting his name, all of the information on the screen turned to English. The time and date were displayed for Earth at the top right corner, and down the left side, meal categories were listed. Noticing that it was 6:00 am on Earth, Zade selected breakfast and then chose coffee, four scrambled eggs, bacon, and oatmeal. From the condiment menu, Zade chose brown sugar and hot sauce. If Zade knew any-thing from his time in the army, it was that scrambled eggs and oatmeal were the two most challenging foods to fuck up. He was hoping this held true for alien food processing units. He had the hot sauce; enough hot sauce can make anything edible.

Everything smells great. Hope this thing gets bacon right, at the very least. I can survive here indefinitely with bacon. If it fucks up bacon, I'm getting off now.

Zade grabbed the tray that the gut truck spat out and headed for his spot at the table across from Jorloss. With some hesi-tation, Zade tried his breakfast. To his surprise, the eggs and bacon were spot on, and only the oatmeal missed the mark. Grabbing the coffee to wash down the meal, Zade began asking Jorloss about the ship. Upon first taste, the coffee didn't seem too different from coffee back on Earth, but the aftertaste was horrific and only got worse as time passed. One sip was all it took for Zade to pitch the coffee in place of some sloop. The prospect of being forced to go without caffeine was far worse than the possibility of getting sick from some alien drink. The sloop was actually pretty good. It reminded Zade of black tea, but stronger. After talking with Jorloss a bit more and finishing his drink, Jorloss informed Zade that the captain wanted to see him. As Jorloss got up to leave, he tossed his tray in a small trash can built into the wall. Zade followed suit.

Shadowed by his robot chaperone, Zade left the galley trying to follow Jorloss's directions towards the command deck. After hanging a left and heading towards the command deck at the front of the ship, Zade noticed the environment had changed. The galley, common area, and quarters all seemed to have some attempt at comfort included in their design. Once Zade left the berthing area, the ship took on a very utilitarian, functional aura. The corridor he was traveling in had just enough light to safely navigate it. The walls were bare metal with the occasional outline of a door breaking the monotonous silver. The floor was only a grate with miles of cable running under it. If he didn't know any better, Zade could have mistaken this place for a submarine or the deep interior of a Navy ship. The hall ended at a short staircase. Zade climbed the six stairs and entered the command deck. Upon entering, he was awestruck. The view was amazing.

The leading edge of the V-shaped command deck from floor to ceiling was a panoramic view of space. Millions of stars in every color were scattered against an entirely black backdrop from white to deep red. To the left side of the command deck, a gigantic, twisting, green and orange gas cloud sprawled past the bounds of the windows. To the right, a quasar extended indefinitely, cutting space itself in half with a perfect purple line as long as the eye could see.

"Amazing, isn't it?" Samix asked from somewhere to the left of Zade.

Unable to respond for a moment, Zade finally managed a quiet "Yes."

Prying his eyes from the panorama in front of him, Zade scanned the command deck. Zade had entered at the back-right corner of the command deck, which was roughly shaped like a triangle, point forward. The back wall was covered in monitors and different system readouts. In the center of the back wall sat Samix in what Zade suspected was the captain's chair on an elevated platform that covered the rear quarter of the command space. Just behind the captain's chair's left shoulder, a man-sized indentation in the wall housed what Zade expected was another one of the SSILF, similar to the one currently shadowing him. Forward of the captain's chair on the lower level of the command deck were four workstations angled toward the center of the room. Zade looked from Samix to the windows and back.

"You can sit at one of the workstations if you'd like. We have time before we start landing procedures," Samix offered.

"O-Ok," was all Zade could manage to stammer.

Without removing his eyes from the view, Zade moved toward the closest workstation to sit. Just as he got to it, Samix locked out the screens and controls. Zade sat engrossed by the view for what could have been seconds or days, the magnitude of his situation finally setting in. Every Sci-Fi book he had read, every game he had ever played, every movie he watched—Zade was living all of them right now.

"Captain Zade...Captain Zade...Captain Zade!" Samix said, finally breaking Zade's reverie. "You need to get up; I am leaving the command deck for some sloop."

"Come on, you guys have the dog and pony bullshit in space, too? Where everyone needs to stop what they're doing to stand and salute when the captain leaves the room?"

"What?" Samix asked, confusion staining her voice. "No. You just have to stand up and leave. I'm going to get a cup of sloop, and I don't want you up here when I am not around."

As Zade stood to leave, he could almost make out the system they were going to. One star was moving independently across the star-scape, a behavior known as parallax displacement, which meant that it was significantly closer to the ship than the other stars. As Zade followed Samix out of the command deck and toward the galley, he tried to figure out how he would word his question to her. He needed her to say yes. Samix turned right and into the galley heading straight for the sloop. After grabbing a clean mug and the pot, she headed to one of the chairs in the common area. Both the galley and common area were deserted. Jorloss must have been in the medical bay working. Zade grabbed a cup and took the seat next to her. After filling both mugs, Samix sat back, gingerly sipping on the drink. Zade, forgetting how hot the drink was, pulled down a big gulp, immediately regretting his choice.

"I'm guessing Jorloss talked you into drinking sloop instead of your local drink of choice?" Samix asked.

"Yeah. He said that the machine couldn't make my drink, coffee, correctly, so I might as well start on sloop."

"Sounds like him. Sloop is one of the only goods we actually carry on this ship. We have enough in the cargo hold to last us a few years."

Samix took another sip of sloop, looking between the cup and at Zade.

"Look, Samix," Zade started slowly. "I have to ask you something. I know I'm essentially just a stowaway on this ship, destined to be tossed back on my planet as soon as you get the chance, so is there any way that I can go planetside when we land for repairs? I would be the first of my species to set foot on a planet other than Earth."

"I don't see why not," Samix said after a minute of contemplation. "As long as you stay out of our way. It's good you asked now, though. You will need to go to the medical bay to get another nanite treatment before you head down the ramp, and we are almost too close for the nanites to complete before we land. It will protect you from some of the poisonous plants native to the planet. After we land, meet us in the cargo bay. From there, we will suit up and head out."

"Awesome. I can head to the med bay right now. How do I get there?"

"Didn't Jorloss tell you how to get around the ship? Every screen on this ship, unless being used for something else, will bring up a map with a marker for your location if you touch it."

Slamming the rest of his sloop, Zade thanked Samix and headed toward his quarters. He wanted to bring up the map by his room to see how to get to the med bay and how to get to the cargo bay, expecting that he would be in his quarters sleeping off the nanite treatment when the ship started its descent.

A cursory glance showed that the ship's main fuselage was disk-shaped, with a triangular protrusion at the front and a rectangular rear section. The vessel was divided into three different levels. The sublevel had all of the machinery and engines in it. That was where the material reclamation systems were located as well. The first level consisted of four lab spaces, all roughly the same size. From a top-down view of the ship, the front left was labeled anthropology lab, the front right was the biology lab, the rear left was the resources and terraforming lab, and the rear right was the robotics and fabrication lab. The rear labs had rolling doors that connected them to the cargo bay, which occupied the ship's rectangular rear section. In every space book Zade had ever read, both terraforming and robotics could require or produce equipment that was too large to fit through a standard man door, which is what he supposed were behind the large doors. On the other hand, anthropology and biology could survive without access to the cargo bay.

The second floor of the ship appeared to be split right down the middle from front to back. The protrusion on the front of the ship was the command deck, with which Zade had already become acquainted. The left side of the ship appeared to be bil-let. Immediately to the rear of the command deck on the left side was the captain's quarters. Following the outer arc of the ship, there were five smaller crew quarters. The space between the interior of the crew quarters and the centerline of the ship was occupied by the galley and common area. On the right side of the second deck, directly opposite the captain's quarters, was the forward staircase and the medical bay, where Zade was first introduced to the ship. There were four offices just behind the medical bay, corresponding to the four labs and the four sci-entists onboard. Separated from the offices by a short hallway running left to right, there were a meeting room and the storage room for the communications, navigation, and probe systems. The cargo bay was two stories to accommodate large equip-ment, so like the first deck, the rear rectangular section of the second deck was occupied by the cargo bay. The cargo bay also housed the back staircase that ran down the interior wall.

Judging by the indicator on the map, Zade was staying in crew quarters number five, the room closest to the cargo bay. After getting his routes memorized, Zade turned and headed toward the galley to crush some food so Jorloss could give him the nanite treatment as soon as possible.

"One last thing," Samix said as Zade reentered the common area. "If you don't make it out with the main body, you are going to be stuck on the ship. We have to close it up for diagnostic testing. And we will need the SSILF that's been shadowing you when we're planetside, so if you stray away from the ship, you're on your own."

Acknowledging Samix with a nod, Zade headed to the gut truck for 15 replica beef and cheddar sandwiches, his favorite from his favorite fast food joint back on Earth. After choking down all of the mediocre sandwiches, Zade headed for the med bay, where he found Jorloss examining a charred arm on a light table. Thinking nothing of it, Zade explained that Samix had approved of him going planetside. He needed the nanite treatment to protect against the poisonous wildlife before they landed and that he had already eaten and was ready for the shots. Jorloss turned slightly, his face giving the same blank stare that Zade had seen at breakfast that morning.

△△△

Zade charged into the med bay right as Jorloss was examining one of Zade's original appendages that were too damaged to repair. Worried about how he would react, Jorloss headed him off before he could make it deep into the med bay. Luckily, Zade was too worried about going planetside to make the connection.

The nanites in both Jorloss and Samix had slightly more functionality than the ones given to Zade. These nanites connected crewmembers to the ship's internal data network, giving them a permanent means of communication. After listening to Zade, Jorloss decided to confirm with Samix before administering.

Samix, did you tell Zade he was going planetside?

Yup.

What nanite treatment do you want me to give him? He's rattling on about poisonous plants.

Give him a treatment that meets the standards of the ones we got before we hit this planet the first time.

Ok.

Make sure you tell him it's for the poisonous plants. I'll fill you in while he sleeps it off.

△△△

"All right, Zade, sit down in that chair while I make up the mix," Jorloss ordered.

Zade sat and waited for Jorloss to finish making up the nanite treatment. Expecting another shot of metal gray goop, Zade held out his arm. Instead, Jorloss moved toward Zade with a slight sedative shot to relax him.

"The nanites were already in your bloodstream, so I just have to reprogram them. The sedative I gave you is enough to relax you but not knock you out. I would, however, suggest you get some sleep before we go outside," Jorloss instructed.

With that, Jorloss turned around and went back to his work, leaving Zade to head back to his quarters. As Zade walked through the common room, a sudden sluggishness came over him, and he decided to rack out, assuming that he would hear or feel the ship begin its descent and thinking that he would have enough time to head to the cargo bay after he awoke.

△△△

Zade was awakened abruptly by Samix's voice over the ship-wide intercom.

"Attention, all crew, we have safely landed and are preparing to depart."

Shit! I must have overslept. Zade thought as he threw himself out of bed and towards the door to his quarters. With the route to the cargo bay memorized, Zade shot through the common area at full sprint. After heading down the hall and through the cargo bay door, Zade could see Samix, Jorloss, and three SSILF staged by the door. Both Samix and Jorloss had just finished securing the helmets of their suits and were preparing to open the ramp. Taking the steps down to the first floor of the cargo bay four at a time, Zade thought he could get to them before they opened the ramp.

"Hold up," Zade shouted as he closed the final distance between him and the rest of the crew.

"Jorloss, close the interior doors and prepare for depressurization. Zade, I told you to be here when we landed. I don't have time to wait for you to put on a suit. Jorloss, final life support check, you good?" Samix said as she turned away from Zade.

With a thumbs up from Jorloss, Samix hit the controls for the ramp, opening it to the atmosphere.

Fuck, fuck, fuck. I don't have a suit on; I'm going to die as soon as that door opens. Either sucked out of the ship or suffocated by unbreathable air. Why are Samix and Jorloss doing this?

"Shit!" Zade screamed as he hit the ground.

After a few tense moments, while the ramp finished descending, Zade could hear raucous laughter coming from above him. Removing his hands from the back of his head and looking up, he could see Samix and Jorloss, helmets in hand, laughing hysterically. Jorloss was doubled over laughing so hard he could hardly catch his breath.

"That's what you get for scaring the shit out of us in the med bay, jackass," Samix said, tears rolling down her face from laughter. "Did you really think we were going to space you for being 30 seconds late?"

"You should have seen your face," Jorloss chimed in.

Zade, red-faced and embarrassed, stood and dusted himself

off. After regaining his composure, Zade began to laugh just as hard as the other two in the cargo bay. The absurdity of the situation was too much to go unappreciated. As the three began to collect themselves, Zade spoke up.

"Y'all think you're regular comedians. But seriously, how am I standing here without any kind of protection? I don't think there is any kind of barrier up. I can feel the wind coming through the door. And this definitely is not Earth. We don't have purple and orange spiky bushes."

"The nanite treatment I administered wasn't for poisonous plants since there are none on this planet," Jorloss explained, a tinge of annoyance in his voice. "This planet is very similar to Earth, with two major differences: the atmosphere has about half as much oxygen in it, and the planet is slightly larger than the earth, meaning it has more gravity. The treatment programmed the nanites to increase your lung capacity to account for the lack of oxygen, and to slightly increase your bone and muscle density, to adjust for the extra gravity."

As Jorloss finished his explanation, a humanoid robotic skeleton stepped up to the group. Initially, Zade assumed that it was just another SSILF. Zade had come to learn that the SSILF were synthetic semi-intelligent life forms created in the robotics and fabrication lab. The ship crew used them for maintenance while on the ship and rudimentary security forces while off the ship. Due to their relatively expendable nature, the SSILF were not capable of true artificial intelligence. They were advanced for human standards, capable of understanding and processing complex tasks like fundamental security, but unable to adapt or operate under any standards not established in their coding. Upon closer inspection, Zade could tell that whatever just walked up to the group was not one of the SSILF. Conceptually, it looked like the SSILF, but the quality was better. Unlike the SSILF's raw metal bodies, this one was painted fire-engine red from head to toe. Zade's pondering was interrupted by Samix's voice.

"Zade, this is Mur," Samix said, introducing the red creature.

Mur was the embodiment of the ship's artificial intelligence. While onboard the ship Mur conducted all navigational and maintenance activities. Mur could then occupy the red body and go with the scientist's planetside to provide additional security or remotely control the ship. It would be staying on board the vessel running a full diagnostic sweep for this mission. The designs of any broken piece found by Mur would be sent to the robotics lab to be fabricated. Samix and Jorloss would be outside the ship running diagnostics on some of the external systems, parallel with Mur's testing, to expedite the pit stop. The SSILF would provide security for Samix and Jorloss outside the ship. Even with all three individuals testing and repairing the vessel, the estimated time to completion was over three hours. Remembering that Zade didn't have the same data link that the others had, Samix continued with a brief planetary description covering all of the threats on the planet. Based on their last visit, Samix knew that there was at least one class one species on the planet, somewhere in their hunter and gatherer stage of development. The ship was located in a remote region of the planet's southernmost continent, significantly decreasing the odds of interacting with the indigenous people. There were multiple predatory and dangerous creatures in this area, hence the SSILF security team. With that, Zade, Samix, Jorloss, and the SSILF security team started down the ramp, leaving Mur to close it and head to the sub-deck to begin testing.

CHAPTER 4

W alking down the ramp with a supply crate he had grabbed to help the team out, Zade began to think about the increased strength that Jorloss had mentioned. Doing some rough math, Zade estimated that the crate he was holding had to weigh upwards of 300 pounds. Impressed that he was carrying it with ease, Zade curled it a couple of times, trying to hash out the extent of his new abilities. At the bottom of the ramp, Zade sat the box down and offered to help carry more items, but Samix and Jorloss both declined. With nothing else to do, Zade did a slow turn, taking stock of the planet.

The ship had landed in a small clearing of purple-tinted meadow, which was surrounded on all sides by thick forest. The forest contained three distinct types of trees—the tallest and most abundant type towered over the other two. The tall trees had slender yellow trunks, topped with red foliage similar to palm trees found on Earth. The second type of tree almost couldn't be classified as a tree at all. The stout, bulbous blue trunks only stood around twenty feet tall, with a diameter at the bottom to match the height. It tapered to a point at the top covered in red spikes. Initially, Zade thought they may have been adolescents because of the dramatic difference in height from the first trees, but Zade couldn't spot one taller than twenty-five feet throughout the tree line. The last tree reminded Zade of some of the spruce he had seen while training in

Alaska. These spruce-like trees were conical with evenly spaced rows of branches all the way up the trunk. Unlike the common spruce that Zade was familiar with, the bottom boughs of these trees were a deep azure that slowly transitioned to orange at the top. Looking up, Zade could see that the atmosphere on this planet shone a beautiful purple instead of the blue that he was used to back on Earth. The sun had dropped just below the far side of the ship. Circling the ship, Zade could see the orange behemoth perched just above the treetops. It was a much deeper color than the Sun. Jorloss informed Zade that it was a K class, one of the smaller types of stars.

After analyzing his surroundings, Zade turned toward his current companions. The low lighting on the ship made finding a good place to study his shipmates almost impossible. Planetside, with beautiful orange light shining down, Zade could really see the crew, starting with Samix. It appeared to Zade that the Xi'Ga were built for space from watching her work. Samix's lithe body and long limbs made her movements seem effortless as she climbed up and down the ship. She moved gracefully, and the blue of her skin shown brightly in the orange light. Zade thought she was quite beautiful. His gaze shifted to her hands. The digits on both her hands seemed to flare out at the end. Zade believed that the tools Samix was using may have been stuck to her hands. Jorloss was the exact opposite. Zade had noticed that he was a stocky, thick creature while under the ship lights, but planetside, standing next to the SSILF and Samix, Zade wasn't even sure how Jorloss could even move around. The last of the crew to be inspected by Zade, in the daylight, were the SSILF. After leaving the ship and setting the equipment crates down, the SSILF had formed a loose perimeter about 100 yards from the ship. They were stationed at twelve, four, and eight o'clock around the ship.

Moving towards the nose of the ship, Zade could see the backside of the SSILF at the 12 o clock position. At roughly six feet tall, it had a bare metal frame with joints in all the same places as a human except for inverted knee joints. The SSILF that was escorting Zade on the ship had no protective paneling because Zade presumed it was meant for ship maintenance. The one Zade was approaching was a combat variant, and although he could see the internal workings of the SSILF from behind, he could not see through its chest cavity like the maintenance variant. As Zade circled to the front of the SSILF, he could see that it had a rigid, white, synthetic panel covering its chest and a faceplate made of the same material. Stamped vertically across the chest piece and faceplate's left side were an identification number, along with the ship identifier.

"Hey Samix, what are the numbers on these guys for?" Zade shouted to Samix, who was perched like a gargoyle atop the command deck, typing away on a small piece of diagnostic equipment.

"What does that one say?" she replied.

"#2034, XES01," Zade read, running his eyes down the front of the SSILF.

Samix explained that the SSILF was the 2034th created in the robotics lab on board the ship. Zade remembered that Samix had informed him that the ship had only been on mission for six months, and he remembered that Jorloss explained that the SSILF were expendable.

These guys went through 2034 robots in six months? It must have been rough going before I came aboard, Zade thought.

Continuing his inspection of the SSILF, Zade identified some kind of long rifle that each was carrying. Like firearms he was familiar with, these were made of the same synthetic material that the protective coverings were made of. A magazine stuck out of the bottom of the rifles. The only difference was that these, unlike regular firearms, lacked any kind of trigger assembly. With just over two hours left in the testing, Zade was satisfied with what he had learned about the crew and decided to head out and explore the woods surrounding the ship.

"Samix, I'm going to take a look around. I'll stay within earshot. I don't want you guys getting wise again if I'm late getting back."

"That's fine. We're going to be a while here. Be careful; there's an animal that lives in the blue and orange trees. Looks like a monkey but actually belongs to the reptile family. It loves to throw rocks down on things below it. The last time we were here, Axis got hit by one, and it took almost a quarter of his nanites to repair the gash on his head."

"OK, Mom," Zade said as he headed into the woods, laughing at the idea of a combat vet being afraid of a little lizard monkey.

△△△

"Why did he call you mother? And what was he laughing about?" Jorloss asked.

"I don't know. Maybe it's a joke his people have. I need you up here. Looks like the data drone system was damaged by the solar flare, and it doesn't look good," Samix replied.

The data drone launch system was a standard system for all Unity exploration vessels. Every time a new astronomical object was discovered by the exploration ship, all sensory, navigational, and manually input data was stored in the data drone. The small warp-capable drones were launched after every discovery to prevent catastrophic data loss from an exploration vessel being destroyed or disabled outside Unity space. Unlike ships, the drones were nimble enough to avoid the gravity wells of astronomical bodies they passed during the flight back to the nearest Unity space station and were not required to make periodic navigational stops. Before launch, the exploration vessel captain could manually choose data they would like to keep stored on their ship. The drone containing all of Earth's data, including galactic location, was no longer attached to the vessel.

Luckily for Jorloss, his family was part of the forest-dwelling subspecies on his planet, meaning that he was born with the same sticky pads on his hands and feet that his ancestors used to climb trees to avoid predators. It made the climb to the top of the thirty-foot-tall ship no harder than a walk in the park. As he made his way to the top of the command deck, Jorloss immediately saw the problem that Samix called him up to see.

"Where is the drone? Why is it not in the launcher?" Jorloss asked as he made his way to Samix's side.

"It looks like the system was damaged by the flare that hit us just before we warped," Samix replied, finishing the last test on the drone system. "The electromagnetic clamps holding the drone in place inadvertently released. The drone must have fallen off the ship just before we warped."

"Don't these drones have recovery protocol?"

"No. Exploration vessels jettison damaged or subpar drones all the time. The Unity didn't want the inconvenience of having to recover broken drones, so they never created a recovery protocol," Samix answered coolly.

"What information do we have on Zade's planet, then?" Jorloss retorted.

"The only data left is Zade's personnel and medical data. It was tagged as such, so it never made it to the drone."

"Zade is expecting the next stop to be his homeworld," Jorloss said, concern creeping into his voice. "If we can't get him there, what do we tell him?"

"I don't know," Samix said as she sat down hard on the canopy of the command deck.

Realizing that the friendly hitchhiker she had on her ship might become violent as soon as he heard that he could never get home, Samix began thinking about her options and figuring out the best way to break the news to Zade. Both Jorloss and Samix finished their external testing in somber silence.

△△△

Finishing early and waiting on Mur, who still had 45 minutes left to complete his analysis, Jorloss and Samix sat on the ship and discussed how to break the news to Zade. As both sat in silent contemplation, Samix heard a high-pitched cackle coming from the woods at the nose of the ship. Samix stood up and moved to the front of the ship to try and see what the noise was coming from, but as she peered into the woods, another cackle erupted, this time to the back-left side of the ship. Startled, Samix turned again, trying to sight the source as another bout of cackling erupted, this time to the rear right of the ship.

"I know what those are," Jorloss whispered, his eyes widening in fear. "They were the second lifeform I saw when we first cataloged this planet. These creatures appear to be the top scavengers in this area. When faced with hunger, they become active hunters. Like other canine species that we have run across, these have perfected the art of hunting in a pack. If they're around, we may not have to explain to Zade why we can't get him back to Earth."

Jorloss and Samix stood and crept closer to the edge of the ship in an attempt to lay eyes on the creatures. All the while, the cackling grew louder and more frantic. Samix knew that there were at least three of these animals, stalking just out of sight, waiting for the perfect moment to attack. Suddenly, the frantic communications of the animals stopped, and the forest became eerily silent. Samix hoped that the creatures have lost interest in the ship and its crew. As she slowly inhaled, three towering shapes launched out of the tree line, one targeting each of the SSILF tasked with protecting the ship's crew. The SSILF at the nose of the vessel had the animal on top of it before it could raise its weapon. After pinning the SSILF to the ground, the animal wrapped its colossal mouth around the SSILF's head, and after two violent shakes, managed to separate it from the SSILF's body. Samix spun to see that the other two SSILF at the rear of the ship had been dismembered by the powerful claws of the other two creatures. As the two animals at the back of the ship finished terminating the SSILF, the largest of the creatures, clearly the alpha, walked out of the trees and began circling the trapped crew.

While the animals were attacking, they had been moving too fast for Samix to get a good look at them. While they were circling the ship slowly, Samix could see what her crew was facing. The creatures stood waist-high, the alpha standing chest height, weighing about 350 pounds apiece. The muscular animals were covered in jet black fur with a green, dappled pattern stretching across their chests and heads. They each had six legs. The four rear legs were slightly shorter than the front two, allowing them to run at full speed while using the four-inch razor-sharp claws on the front paws to swipe at prey. The creatures' mouths were misshapen and full of dagger-like teeth, which stuck out at wild angles. These creatures were known to be aggressive, strong, and cunning, and now Samix and Jorloss were trapped by them.

ΔΔΔ

Just after venturing away from the ship, Zade decided to carve "Alex was here" into the trunk of one of the fat blue trees. Zade continued deeper into the forest, admiring the scenery and looking for wildlife. After walking for a short time, Zade came upon a swift-moving creek covered with red algae. It was home to beautiful, fluorescent fish that glowed vivid pinks and greens. Not knowing what the water might contain and not really wanting to have wet feet, Zade headed upstream to try and find a place where he could jump across. Luckily, after only a couple hundred meters, the stream sank into a rock fissure narrow enough to cross. Zade continued into the forest and shortly decided to sit beneath one of the spruce-like trees to rest out of the sun and take in the landscape.

As Zade sat down, he felt something hit him in the top of the head but thought it was nothing more than some cone or seed pod that had fallen out of the tree. As he marveled at the serendipity of his current predicament, his train of thought was interrupted again by something hitting him in the top of the head. Zade looked up and locked eyes with a baboon-like creature covered in alligator skin. As Zade jumped to his feet and put distance between himself and the tree, the monkey made his way further up the tree. Zade stood and watched as the creature began pulling rocks and nuts out of a small hollow in the trunk and began hurling them at Zade as fast as his arm would move. Not to be outdone by a primate, Zade began collecting rocks to return fire. Zade's third projectile connected with the monkey's chest, knocking him out of the tree. It hit the ground and laid still.

Afraid he may have killed the creature, Zade moved closer to investigate. At four paces away, the monkey sprang to its feet and charged him. Before he could react, the monkey was on top of Zade, throwing wild haymakers at his face. Struggling to regain his feet while defending himself, Zade managed to put a small amount of distance between himself and the creature. As the monkey tried to close the space again, Zade prepared himself for a second round and was ready. When the monkey was in range, Zade gave it a sharp kick causing it to go airborne and land a few feet away unfazed. The creature charged again, and the ensuing fistfight backed Zade all the way up to the red creek he had passed just minutes prior. Tired and unsure about his chances of beating this scrappy alligator-monkey, Zade jumped the creek and prepared to make a break for it. After clearing the stream, he jogged away. Zade turned to see the monkey on the opposite bank. Zade could have sworn the monkey began making obscene gestures, but he turned his head to watch where he was running.

As Zade neared the landing site, he could tell something was amiss. When he had left, he could hear Samix and Jorloss well into the forested area. Now, almost in view of the ship, all he could hear was heavy panting and occasional laughter. Slowing to a walk and crouching down, Zade covered the last bit of distance until he could see the ship. His heart dropped into the pit of his stomach as he crept closer to the ship. The only two people in the universe capable of getting him home had been treed by four giant, black, six-legged hyenas. The hyenas were circling around the landing gear; between the hyenas and Zade laid the torso section of one SSILF.

If I can get to the SSILF, I can get its weapon and dispatch these mangy dogs.

He could see four hyenas, one being markedly more prominent than the rest and appearing to have slightly misshapen legs running down its left side. As they patrolled around the craft, there was a small window when both he and the SSILF were in the hyenas' blind spots. Planning to sneak up to the SSILF body when the hyenas couldn't see him, Zade would grab the weapon and retreat back to the tree line. Then, Zade would engage the animals from the trees' safety, starting with the alpha and finishing with the runt.

Satisfied with his plan, Zade sprang into action. As the last hyena turned towards the front of the ship, Zade ran to the SSILF and grabbed the weapon clutched in its hands. After a sharp tug, Zade realized that it was somehow attached to the SSILF. *Seriously Murphy?* Zade thought as he elected to carry the whole damaged robot section back into the trees, out of earshot of the animals. Once safely separated from the predators, Zade managed to pry the weapon from the robot's grasp, a task made difficult by dozens of tiny wires extending from the SSILF's palms to the weapon's stock. Doing a quick inspection of the gun, Zade first checked the display located at the rear of the upper receiver; it showed a green battery. Not knowing what exactly he was looking at, Zade figured that a green battery must be a good thing and moved on to the magazine. After getting it to release, he saw that it was filled with tiny BBs.

Come on, guys. I know you're an exploration ship, but BB guns for potentially hostile unknown planets?

Slapping the magazine back into the weapon, Zade's final check was for some kind of trigger. The only control Zade could find on the whole gun was a tiny button located under the thumb of his front hand. He figured that if he stayed concealed in the trees and that the button fired the weapon, he would be good, and if the button did nothing, he could make up a new plan. Taking a deep breath and calming himself, Zade moved into position. The weapon had no sights, but aiming the best he could at the alpha, Zade pressed the button. The weapon exploded with a deafening roar, and the alpha disappeared in a pink cloud. Based on the carnage, Zade knew he was holding a railgun. Before the others could react, Zade lined up the next target and pressed the button, nothing. As he squeezed the trigger the first time, Zade was shocked to see a 30 second timer begin counting down in his right field of vision.

Attention: your actions have been deemed detrimental to the survival of this ship. If you do not cease aggressive activities within 30 seconds, the nanites in your bloodstream will be forced to remove the threat by terminating you, said a computerized voice, which seemed to come from inside his head.

All right. Fuck you, Murphy! Now you're just screwing with me.

Examining the weapon, Zade could see that the once green battery on display was now a soul-crushing black with a red X through it. The weapon was out of power. While Zade was trying to fix the weapon, the remaining three hyenas had caught his scent and were now staring straight at him. Attacking one at a time to preserve the hierarchy, the first began to run towards Zade. Out of options, Zade jumped to his feet, flipped the weapon, so he was holding it with both hands on the buttstock. As the creature closed, Zade took two steps forward, closing with the animal before it could lunge, and swung as hard as he could. The weapon connected with the animal's head with a sickening crack. It hit the ground and wasn't moving. As Zade was grand slamming the second hyena, the third had moved into position behind him. Hearing it approach, Zade turned just in time to lodge the weapon in the maw that had been aimed at his head. Although the weapon stopped the killing blow, the creature buried its razor-sharp claws into Zade's shoulders and drove him to the ground. Struggling to maintain control of the weapon, Zade grabbed the ends protruding from either side of the animal's mouth and twisted. The weapon broke in half, but only after Zade heard the satisfying snap of the creature's neck. As the weapon broke in half, the countdown timer, now down to eighteen seconds, disappeared.

Three down, one to go. Also, ask Samix why she put a kill order out on me.

Zade regained his feet, still holding the two pieces of the weapon. Looking at the remaining beast, Zade could tell it had become slightly indecisive. Using the animal's hesitation, Zade looked at the pieces of the weapon he held. The barrel section had broken free from the upper receiver leaving a sharp point. Tossing the rear half of the weapon, Zade squared up with the last beast. Learning from the last one he had killed, Zade knew that this one was going to lunge for his head; this time, he would be ready. Seconds felt like hours, but the creature finally lunged at Zade. Sidestepping the attack, Zade jumped into the air and drove the pointed end of the barrel into the top of the creature's head with all his might. As the beast slid through the grass, obviously dead, Zade could see that with his new strength, he had driven the barrel clean through the head, leaving only the section he was gripping exposed at the top.

After dispatching the last hyena, Zade moved to the ship to check on Samix and Jorloss.

"You guys good?" Zade asked.

When neither replied, Zade looked up to see both, mouths agape, nodding their heads in shocked silence. After realizing that neither had been hurt, Zade made his rounds, ensuring that all four creatures were dead. Confident that none were going to spring back into action, Zade began to examine the almost forgotten wounds he had received from the third animal. To his surprise, none of the eight jagged cuts bled more than a couple of drops. Moving his sleeve out of the way, he could see that each had been sealed with a gray film.

"It's the nanites," said Jorloss, walking up behind Zade. "Their basic programming includes repairing any injury that threatens their host's survival. When we get back on the ship, you're going to need replacements."

"These little guys come in handy," Zade said, staring at his arm in mild disbelief.

Samix had disembarked from the top of the ship and looked at the dispatched animals. She walked toward Zade, unable to even meet his eyes.

"You...You handled four apex predators with nothing more than a club," Samix said meekly. "You saved our lives."

With that, she shuffled aimlessly back to the rear ramp that was now opening. Mur had completed his tests. The crew cleaned up their equipment and the broken SSILF, which would be sent to material reclamation, and boarded the ship before any other wildlife came to see what all the excitement was about. Jorloss and Zade headed to the medical bay to replace the nanites Zade had lost due to injury, while Samix quietly headed to the command deck. As Zade stepped into his shower, he felt the ship take off and head for high orbit.

CHAPTER 5

After his shower, Zade tried to sleep, but rest evaded him. With his mind spinning about the events that had occurred earlier, he stepped out of his room, grabbed a quick meal from the galley, and retreated to one of the overstuffed club chairs in the common area. The lights had been dimmed as the ship was just entering its night cycle. From his time aboard, Zade figured that the ship followed a lighting and ambient noise pattern that must have represented the Unity planets' day-night cycle. Bereft of a watch since he came aboard, Zade could only estimate, but it seemed that the ship had a daylight period of about sixteen hours and a night period of about ten hours.

Now sitting in the darkened common area, Zade replayed the events of the past day. For the first time since he had first set foot on an active battlefield, he actually felt alive. Everything about this new experience was precisely what he had been missing back on Earth. The never-ending string of boredom and disappointment Zade felt during his time in the military highlighted that even the most adrenaline-filled, dangerous job—being a combat officer deployed forward to a warzone—wasn't enough to satiate Zade's appetite for excitement. However, the short time aboard the XES01 had excitement at every turn. Since leaving Earth, Zade had been introduced to two separate alien species. He was made near superhuman by advanced biomedical technology and engaged in single melee combat with gigantic space dogs. Zade wondered how he would go back to his everyday life on Earth.

Not one to make snap decisions, Zade began thinking about the options staring him in the face. Staying on with this crew meant relegating himself to the possibility of never seeing anyone he loved back on Earth ever again. Zade knew he didn't understand how the ship's warp engines worked, but as an aspiring engineer and physicist, he understood the concept of time dilation. Zade knew that while the vessel was in warp, moving faster than the speed of light, time for the ship and its crew nearly stood still. The three-day warp the ship just made to and from Earth, from the perspective of the planet itself, could actually have taken hundreds of years. Zade knew there was a distinct possibility that when he made it home, the planet could have changed significantly, and most of the people he loved could be dead. Hell, Zade thought, they might already be gone after the first trip. Pushing the melancholy prospect from his mind, Zade reasoned through what it would mean if he had only been gone for the duration of time that he spent aboard the ship. Zade knew that he could never go home.

If Zade were to return six days after he left, he would face one of three very unpleasant scenarios. In the first scenario, Zade would be returned, preferably to Manas, where he would be greeted by senior military leadership, who would be both relieved that Zade was back and pissed that he had been missing. No one would believe his tale, and under pressure from the major, Zade would be charged with desertion, stripped of his rank, and thrown in a military prison for the rest of his life. The second and equally unappealing option would be that people would hear his tale. He would either be thrown in a mental health facility where he would spend the remainder of his overmedicated life in a padded room, or in the third scenario, he would be carted off to a secret military facility where he would be interrogated and experimented on. The latter option was much shorter than the last two because the military would most likely dispose of him after extracting information and testing him. Any way he cut it, Zade could see no happy ending resulting from getting dropped off on Earth.

As Zade stood to refill his mug of sloop in the galley, Samix's voice rang over the ship's intercom system. She was calling Zade up to the command deck. Leaving his unfilled cup behind, Zade headed up to the command deck, where he found Samix staring out the windows at the planet below. As Zade made his way next to her, he could tell that she was sad. It was the kind of sadness that comes with telling someone bad news. The sort of despair he had only seen on his parents' face when they were about to tell him that the beloved family dog had died. As Zade waited for her to speak, he could feel a shred of anxiety settle in his soul.

"Thank you for what you did for us down there," Samix said, motioning toward the planet. Clearly, it wasn't what she had in mind, but she couldn't seem to force herself to say what was bothering her. She looked toward him and away quickly, trying to avoid eye contact. Zade noticed how beautiful her eyes were in the short time their eyes met.

"No problem. You guys were my ride home. Couldn't let anything happen to you," Zade replied, trying to lighten the mood.

Zade could saw a solitary green tear roll down Samix's face.

△△△

Samix couldn't figure out how to break the news that there was no way they could get Zade back home. After being freed from the top of the ship, Samix immediately headed to the command deck to recover any navigational data on Earth, hoping that, against all odds, any data had been stored on the ship. The hope was for naught; after hours of scrubbing through system logs, she couldn't find any information on Earth.

A deep sense of leader's guilt settled on Samix. Although unknowingly, she had changed Zade's life in her mind, and she felt responsible for his well-being. A myriad of possibilities began to fly through Samix's mind. What if she had grabbed the location of Earth before the ship jumped? What if she had overridden the evasive jump protocol? What if she had done a better sensor scan before landing?

What's done is done. Beating myself up isn't going to make anything better, Samix thought as she started to craft options for what to do next. The first thought she had was to ask Zade to stay aboard as the head of the robotics and the security chief. She had looked through his file and was impressed by his academic prowess. Zade had completed training as a mechanical engineer focused on robotics before attending a military academy.

Further highlighting his mental acumen, he completed the program, usually taking four years, in half the time. Samix had no reservations about Zade's ability to manage the lab on the ship. As for the security position, before planetfall, Samix had already found that Zade was unknowingly a contender for some clandestine military program on Earth, meaning that he was one of the best warriors on his planet—an assessment solidified by his actions to defend her and Jorloss when they had been attacked by the beasts during the repair stop.

Only once in her life had Samix seen a warrior best such opposition. It was at the Carlas, the gladiatorial games, of Xi'Ga. Xi'Ga was the homeworld and namesake of Samix's species and the planet of her upbringing. As a child, her father would take her to the games, where she would dream about one day becoming a great warrior like the individuals performing for the crowd. The games that Zade's actions remaindered her of had happened on her 90th birthday. Just out of adolescence, her father took her to the games to celebrate her acceptance into the Unity Standard Military Academy command program. The competitor, a Marlog, had bested five ultra-aggressive, 400 pound, poisonous, armored, amphibious creatures from Jorloss's planet, Lassf, while entirely unarmed. The Marlog were renowned across the Unity as the best warriors alive. A large bipedal species that dwarfed the Xi'Ga, the Marlog, was dark grey with black armor plates covering their vital organs. Although the Xi'Ga regularly outfitted the Marlog with the latest weapons and utilized them as mercenary protective forces, the Marlog were capable of unarmed combat thanks to a retractable claw that ran the length of their forearms. Few warriors could measure up to the Marlog, and those who had the physical prowess to best one lacked the mental agility to adjust their tactics while in combat. Those with mental agility often lacked the physical prowess. After watching him work planetside, Samix had no doubt that Zade embodied the right balance of strength and intelligence and would have fit perfectly into the Marlog society; he could significantly augment the survivability of the mission.

The second option she had come up with was the possibility of returning Zade to a planet like his own. Looking through the profile data of the worlds found prior to the incident on Earth, Samix found one with an atmosphere that would support Zade, and it had a species similar in both looks and development as humans. Given the proper backstory and timing, Zade had the potential to live out a long, fulfilling life amongst the people of the planet. With options at the ready, she had to tell Zade that he might never again be able to go home, resume his old life, or see his people.

"We were able to identify all of the damage the ship sustained from the solar flare," Samix started slowly, gazing at Zade. "But the data drone we had on Earth was dislodged from its mounts."

She then began to explain what the drones were used for and why they were a primary piece of equipment on exploration vessels. She explained that the only information pertaining to Earth was Zade's medical file, which was kept in a separate system to prevent corruption or ship-wide power outages from disallowing the medical staff access.

"The chance of us running across the signal bubble from your planet is almost zero. There is no way for us to get back to Earth," Samix said quickly. "I'm so sorry."

Even after deciding that he wanted to stay aboard and help, the news hit Zade like a punch in the gut. Not wanting to go back was far different from not being able to go back, the latter being significantly worse. For Zade, the desire was a choice, but the ability was not, meaning that any limitation based on ability made him feel helpless. Zade stood next to Samix in silence, stunned by the revelation.

After letting the news sink in, Samix began again, "You do have a couple of options. The first and best option for our mission..." Samix trailed off momentarily.

"I would really like for you to stay on as a crewmember," she continued. "I have already lost a crewmember to hostilities, and we need someone like you to organize security. Option two is that we can drop you off at a planet whose species closely resembles your own. From there you could do as you like. I know it's a hard choice; we will stay in orbit until you come to a decision."

Samix headed out quickly, leaving Zade on the command deck for the first time by himself, where he sat staring out at the stars. Exhaustion finally came, and Zade headed to his quarters. For two days, Zade retreated into the structured, recognizable safety of his own mind, where he mulled over his situation, leaving only to get food from the galley, which he carried back to his room to eat in quiet isolation. Finally, the despair and disbelief gave way to anticipation and curiosity, and Zade realized that his vacation in the stars had become his destiny. He headed out of his quarters with a new outlook and an answer for Samix.

To his surprise, sitting at the table in the galley was a figure he had never seen before. This minuscule individual, too short to even touch the ground while seated, had rich dark reddish-brown skin covered partially in coarse, thin hair. Atop his head sat two swiveling ears, half as long as his body. Approaching carefully, Zade gave the being a wide berth as he moved to grab a cup of sloop. Turning towards the table, Zade was startled by the being's face. Sitting where his eyes should have been were two deep pits, and in place of a mouth, it had two solid stone plates.

"Unless we picked up another hitchhiker, I'm guessing you're another crew member," Zade said as he sat at the end of the table.

"The name's Axis. Just got out of my quarters; I was pretty under the weather. You must be Zade, the only hitchhiker we have picked up," Axis replied.

"Yup. I was told that you guys couldn't get me home. I was just heading up to the command deck to talk to Samix about what I want to do."

"Wouldn't mind seeing you stick around if half of what Samix has said is true. This ship is full of scientists and thinkers. After the incident with Farn and the incident you were involved in, it wouldn't hurt to have someone defending us. My thoughts, at least. Pleasure meeting you," Axis said as he jumped down from his chair and headed to his room.

△△△

After finishing his drink, Zade headed for the command deck to talk to Samix. Samix was nowhere to be found, and only Mur was present. Mur was sitting in the captain's chair and said nothing as Zade entered the command deck. As Zade turned to leave, he could have sworn that usually stone-faced Mur was wearing a frown. Zade's next stop was the medical bay, where he found Jorloss engrossed in his work. Jorloss only spared a brief moment from his job to inform Zade that Samix was in her quarters. Zade walked across the hall and knocked on the door to the captain's quarters. After hearing movement inside, the door slid open, revealing how much it paid off to be the captain. The captain's quarters contained a full bed, a marked improvement from the twins in the rest of the crew quarters. Just past the sleeping area was a small living area complete with a couch, desk, and two bookshelves, packed to capacity with other literature. Like the crew quarters, the captain's room had a functional bathroom area with linens and air dryers. Samix was sitting at the desk reading a book from one of the book-shelves. Samix put her book down and turned to face Zade.

"Even if you had the navigation data, I couldn't go back to Earth," Zade said vehemently. "I would most likely spend the rest of my life confined or worse. And I defiantly don't want to be dropped on the next habitable rock like some errant stow-away. I want to stay aboard as part of the crew."

Overcome with happiness, Samix hustled over and gave Zade a hug. He was pleased to know he had made the right choice in her mind. Leading him over to the couch to sit, Samix began explaining, in detail, the operations of the ship and how Zade would fit in, the excitement in her voice now evident. The XES01 followed a strict process while exploring. The vessel would warp to interstellar space to conduct a deep space scan. This scan would identify anomalies and unique planets based on spectrometry and other sensor readings. After the scan data was compiled, all special items and planets of interest were identified, Mur would plot the most efficient warp path to examine each. As the ship arrived at a world, it would maintain high orbit. The first orbit would map the topography of the planet. The second and third orbits were used to collect the atmosphere and planet's composition, respectively. The fourth and last orbit would catalog any plant or animal life on the planet. Viewing the data, the scientists aboard would decide whether or not they needed to land and collect more information. If a spot of interest was identified, the ship would move into a geosynchronous orbit, staying directly above the point of interest while the crew prepared to land.

These landing parties were going to be led by Zade. As the new security expert aboard, it would be his job to identify any threats, make and outfit the SSILF, and provide security for the scientists doing data collection. After explaining the main exploration methods, Samix stood, motioning for Zade to do the same, and headed for the door.

"Now, we're going to head down one deck, and I will show you your lab," Samix said, leading Zade out of her quarters and towards the rear of the ship.

Walking past the galley, Samix pointed to a row of innocuous doors explaining that they led to each scientist's office. The one closest to the outer hull was unclaimed, and Zade could use it if he chose. Pointing to a door across from the offices, Samix noted that it was to the ship's ready room, where all mission briefings and debriefings would occur. Walking past the ready room, Samix led Zade down the rear stairs to the cargo bay. Turning back towards the front of the ship, Zade could see a standard man door set in the center of the wall with two enormous rolling doors on either side of it. Samix informed that the left rolling door opened to Axis's terraforming lab, and the right opened to the robotics lab. Walking through the man door, Zade could see four doors down the hallway: two to the left and two to the right. Stopping at the first door on the right, Zade read the placard: "Robotics and Fabrication." Identifying the other three labs before entering robotics, Samix informed Zade that the front left was the anthropology lab. The front right was the biology lab. As stated before, the rear left was the terraforming lab.

The inside of the robotics lab was a sight to behold. The walls were covered with different blueprints and design sketches. Against the far wall, four different SSILF, all clearly different variants, were lined up. Directly in front of Zade, in the corner by the robots, there was a small workstation complete with six displays, three on each wall. Turning clockwise, Zade could see tables in the center of the room, one of which had the burnt remains of his army equipment piled on it. His visual inspection finished with the wall closest to the center of the ship. Across from where he was standing, different manufacturing equipment lined up against the wall, near the rolling door at the rear of the lab. Samix explained that the three cylindrical manufacturing machines towards the back of the lab were for fabrication. They could fabricate any equipment that the ship needed, including fully functional SSILF. The machine next to the tubes was a disassembler, which Zade could use to replicate any equipment, not in the lab database. All he had to do was place the device into the machine, where it would be broken down and mapped. After all the required information about the workings and material of the device was logged, it would be re-assembled. Next to the disassembler was a smaller fabrication machine used to make smaller, more delicate parts for the ship. The last piece of equipment in the row was a modification machine. It was used to improve or modify any already existing piece of equipment.

Walking to the computer station, Samix explained that any-thing that Zade could draw or design on the workstation could be created in the lab. Zade just had to provide the idea, and the ship's material reclamation system provided the materials. Samix explained that after Zade went to see Jorloss, he wouldn't even need to be in the lab to create things. The nanites' cerebral linkage would link him to the design systems.

"Speaking of nanites," Zade said sarcastically. "Now that I am a full member of the crew, will you be lifting the kill order you programmed into them?"

Trying to convince Zade that he was mistaken, Samix assured him that she had ordered no such thing. Undeterred, Zade ex-plained how during the fight, when he picked up the railgun, he could hear Mur's voice informing him that his aggressive actions would be met with termination and how a 30-second timer appeared in his right field of vision. Disgusted by the idea of executing Zade for taking action to protect the crew, Samix assured him that she would look into it after she finished show-ing him how the lab worked.

"It shouldn't have done that if you were trying to protect us," Samix said, flustered and under her breath. "It should have only done that if you had tried to harm us."

Zade smirked as she went back to talking about the equip-ment around him. He could swear her cheeks turned a darker shade of blue as she avoided eye contact. Walking to the pile of his old gear, Zade could see how much damage he actually took as his body broke through the atmosphere, trapped on the side of the ship. The side of his IBA not trapped against the side outside of the hull was completely burnt away, leaving only the material protected by his SAPI plate. The M4 that had been strapped against his chest had taken enough heat damage to warp the barrel, and the rounds in the magazine had cooked off, leaving only a twisted hunk of metal where the front of the lower receiver should have been.

Not everything was a loss, though. When he got pinned, his leg must have been turned enough to protect his 1911 because the only damage it sustained was a large gouge in the slide. Everything in his butt pack survived as well. Sliding the kit towards him as he flipped it over, Zade unzipped the bag. As soon as he opened it, a wolfish grin spread across his face. Inside were two hockey puck demo charges, two extra magazines for his sidearm and his primary, and most importantly, his iPod. As he removed each item from the pack and placed it on the table, he explained what it was used for to Samix, who seemed particularly curious about the iPod. Things were starting to look up. Now, at least, he could continue his pre-mission ritual of listening to his combat playlist. Turning it on, he flipped to his favorite song and stuck the earbuds in. After noticing Samix inquisitively looking at him, he handed her one of the earbuds so she could listen.

"Horrible, angry noise," Samix said, clearly not impressed. She tossed the earbud back to Zade. Chuckling to himself, Zade wrapped up the iPod and pocketed it, anticipating going back to his quarters so he could listen to it. To end the tour Samix, asked Zade which weapon was his favorite.

Well, I am a fan of the M4, but with rail guns available, it seems I'd be a little outclassed. Plus, I was pretty lucky to be carrying a .45 Colt 1911 instead of the issued Beretta M9. Thanks, douche major who thought he was special forces, Zade thought as he picked up the sidearm.

Samix took it from him and headed to the disassembler. After placing the weapon inside the machine, the door closed, and the machine whirred to life. Samix led Zade to the workstation, where a perfect model and set of design specs came on the screen.

"Is it damaged at all?" Samix questioned.

"Yeah. This is supposed to be smooth, like the other side," Zade replied, pointing to the large gash in the slide. Samix used the cursor to circle the damage, spin the gun, identify the mirrored surface and clicked match. All of the damage was corrected, and Zade was looking at a beautiful new pistol. With one final adjustment, demanded by Zade, Samix hit the produce button, and the small fabrication machine behind them began its work. After five minutes of work, Zade held his new ivory-handled 1911. Not quite Patton's revolver, but it would do just fine. Unable to wipe the shit-eating grin off Zade's face, Samix headed to her quarters to investigate Zade's kill order claim, informing him to meet Jorloss as she stepped out of Zade's lab.

△△△

Leaving Zade to ogle the new weapon that they had created, Samix headed to the command deck to investigate the kill order that Zade was talking about. After sifting through hundreds of pages of code and protocol, Samix finally found what she was looking for. A tiny piece of code hidden amongst the basic operating protocol for the nanites instructed them to terminate their host if he started exhibiting behavior that would jeopardize the crew's survival. Unsure how to process the information, as Zade was the first sentient being allowed on the ship other than the crew, Samix began deleting the code. The code's presence didn't surprise Samix; every bit of programming was intended to protect the crew and ship, and destroying an internal threat was simply part of that programming. What did surprise Samix was that the judgment to determine what was and was not threatening was left to the ship's AI, Mur, and not her as the captain.

After completely deleting the line of code, Samix began to

scroll through the rest of the protocol to make sure she didn't accidentally alter anything else. Just before the chunk of code that contained the kill order scrolled out of view, Samix could see the kill order code repopulate. After a second attempt to remove the code Samix, now aggravated, changed her authorization to the administrative level and again tried to remove the code. After three failed attempts as admin, Samix relegated herself to getting the AI's help.

Communicating directly through her interface, Samix explained what she was trying to do to the AI. The cold robotic voice betrayed no emotions, but there was something about Mur's behavior that rattled Samix. Mur was arguing against removing the code, which he explained as an entirely precautionary measure. Samix explained how Zade had risked his own life to protect both herself and Jorloss while the ship was completing repairs and how he was not a threat to the vessel or the crew. After having the conversation to rationalize her judgment, a conversation that no captain should have to have with a ship AI, the termination code was removed.

△△△

After securing the new weapon in one of the drawers at the workstation, Zade exited the lab. Heading towards the nose of the ship, he first stuck his head in the biology lab to see if Jorloss was doing any work. With no sign of life in the lab, Zade headed up the stairs to the medical bay, the only other area on the ship where Jorloss worked. Stepping inside the medical bay, Zade could see Jorloss peering into a microscope, clearly fascinated by what he was looking at.

"Samix said you had something for me now that I'm part of the crew," Zade said, interrupting and startling Jorloss.

Motioning for Zade to climb onto one of the exam tables, Jorloss said, "the nanites in your bloodstream now are one of the earliest versions created. In Unity space, they are given to every citizen as part of a free inoculation program. The nanites that this crew uses are the 17th version of the technology, and only given to exploration crews."

After having Zade take off his blouse and shirt, Jorloss hooked him up to a filter machine that would remove the old nanites from his blood and replace them with the new variant, all while explaining, in minute detail, what the nanites were and how they worked. The new variant nanites were microscopic cylindrical robots that could transfer material and data to any part of Zade's body. The backside of the nanite consisted of four flagella that, while powered, would act as small tails to steer the nanite around Zade's body. As the nanite ran low on power, it would anchor its nose to the blood vessel wall and use blood flow to spin the flagella and recharge its energy source. Unlike Zade's current nanites, the new versions could be programmed internally by the host, who simply had to think about what he wanted the nanites to do. This feature was mandated for exploration crews to expeditiously adjust their own physiology to accommodate the many different situations they would face.

Zade learned that the nanites were programmed to maintain the host's optimal health, and in many species, they were able to prolong the life of the host almost indefinitely. Zade would have to be fully sedated and hooked up to an IV for the nanites' initial work, work that was standard for any exploration vessel crewman. The IV was required because of the significance of the changes. Zade would not be able to intake enough material to supply the changes. The modification would consist of two stages. The first stage was a preparatory stage where the nanites would manipulate Zade's physiology to match a perfectly healthy human. While orbiting, Jorloss had collected all data about the biology, physiology, and genetic disposition of mankind, all of which was stored in the medical bay. This information was then compiled to create a profile for the species that would be the metric to determine if the nanites would have to change anything. Any of Zade's old injuries or persistent imperfections would be corrected before the nanites moved into stage two. As Jorloss finished explaining stage one, Zade began to think of the chronic injuries that had plagued him since college. He had broken his collar bone playing football for the Army team, and to this day, it bothered him. Every time he tried to reach behind him, a consistent pain shot down his left arm. Zade had also partially torn his ACL on his second deployment and put off surgery until he could complete his last deployment. Zade's eyesight was also less than perfect, not bad enough to need glasses but not good enough to allow him admittance into the aviation branch, which had been his ultimate reason for joining the Army. Nodding for Jorloss to continue, Zade laid back and began to ponder the prospect of a life without chronic pain from past sports injuries.

Jorloss explained that after the nanites prepared and perfected Zade's body, they would begin developing the cerebral interface that would connect Zade to all Unity data networks. Pulling down the neck of his uniform to expose a black spiral tattoo, Jorloss explained that the nanites would use a metallic material to create a data transfer antenna just under the skin, which would connect him to the network. Since Zade already had tattoos, the nanites would replace the black ink under Zade's skin with the new metallic material. In Unity space, Zade would always have access to network data. Zade would have access to ship data on this mission as long as the ship was in the same solar system as him. After the antenna was complete, the nanites would move to Zade's brain and begin creating the interface. Each interface was different because no two brains were identical, but there was a basic pattern to the work. The interface had three main components: data transfer, optical augmentation, and audio processing. The data transfer was the most complicated. Any data that Zade pulled off the network would be routed into the appropriate portion of his memory, allowing him to recall it at any point. The inverse of this allowed Zade to remember data for transfer to the network. The interface would find the data in Zade's memories, convert it into network format and transmit it.

The optical augmentation was the most awe-inspiring for Zade. The cerebral interface could take any video feed and route it to the optical center of Zade's brain via his optic nerves. It would appear as a slightly transparent overlay in his field of vision. Like the data transfer portion of the interface, what Zade was seeing could be uploaded to the network in real-time if he chose to do so. The possibilities of this technology made Zade's head spin. He could use it to monitor what the SSILF saw on security details. He could mount sensors on his weapons, so a targeting reticle would appear in his field of vision based on where the weapon was pointed, significantly reducing target acquisition time. The possibilities were endless.

The final portion, audio processing, Zade realized was what he had seen when Jorloss would stare off into middle space, looking like he was having a conversation with someone. The audio processing portion transmitted data along the nerves that connected the eardrum to the audio center of the brain. It would seem like the sound was coming from a set of headphones to the user. It was mainly used to listen to reports and communicate with the other crew members. By simply thinking about who he wanted to share with and thinking about what he wanted to say, Zade could send his message, in real-time, right to the mind of the recipient and vice versa.

To close his explanation of the nanites, Jorloss covered some of the personal touches he had programmed in. At first interaction, Zade thought Jorloss to be a biologist with a limited understanding of technology. This couldn't have been farther from the truth. Based on some of Jorloss's personal touches,

Zade quickly realized that Jorloss was not only highly tech-savvy but extremely paranoid about "big brother" watching over him. The first modification that Jorloss had made was a bit of programming that made the remote monitoring of any individual by tracking their nanites optional. With any other variant of nanites, the Unity could remotely monitor an individual while in Unity controlled space because the nanites would send out location data. The Unity claimed the data was used to apprehend criminals and help stranded citizens, but Jorloss wasn't buying it. He removed the code that caused the nanites to send out tracking data. Secondly, Jorloss knew eventually everyone would move out of the exploration command, and as their nanites were used to repair damage, new conventional versions would replace them. This would reduce the functionality and the host's capabilities. To prevent this, Jorloss coded in the ability for the version 17 nanites to reprogram any lesser nanites, making them exact replicas of themselves. His latest change replaced the current data encryption. It was challenging but not impossible to break. His new encryption, based on each host's DNA and genetic markers, was unique and impossible to crack. Now entirely comfortable with what was about to happen, Zade gave Jorloss the go-ahead.

"After this is done, we need to sit down and discuss any elective modification that you will need to make," Jorloss said as the sedative began to kick in.

Zade drifted to sleep, thinking about everything he could do to his body to make him the perfect warrior. The process took three days, in which time Samix had moved the ship into interstellar space and begun scanning for any bodies of interest.

CHAPTER 6

Waking up in the cold, sterile medical bay gave Zade a deep sense of déjà vu. Propping himself up on his elbows to look around the bay, Zade saw that he was alone. As he laid back down, Zade wondered if Jorloss would be angry if he took the different tubes out and went to the galley for some sloop. Then Zade remembered that he didn't have to wonder. He could just talk to Jorloss from here. Excited to try out his new hardware, Zade pictured Jorloss.

I'M AWAKE. WHY WASN'T THERE A CUTE NURSE HERE TO GREET ME? Zade thought, with the picture of Jorloss clearly fixed in his mind.

I'm down in the biology lab. Let me clean up down here, and I'll be there. You should really work on relaxing when you use the communication. The harder you focus on your transmission, the stronger it comes across. You yelled so loudly that I dropped a beaker, retorted Jorloss, his voice popping into Zade's head.

Fueled by the communication success, Zade began to explore his other abilities. As he sat and waited for Jorloss, Zade focused on connecting with the ship's sensor array and navigation readouts. After a few minutes and as many failures, an image of the starscape surrounding the vessel appeared in Zade's left eye. A navigational map with a pulsing red dot, indicating the location of the ship, appeared in his right. The view outside the ship, although different, was no less beautiful than the one he saw when he first set foot on the command deck. The ship was currently sitting in a blue and green gas cloud's inner edge. The brilliant spectacle resembled a spiral pattern where vivid greens intertwined with cold blues. Wondering where such a beautiful sight was located, Zade shifted his attention to the navigational map. The ship was currently located just outside the Oort clouds of six different stars. Based on the progress indicator at the bottom of the map, 20 percent of the space within the sensor range had been scanned, and three bodies of interest had been found. Looking at the map more closely, Zade could barely make out three tiny, red crosshair emblems in the surrounding space.

Content with what he had seen, Zade pulled up the feeds of the internal cameras. Samix was on the command deck, Axis was in his lab, and Jorloss, having finished cleaning up the broken glass, had just exited his lab and was headed for the medical bay. Zade watched him walk through the ship, changing the camera feeds in his field of vision as Jorloss moved out of the frame he was currently observing. For some reason, he had elected to use the rear set of stairs, and as he was nearing the galley, Zade shot him a message:

Could you grab me a mug of sloop? I'm parched.

Watching Jorloss on the feed, Zade saw the slightest change in his stride, indicating that he received the message. After making a pit stop at the galley to grab two mugs of sloop, Jorloss entered the medical bay. The men exchanged pleasantries as Jorloss set the cups down and unhooked Zade from the machinery. After helping him to a seated position and handing him one of the steaming mugs, Jorloss pulled a chair over and sat facing the bed. It amazed Zade that he still felt the need to vocalize his thoughts even with the new communication abilities. As he sipped on the delicious brew, Zade explained what he had been doing as he waited for Jorloss. Surprised at Zade's aptitude, Jorloss explained that successful communication took most crew-members days to master, and successfully tapping into sensor feeds took weeks.

After explaining that the ship would maintain its current position for at least another 72 hours, Jorloss broached the subject of elective modifications. Usually, Jorloss would be hunched over a display of the human body, with every bit of data about human physiology flanking the rendering of the human body. Jorloss elected to view the data via Zade's new interface in order to familiarize him with the sensation. After explaining what Zade had to do to pull up the image, Jorloss began listing the ideas he had come up with—ideas he felt would improve Zade's ability to defend the ship and its crew. Some were mild, like enhanced lung capacity and cardiovascular efficiency to improve Zade's endurance, while others were extreme, like the idea for inverted knee joints like a SSILF to improve Zade's speed and agility. After finishing his list, Jorloss explained that they were only suggestions, and he required Zade's input before making any final decisions.

"Changing anything without your input for enhancements," Jorloss stated, "would be like trying to make one of those demonic hyenas better without taking into consideration that it is a hunter. You have to know what purpose it has and what its intentions are first."

Zade chose to go through many changes that wouldn't change his appearance drastically. There was a level of pride that came with being the first of his kind interacting with the Unity. Changing his appearance, and thus others' perception of what mankind was, seemed to cheapen that meeting. After two more mugs of sloop, consumed while thinking about and talking through improvements with Jorloss, Zade finally had his list. First and foremost, as the security officer, he wouldn't be afforded the luxury of sleeping through any changes like the scientists could. He was required to stay awake and prepare for the mission, so he wanted some kind of pain block that would allow him to function as his body changed. After the pain block, Zade realized that any lack of physical ability could be compensated for with technology, so he suggested an increase in muscle density to allow him to carry the things he needed to complete the mission.

After three deployments, Zade knew that the human body was not meant for the rigors of constant fighting and would eventually breakdown, no matter how well it was taken care of. Therefore, Zade had two more requests. First, he wanted his skeleton reinforced with some kind of rigid material to prevent debilitating skeletal injuries during combat. This idea stemmed from memories of battle where his men had broken bones from nearby explosions or from jumping down off of a vehicle. No matter how small the break, it always put them out of commission. The second augmentation he wanted was to include some kind of damage-resistant material in his skin to prevent injuries like the ones he sustained during the repair stop.

The second category of improvements Zade wanted to address were those surrounding perception. Again, based on his combat experience, Zade knew that noticing the most minor details and being able to see the enemy before the enemy could see you were two of the major contributing factors in an individual's survivability. Knowing that hypersensitive sensory organs could also be overloaded in some situations, Zade wanted these augmentations to be scalable. First, he needed to improve his hearing for quiet situations where he needed to notice movement. This hearing augmentation had to be controllable because hypersensitive ears could be overwhelmed by loud noises during the chaos of combat. Secondly, Zade wanted to improve his sense of smell. Zade explained to Jorloss that warriors needed to rely on all of their senses in battle, and not improving one would be the equivalent of intentionally handicapping oneself. The last and most ambitious augmentation had to do with his vision. Zade admittedly didn't know how to accomplish the augmentations, but he wanted them nonetheless. He explained that the human eye had two different types of cells on the back of it called rods and cones. The rods were used in high visibility situations and picked up colors; the cones were used at night to gather ambient light. Since humans were primarily daytime creatures, they had all but lost their ability to see at night. He wanted some way to see better at night.

Furthermore, Zade knew how useful infrared could be in low visibility situations. He knew that some of the most successful predators on Earth could sense heat and overlay the infrared data on the visual picture obtained from the eyes. Zade's final suggestion was infrared sensing pits to help sense threats after dark.

Jorloss sat quietly as Zade explained everything he wanted, making a list of the improvements. After Zade had finished, Jorloss explained that Zade could complete the pain block and increase muscle density entirely on his own. Jorloss explained that all Zade needed to do while addressing the nanites was to explain that he wanted the ability to close off the ends of pain receptors just as they were triggered, thus shunting the associated pain. He further explained that any knowledge of human biology would help create a detailed set of instructions and improve the success rate of the change. The same method would work for the increase in strength. The nanites would develop the process required and, upon completion, would output a readout consisting of the macronutrients necessary. The readout would be displayed in Zade's field of vision. Zade would need to ingest the required materials, and as soon as he did, the nanites would begin their process.

As for the sensory upgrades, Jorloss explained that Zade should never try any modification on his own because, if done incorrectly, it could disable him altogether. The ship had state-of-the-art medical equipment and could create the program required to accomplish the modification with no risk of failure. Jorloss continued by saying that Zade could complete the skeletal augmentation independently. Still, Jorloss would have to determine what material could be used to strengthen Zade's bones without adversely reacting with his body. For example, if nickel was used, it would seep into Zade's blood and blind him. Jorloss finished his explanation by telling Zade that he could start on the two augmentations while he researched the best way to accomplish the rest of the changes Zade wanted. He informed Zade that he would notify him and upload the programming to Zade's nanites as soon as he created a way. As Jorloss moved over to a workstation, he began researching different approaches to successfully complete the procedures. Zade remained in the medical bay. With Jorloss working, Zade went into painstaking detail as he instructed his nanites on the nerve block. Satisfied with his instructions, the nanites output the materials list in Zade's left eye. He needed to intake 400 grams of protein and 100 grams of fat.

Looks like it's time for a steak, Zade thought as he left the medical bay headed for the galley. As Zade was finishing the prime rib and mashed potatoes drowned in butter, sour cream, and gravy, which he had ordered from the gut truck, Samix walked into grab a meal. As she stood, back towards him, ordering food, Zade just sat and enjoyed the view. Realizing that he had been away from women for at least nine months while he was in Afghanistan, and however long he had been on the ship. His mind wandered to Samix.

She clearly looks like a woman. I wonder how much her body matches a human. Aw, who am I kidding? After nine months of being deployed with nothing but sweaty, smelly Joe's, I'd low crawl naked through a mile of barbed wire and battery acid to see what's under that uniform.

Based on Samix's reaction, Zade clearly had not yet mastered his new ability of telepathic communication. Samix spun on her heels and glared at Zade. With eyes shooting daggers toward him and a painfully obvious bright blue flush across her face, she stormed over and backhanded Zade out of his chair.

"Remember, you ass, that I am still the captain of this ship," she roared as she stomped out of the galley back toward her quarters or the command deck.

It was hard for Zade to forget from the floor where he was lying, stars dancing across his vision. Picking himself up off the floor, still dazed, he headed to his quarters. As he entered his room, the slight itch under his skin signaled that the nanites had started working. Not at all abashed about being put in his place, all Zade could think about was the tingling and the purpose it served.

Why couldn't I have thought that after the nanites finished the pain block?

Zade wanted to grab a shower and lay down. Even after being asleep for three days, he still seemed tired. Forgetting that the dresser only contained uniform items, Zade headed over to find a pair of shorts to sleep in. As he neared the dresser, he noticed a small black box, no larger than a pack of cigarettes, sitting on top of it. As he picked it up to examine it, a message appeared. It was from Samix. It explained that Zade was authorized to have a personal storage device aboard the ship as a crew member. It was directly connected to Zade's interface, and like all of Jorloss's nanite technology, it was encrypted with his DNA so only he could access it. As Zade looked at it, he completed a mental search of the items and signals in his room, finding it labeled "Alex Zade: Personal Storage." Investigating the contents, Zade found that Samix had transferred all of his music off the iPod to the device, which allowed Zade to listen to it from anywhere.

Now feeling guilty about what he had said to Samix—*Well, thought to Samix, really*—Zade made a mental note to apologize and thank her for the device. While scrolling through his music, Zade noticed that the device had an enormous, if not unlimited, capacity. Selecting one of his relaxing playlists, "Space Oddity" started playing as he searched the drawers to find they contained the same items as the last time he had looked.

Before showering and sleeping, Zade decided to make some personal effects. He headed for the fabrication lab. After entering the lab, he grabbed the chair at the workstation and moved it to the center of the room. Determined to master his interface, Zade connected with the fabrication database and began queuing up the items he required. First on the list was a towel like the ones he saw in Samix's quarters. The air dryers were novel at first, but being dried off by a harsh wind was growing old. As the small fabrication machine began to create two towels, Zade began the slightly more complex process of producing items that were not in the database. First was a pair of shorts to sleep in. After moving into the creation portion of the fabrication program, Zade tried to isolate, in his mind, an image of silkies. Three failed attempts later, the fabrication machine began work on four pairs. Having gotten the hang of a simple creation program, Zade decided to move on to a more challenging item. The material selection of the shorts had given him enough trouble that Zade was dreading trying to create the next two things he required. The next thing, to his surprise, only took one try. Maybe it was because he had understood the program better, or perhaps because he had used it since childhood, making the memories clearer; he couldn't be sure the reason. As he slid the chair back to its home, his toothbrush dropped out of the fabrication machine into the collection tray at the bottom.

Grabbing his sundries, Zade headed back to his quarters for a much-needed shower. As he walked back to his room, he noticed that he had become desensitized to the nanite itch, which now seemed to be barely perceptible. He only saw it when he focused on it. Curious about the nanite progress, Zade inquired and received a notification that they were already 40 percent complete. Because he wanted to get as many changes as possible completed before landing on the next planet, Zade instructed the nanites to notify him when they were complete. After showering, Zade climbed into bed, changing his music to a sleep playlist consisting of nothing but relaxing classical music. After instructing the music to stop playing when he fell asleep, he brought up the room controls and turned out the lights.

A soft chiming pulled Zade out of his dream. Before he even opened his eyes, he read the message that the pain block was complete. Climbing out of bed, Zade turned the lights in his room up to a soft glow. After pulling up the increased muscle density program he had developed while sitting in the medical bay, Zade checked the ship's clock; it was just past midnight. Still waiting for the nutritional requirements, Zade pulled up the interior feeds and noticed none of the crew were present. It meant that they were all in their quarters, where there were no camera feeds. As he read through the nutritional requirements, a deep-seated sickness grew in the pit of his stomach. Initially, Zade thought it was cool that all he had to do was eat to change his body, but after reading the gross amount of protein he would have to intake for this change, he considered doing the rest with IV nutrition.

Since everyone was still asleep, Zade headed to the galley wearing only his shorts. Sitting at the table, Zade tried to figure out how he would ingest the amount of protein required for the nanites. As a thick-built army officer who was into weight training, Zade knew the protein content of an inordinate number of foods. Based on the requirement, he would have to eat over 100 chicken breasts or almost 300 eggs, both feats of god-like constitution that he didn't have. Thinking about the situation, Zade decided to approach the problem from a different angle. He had built the initial code under the assumption that the only way to increase his strength was to increase his muscle density and thus created a program to increase the number of muscle fibers he had. Trying a different approach, Zade carefully described the muscular and skeletal systems, then simply stated that he wanted to increase its functional capability, leaving the nanites to compute the best way to achieve the goal. After a short while, a list of nutritional requirements popped into view, this one containing a more manageable amount of food. After seeing the requirements, Zade accessed the gut truck remotely and searched for what he needed. Toward the bottom of the food list, he found a nutritional drink in the miscellaneous category. After selecting it, Zade was required to input the dietary values required and desired concentration, which he did. Unlike the original program that required only protein, this new program required protein and calcium. Zade selected the maximum allowable concentration and waited for the machine to produce the drink. The drink, which Zade estimated to be just over a gallon in size, had a smell that would knock a possum over.

Taking it from the machine, Zade steeled his will, sat down, and took the first sip. The drink had the consistency of a thick milkshake, but it didn't taste as bad as it smelled. He knew that he couldn't hold over a gallon of liquid in his stomach, so he made one last tweak to the nanite programming, which instructed them to begin using the intake as it became available as opposed to waiting until all resource requirements were met before starting the work. He hoped that the nanites would empty his stomach as fast as he could fill it. An hour and a half later, and feeling less full than he thought he would, Zade finished his herculean task and headed back to his quarters to sleep until morning.

Just as the ship slid into its daytime cycle, Zade's nanite completion notification awoke him. Anxious about the outcome of a nanite-defined augmentation, Zade just laid in his bed and opened the two messages he had received while sleeping. The first was from Jorloss, who said that he had found a way to successfully complete the rest of the requested modifications. It instructed Zade to meet him in the medical bay at his leisure. The second was from Samix and was addressed to both himself and Axis. It informed them that initial scans had identified a planet that may require a landing team consisting of Axis, the security officer, and his team. The message also set a reminder for the required eleven o'clock meeting in the ready room that Samix had set up.

I must have really gotten under her skin. She has never identified me by my position alone.

With nothing left to use as an excuse to stay in bed, Zade gingerly swung his legs over the side of his bed and stood. Realizing that he was still capable of locomotion eased his anxiety slightly. To test the extent of his increased strength, Zade turned and grabbed the lip of his rack. The bed was firmly secured to the floor, which he had learned during a previous attempt to rearrange his quarters. Straining against the weight, Zade struggled to stand erect without losing his grip on the bed. Just as he began to worry that the nanites failed to improve his musculature, he heard and felt the bed break free from the floor. Setting the bed back down, Zade could see where the sound of metal screaming under duress came from. There was a jagged tear in the floor paneling right at the edge of the bed. Delighted that the nanites worked and terrified at what would happen if Samix found out that he had damaged her ship, Zade left the room to get his morning sloop.

According to the ship's clock, it was only seven a.m., so Zade planned to talk with Jorloss before he had to meet Samix and Axis for the briefing. Working on his second cup of sloop, he read over the specifications for the different SSILF models. A flash of movement caught his attention, and he turned his head to see Axis walk into the galley.

"Any idea what this meeting with Samix is about?" Zade asked as he watched the settler order his morning meal.

"I would imagine that there is something on the planet that I need to see, and you're coming along to make sure I make it back to the ship," Axis said, grabbing his meal.

Zade had noticed that Axis only occasionally ate in the galley. He took his meals in his lab or quarters most of the time. This morning was no different. After answering Zade's question, the tiny alien headed back to his room, leaving Zade alone in the galley. Finishing his drink, Zade pulled up the medical bay video feed to make sure Jorloss was there before he walked all the way across the ship. Jorloss was in the medical bay working at his station when Samix walked into the medical bay and began talking to him. Zade wanted to hear what was going on but had not yet mastered the ability to route video and audio simultaneously through his interface. As Zade tossed his cup and headed towards the medical bay, Samix left Jorloss and headed back to the command deck.

As he entered the medical bay, Jorloss looked at him with a broad smile. A smile from any of the other crew members would not have bothered Zade, but Jorloss's amphibious features and an almost comically oversized mouth made the gesture slightly unnerving. Jorloss immediately launched into his findings. Starting with the improved hearing, Jorloss explained that he could have Zade's ear canal redesigned to better capture and magnify the sounds that made it to his eardrum. Smell was the second easiest one to correct. He explained that the highest concentration of cilia and scent receptors was in the nose. He could improve Zade's sense of smell simply by covering the walls of his sinus cavities with the same receptors. Jorloss finished explaining the group of easy fixes by explaining that high-density bundles of carbon nanotubes, formed into a mesh, could be used to reinforce Zade's bones.

With the easy fixes explained, Jorloss motioned for Zade to look at the display he was working on. The monitor had side-by-side pictures of the human eye. As Zade neared the display, he could see that the images were not the same. Jorloss explained that the right display was that of Zade's current eyes, and the left was that of Zade's eyes after improvements had been made. The most noticeable difference was that the nictitating membrane, or the small pink triangle in the inside corner of the eye, had been replaced with a small pit. Jorloss explained that it was initially a transparent protective third eyelid that humans could use when swimming. Because the species evolved out of using it, Jorloss planned to replace it with the heat-sensing pits to give Zade infrared overlays. Impressed with Jorloss's ingenuity and dedication to honor Zade's wish to remain looking like a human, Zade approved of the enhancement. Jorloss zoomed into the display until Zade could see the cones and rods at the backs of the eyes; he beamed with a pride Zade had never seen from him before.

At first look, Zade could see that the left eye contained hundreds of times more rods than Zade's current eye. One inquisitive look from Zade was all it took for Jorloss to launch into an explanation. Jorloss had originally been stumped about how to make the low light visibility controllable until he started thinking about some of the nocturnal plants that adorned his homeworld. These plants would close when they sensed light, and as the sun went down, they would open. Using this framework, Jorloss had designed new cells that would act as rods and enhance daytime vision when in high light conditions. As light levels went down, these cells would open into cones, thus improving low light visibility. The only drawback was that as the cells opened into cones, Zade would lose the ability to see color. Zade could not have been happier with Jorloss's work.

The only thing that Jorloss wasn't able to do was improve the toughness of Zade's skin. It was possible, but it didn't meet Zade's requirement about not changing his appearance. Zade was excited to get the final round of changes started, but he informed Jorloss that the procedure would have to wait until after his meeting with Axis and Samix at 11. Since there was still a couple of hours until his meeting, Zade first swung by his room to grab his uniforms before heading to his new lab. To gain practice with the lab equipment, Zade began making minor changes to his uniforms to make them more applicable to ground combat. After reducing their weight and increasing their UV, tearing, and fire resistance, Zade was happy with their design. Tagging them as his uniforms in the database, Zade donned one of the new uniforms and headed to the ready room for his briefing.

Zade had left a small ship clock readout in his field of vision, and because of the old army saying, "if you're early, you're on time," he was the first person in the ready room. While he waited the last 15 minutes for the others to arrive, Zade put his feet up and began looking through the database's weapons designs. After Jorloss was done changing his body, Zade would have to start developing a usable kit for both him and the SSILF. Zade was so distracted by modifying the current railgun design to include its own power source that he didn't even notice Axis and Samix walk into the room.

"If you're not too busy, could we get this meeting started?" Samix chided.

While shooting a scowl of his own at Samix, Zade shifted his attention to the meeting and sat attentively, waiting for Samix to begin. Samix started the brief by explaining that the deep scanners had identified a planet that may have high concentrations of exantium in it. As Samix droned on about the different materials in the crust, Zade queried the ship data stores about exantium and found that it was a robust and lightweight metal used by the Unity in all spacecraft. Zade shifted his attention back to Samix as she was closing out the list of other possible minerals on the planet. The planet had a climate signature similar to ones that supported large reptilian life. Samix closed with the mission statement and timeline. Zade was to use a team of SSILF to escort Axis to the surface, where he would run tests and identify the estimated concentration of exantium. The target planet was one of four of interest and would be the first stop after the deep space scan was complete. Estimated time until orbit was 72 ship hours. Samix finished, waited for questions, and headed for the door.

Zade hustled past an anxious Axis who was rambling off questions to himself as he tried to catch up with Samix.

"Captain, you have a minute?" Zade asked as he jogged up beside her.

"You have my ear until I get back to the command deck, security officer," she replied icily.

"I just wanted to apologize for what I said...though earlier. It was just some dumb trooper humor. It won't happen again."

"Noted, security," Samix said as she entered the command deck, closing the door behind her.

Zade, still standing at the bottom of the stairs that led to the command deck, turned and headed to the medical bay. Knowing the routine, Zade ditched his blouse and undershirt on a nearby chair as he climbed into the medical bed and waited for Jorloss to prep him for the nanite work.

"How long have you known the captain?" Zade asked.

"We've been friends since childhood. It was just dumb luck that we got stationed on the same ship. Why?" Jorloss answered as he did a final review of the program.

"Just wondering. Does she hold a grudge?"

"You're worried about her being angry at you for what you said."

"What the hell? She told you about that?"

"Yea, told me over dinner that night. It seemed a little crude but funny if you ask me. You know she *is* one of the better looking Xi'Ga. Not sure why you'd run away through miles of razors and acid if you saw her naked. The women of your species must be amazing," Jorloss said, shaking his head as he started the anesthesia.

With the anesthesia starting to take hold, Zade realized his joke must have translated wrong. Samix thought Zade had made a joke about how hideous she was.

"Wait…no. That's not what I…." was all he got out before he dozed off.

△△△

Zade awoke from the second and final bout of nanite changes to Jorloss hovering over him with a worried look.

"You were under longer than expected. The ship is already in its final orbit," Jorloss said as soon as he saw Zade's eyes open.

Zade had hoped to have enough time to redesign the SSILF he would use for the landing party before the actual landing. Based on what Jorloss told him, he didn't suspect he would have the time. Jorloss insisted on running a function check on Zade's new senses, and, although initially irritated, he consented. After the checks, he was happy that all sensory improvements had an on-off switch, especially the smell and infrared.

After Jorloss was satisfied that everything was appropriately implemented, Zade headed to the robotics lab to get ready for his first mission. As he turned out of the front stairwell, he could see Axis waiting by the door to his lab. As Zade closed with Axis, the tiny alien flew into a storm of scatterbrained questions about the mission and why he couldn't get into the lab to get SSILF to help him move his equipment. Zade opened the door while he calmed Axis down. After stepping into the lab, Zade headed to two of the maintenance SSILF on the wall and asked Axis if they would be sufficient.

"Well, I need all of them. I have a lot of equipment."

"Axis, I need to keep some on board in reserve. How much stuff do you have, and how quickly do you need them to move it?"

"All the equipment is ready to move into the cargo bay now, and there are six crates."

Jesus, just like a POG. Take enough shit on a mission to start a small community.

"All right. I have to fabricate more for the security party anyway. I will send three to your lab as I complete them. Two haulers and a loader. If there's nothing else, please get out; I have a lot of work to do."

Obviously satisfied with Zade's plan of action, Axis made his way out of the robotics lab, leaving Zade to begin on the laundry list of tasks for the mission. First, Zade pulled up the specs for the maintenance variant SSILF. After replacing the arms with a second set of legs, Zade bent the SSILF over, turning it into a new variant which he called a pack mule. Zade would fabricate two of these and use them to carry Axis's gear. As the two large fabrication tubes began work on the pack mules, Zade connected with the one maintenance variant SSILF in the lab. Quickly wiping any earlier programming, Zade instructed the machine that this SSILF's primary mission was to load and unload the new pack mules and informed it that it would take all orders from Axis. After briefing the SSILF, Zade pulled up the specs for the new railgun he had been working on. So far, it was the exact same weapon that the combat SSILF carried with the addition of a self-contained power source. The power source could power 200 shots; he figured he would go through almost three power sources per magazine of pellets. He then adjusted the stock to more closely resemble firearms he was used to, which had trigger assemblies. The last thing he included before fabrication was a targeting sensor that, when paired with his interface, would display a targeting reticle in his field of vision when pointed in the same direction he was looking.

Zade sent the model to the small fabrication machine as he grabbed the 1911 from his workstation. The weapon currently had an eight-round magazine in it, and Zade found that both extras were still in working order. Zade took everything and started a layout on the table closest to the rolling door. The pack mule SSILFs and railgun finished at the same time. After adding his new primary weapon system to his layout, he instructed the pack mules to follow the maintenance SSILF to the terraforming lab. Just as he finished moving the two additional power sources for the railgun, he received a message from Axis.

Wow! These are brilliant. By adding two extra legs, you have essentially doubled their carrying capacity. I can't believe we didn't think of it earlier. What are you going to call them?

Pack mules, Zade replied without removing his attention from the combat SSILF he was designing for the mission.

After seeing how useful they were in combat last time, Zade planned on using them as forward observers to identify threats.

After identifying the threats, he would be able to engage or maneuver as needed. This particular variant still carried a weapon, but that is where the similarities stopped. He improved the sensor suite and movement speed on the new observer models and finished by coating the whole SSILF in paramagnetic paint, which would act as adaptive camouflage. Once on the ground, he would send the observers out in every direction to act as a perimeter, and as they spotted movement, he would be alerted. While watching their sensor feeds, if a threat was spotted, he could instruct the SSILF to engage or do nothing and allow him to engage the target.

After instructing the two large fabrication tubes to begin fabricating three of the observer SSILF in each, Zade started looking at ancillary yet necessary equipment that he would need for the mission. After sending designs for a sling, load-carrying belt with appropriate pouches and thigh holster, and a couple of signal flares to the small fabrication machine, he received a message from Samix informing him that the last orbital scan was complete and he was required in the ready room for final brief.

Zade entered an already buzzing, ready room. On his way up, he felt the harmonics of the ship change, indicating that they had started through the atmosphere towards the surface. Everyone on the crew was present, except for Mur. Upon seeing Zade, Samix began to explain the situation and objective. The planet was currently going through some dinosaur period, and the dominant species consisted of giant reptiles. The world averaged 100 degrees Fahrenheit which made it ideal for the creatures. This planet also seemed to be undergoing some geological changes, as there were hundreds of underground vibrations recorded during the orbits. The ship would be landing in the only accessible area near the research site, about three kilometers away. Axis and the security team would have to move to the research site on foot, while Samix, Jorloss, and Mur stayed with the ship for control purposes. She turned the floor over to

Axis, who explained that he would only need an hour at the site to collect the required information. After Axis's portion of the brief, Samix instructed Zade to brief the security plan. Zade informed everyone about how he intended to use the new SSILF as observers. He would be going out with six, but there were three extras in the lab if they were needed. After Zade completed his portion, Samix informed the crew that they had twenty minutes until landfall and headed back to the command deck.

As Zade and Axis headed back down to their respective labs, they brainstormed possible situations that could arise. Although Axis appeared to be a simple scientist, he had decided to carry a defensive side arm after his last landing. Zade entered the robotics lab and was startled to find that none of the observer SSILF were standing by the rolling door. Moving towards the now quiet fabrication tubes, a sense of panic began to form in Zade's stomach. As a last-ditch effort, Zade decided to look for any heat signatures in the lab. After bringing up the thermals, he could see the six heat signatures lined up across the back of the lab. They had their camouflage on, and even though Zade was only two feet away from them, he couldn't see them without his new thermal vision. Zade instructed the SSILF to turn black while he kitted up. After one final inspection of the SSILF to ensure they didn't have any defects, Zade engaged their camouflage and headed into the cargo bay to meet up with Axis.

CHAPTER 7

Trailed by the cloaked SSILF, Zade entered the cargo bay. Axis was already stationed by the rear ramp reviewing the equipment he had loaded on the pack mules. As Zade walked up beside the small alien, he could tell that Axis was anxious about going onto the planet.

"You ready for this?" Zade asked.

"Just another walk in the park," Axis replied nonchalantly, his body language and nervous ticks betraying his worry.

"We'll be fine. Just stay inside the security and focus on getting your work done," Zade said, trying to calm Axis.

Either Axis was too nervous to notice that Zade appeared alone or had complete confidence in Zade's abilities. Either way, Axis didn't seem to have a problem with the team lacking any additional SSILF help. While the two waited for the ship to land, Zade did one final check on the SSILF, first on the camouflage by cycling it on and off, and next on the sensor feeds by viewing them sequentially through his interface. Just as Zade finished the sensor check, Samix walked into the cargo bay.

"We are not going to be able to land; the tectonic activity is too strong," she informed the landing party.

"So, what are we doing then? Do we head back into orbit to

wait the tremors out?" Zade inquired.

"No luck. We're going to keep the gravitational drive engaged and stay at a hover."

Zade could feel the atmospheric buffering on the ship stop as she finished. The ship had finally broken through the atmosphere and was on its final approach. Another few minutes passed before the ramp began to lower. Zade walked to the end of the still moving ramp to survey the landing zone. The first thing he noticed was how fast the clouds on this planet were ripping across the sky. Next, he took a quick survey of the dense jungle surrounding the landing zone. Zade also used his thermals to scan the area as well. He did not actually expect to notice any giant reptiles but was mildly disappointed he couldn't see any. It was going to be an arduous trek to the site. The jungle was exceptionally well developed due to the high temperature, long days, and oxygen-rich atmosphere of the planet.

Satisfied that he wasn't going to be sending any of the SSILF directly into the jaws of a waiting velociraptor, Zade ordered them off the ramp to set the perimeter. The camouflage worked exceptionally well, and as the SSILF landed, the only way to identify them was by the slight disturbance their bodies caused as they crossed through blowing debris. The improved speed of the new observer variants was impressive. They had a 500-meter perimeter established before the ship even settled into its final hover height. Happy to see that the observers' feeds were unpopulated, Zade stepped off the ramp into the maelstrom caused by the ship's engines. Looking back up at the open ramp, expecting to see Axis, Zade noticed that the ship was hovering at just over three stories above him. The skeletal and musculature improvements made the jump feel like nothing more than stepping out of the back of a pickup truck.

While watching the ramp for the other half of his landing team, Zade saw a frightened blue face peak over the edge of the ramp. Samix, worried that Zade had inadvertently fallen, peered down into the fray. Zade waved at her to indicate that he was fine and motioned to send Axis and his equipment down.

I thought you fell off the ramp. Why the hell did you jump from this far up? Samix snarled in Zade's head.

Just wanted to see how the new modifications were working. Plus, I needed to be down here to pull security before Axis came down. Where is the little guy?

He's trying to find a way down. He, unlike you, is not dumb enough to just jump out of a moving spaceship.

Tell him to send the SSILF out the door. They're capable of making the jump, and their impact-dampening hardware will protect the equipment. On a different note, do you have something on board that we can use to cut through this jungle? I didn't think to make anything in the lab.

After Samix's face receded back into the cargo bay, Zade began a quick patrol around the perimeter of the landing zone. As he walked around the outer edge of the landing zone, Zade peered into the dense foliage. The jungle was dark. The trees blotted out almost all of the sunlight. Since he had touched down, the planet below his feet was constantly vibrating. From what he could gather, the vibrations were changing frequency and intensity, but most importantly, they seemed to be coming from the opposite direction of the objective. After completing a full sweep, Zade headed back to the ramp. Entering the maelstrom under the ship, Zade could see three distinct heat signatures below the ramp. Samix had sent the pack mules and maintenance variant out while Zade was patrolling.

Zade moved the SSILF out of the way just as a rope dropped down from the lip of the ramp. Zade made a mental note about changing the pack mules' head structure. The two on the ground still had humanoid heads and faces. It made their necks bend at a grotesque, unappealing angle that made them eerie to look at. As soon as Zade got back on the ship, he would change them to more closely resemble the head of some naturally four-legged animal. Zade turned to see the rope dangling from the ship and immediately shot a message to Samix:

If we have ropes, why are we parked so far away from the site? You could have just flown us over it and let us rope out of the ship.

For two reasons, first, roping into an objective is a direct-action tactic, taught only to troops at the Military Academe. Second, I figured a pleasant jaunt through that miserable jungle would give you time to reflect on both your position and station aboard this ship.

Are you serious about yourself right now? I have already apologized for the thought. Plus, sticking me down here, I understand, but risking the safety of one of your scientists?

Samix disconnected the rope Axis had used to get to the planet with a smirk and hit the button to close the ramp. On the ground, Zade saw the rope come loose and stepped over to pull Axis out of the way of it. Axis had started to unbuckle his harness after making it to the ground while standing directly under the now freefalling rope. Axis's frustration at being handled turned to surprise as he watched the rope slam into the ground, leaving a large divot right where he had been standing. Setting Axis down, Zade headed to the pack mules. Two machetes had been hastily attached to the top of the crates of equipment.

After handing one of the machetes to Axis, Zade checked on the observers. Seeing clear screens, Zade began heading towards the objective with Axis behind and the SSILF bringing up the rear. Based on the sun's location over the horizon, Zade estimated that they had, at best, four hours of sunlight left, so he set a hard pace.

It seems passive-aggressive knows no bounds. At least this punishment is just a walk in the forest; if I had done that back home to a female superior, the penalty would have been worse.

ΔΔΔ

Samix, proud of herself for putting Zade in his place about his insolence, disconnected the rope Axis used to get down to the planet, closed the ramp, and headed to the galley. With the ship hovering above the planet, she would not be needed on the command deck until Axis and Zade returned to the ship. Mur would continue monitoring the team's progress and running further tests on the planet, meaning that she could relax for a while.

As she headed to the galley, a ship alert popped into her field of view. Mur had finished analyzing the crust vibrations and noted that, unlike normal tectonic activity, which propagates from a single point, these vibrations seemed to be moving down fault lines. Excited that she may have found a unique planet whose tectonics were different from any other known rocky world, Samix ensured that the data was uploaded to the data drone. Samix walked into the galley where Jorloss was already eating.

"So, what are you going to do with the couple hours of downtime we have?" She asked.

"I'm going to keep studying Zade's biology," Jorloss answered. "His body has taken to the nanite modifications better than any species I have ever seen."

"Speaking of Zade," Samix chuckled, "you should have seen his face when he realized his long hike was because of his smart mouth."

"Oh... I meant to tell you. Zade and I talked about that little incident before he went down for his last nanite treatment. Just as he went to sleep, he was trying to argue a point. I decided to take a look at the data. I pulled up the message, and there seemed to be some kind of translation error. It wasn't an insult at all; I think it was a compliment," Jorloss said, just before heading back to the medical bay.

As Jorloss headed out of the galley, Samix pulled up the statement she remembered Zade saying. Sure enough, it was a compliment with the corrected translation, albeit a compliment wrapped in dark, dirty, troop humor. Samix contemplated what she had done. She had sent this human, the one who saved both her and Jorloss from certain death, out on a romp through the jungle of a dangerous planet. Samix could only sit and think about the best way to resolve this issue. She was the top graduate from the Academe and the only candidate to make it into the exploration branch. Based on her stellar performance during shipside training, she was hand-selected as one of three captains to command the Unity's experimental ships, and she had let a perceived slight cloud her judgment.

She vowed then never to let personal issues ever play into her decision-making again. The exploration corps, the crew, and her reputation deserved better from her.

$$\triangle\triangle\triangle$$

Zade led the group to the edge of the clearing, constantly checking the observers' feeds as he went. The six observers would maintain a 500-meter perimeter around the landing party, which meant they would move as the group did. With one final check, Zade unsheathed the machete and began clearing an entrance into the jungle. He hoped that once the group got past the edge of the clearing, the underbrush would thin, allowing quicker movement to the objective. To his dismay, the underbrush was as thick in the depths of the jungle as it was on the edge.

The progress was slow as Zade had to clear a path for the team. Axis lacked both the physical capabilities and mental toughness to perform any duration of manual labor. After only 15 feet or so, Axis had decided to let Zade do the work, sheathed his implement, and climbed on top of one of the pack mules to ride the rest of the way.

As Zade was clearing a path, sweating in the harsh climate around him, Axis rambled about anything that popped into his mind; most of his stories were about his homeworld and his species, who called themselves settlers. They evolved on a planet that was far too small to support a large population. Thus, the species evolved to use as little energy as possible and survive in the harshest conditions. As their home planet became more crowded and stressed, the settlers began genetically modifying their population to reduce demand. The first stage of modifications reduced their size substantially, which reduced the number of resources they required. Although the improvement prolonged the life of the planet, it wasn't enough, and the settlers had to resort to more extreme changes. In a second attempt to extend the survival of the species, the settlers changed their genetic code, so their eyes were replaced by infrared sensing pits. The pits still allowed them to sense predators, but by removing their visual equipment, they reduced their energy demands by 15 percent. Realizing that the planet was still dying, the settlers began searching for answers away from their homeworld. The settlers developed terraforming technology to colonize the asteroids surrounding their world, the exodus that gave rise to the new name of the species. As a final attempt to save the species, one last genetic modification was made in the group bred to colonize the asteroids. This generation would have the systems to gain nutrition directly from the minerals and ores of their planet, which was the purpose of the strange mouth that Zade had noticed. As the settlers ate the local ores, their skin changed color, giving them natural adaptive camouflage, which was an unintended benefit of their plight.

Upon arrival to the newly terraformed asteroids, the genetic modifications paid off, as the atmosphere and ecology were still too weak to support the settlers' earlier bodies. Understanding that they were running out of time, the new settlers began to tinker with the terraforming equipment to expedite the process of creating usable land. In addition to learning the inner workings of terraforming, the Settlers had hundreds of different asteroids being terraformed at the same time. This allowed them to refine the process, increase the number of applicable planets, and increase the terraforming process's success rate from 10 percent to nearly 99 percent. By keeping the terraforming techniques and methods secret, this once doomed, almost extinct species became one of the most powerful factions in the Unity, providing services to any species looking to expand their habitable region for the right price.

Luckily, as the team crept through the jungle, Axis babbling away through the communicator, Zade didn't notice anything on the perimeter feeds. What did worry Zade was that the tremors seemed to be getting stronger; Zade tried to tell himself that it was stronger and not closer. He could feel his uneasiness building with the quakes.

"Axis, could you take a break from your leisurely ride through the woods and pay attention to the tremors? It feels like they're getting stronger."

"Excuse me, I'm a scientist, and unlike you, I never grew a fondness for mindless labor or this much walking," Axis stated. "I have to say, though, you did a great job on this new SSILF. I can't feel a thing up here."

"I appreciate the assist, you eyeless alien midget," Zade replied sarcastically.

Axis burst out laughing, placing a limb across his midsection but not jumping down from his throne.

It took another two hours before Zade's interface indicated that they had reached the site. The jungle loosened slightly at the sight because the bedrock was too close to the surface to allow any deep-rooted plants to grow. Just north of the site, running northwest to the southeast, was a cliff that towered 200 feet above the landing team. By the time the team reached the site, the sun was low on the horizon. Zade knew that by the time the group started making their way back to the ship, it would be dark. Running a short program on his interface, Zade had luminous, green waypoints evenly distributed along the length of the path the team had just cut through the jungle. It was a secondary safety measure, but Zade would be able to see the course even in the pitch black that would cover the planet's surface when night fell

Axis jumped off the pack mule and ordered the maintenance SSILF to unload the geological equipment. As Axis got to work, Zade repositioned the observers. The cliff would provide a fantastic watch position; Zade ordered one of the SSILF observers onto it. The ridge also limited the avenues of approach to the site, so Zade consolidated the remaining observers on the sides of the objective that was open to the jungle. Zade set all of the observers to scan their sectors and alert him of any movement or lifeforms in their field of view. After patrolling the area and monitoring the observers' sectors to ensure they interlocked, Zade propped himself against a rock outcropping and dozed off.

△△△

The tremors had grown strong enough to knock Zade onto his side and wake him. Night had fallen, and the worksite was blanketed in the inky blackness that only arises on a moonless night. Standing, Zade looked around and saw Axis, seemingly oblivious to the strange and worsening conditions on the planet. Zade checked all of the observer feeds, but nothing was out there.

Are you guys alright out there? It looks like the earthquakes are moving along fault lines towards your position, Samix asked over Zade's interface.

Since when do earthquakes move? Zade responded.

It's a new phenomenon; we've never seen it before this planet.

The unease settled back into the pit of Zade's stomach. He had never done any work in geology, but he did know the basic principles surrounding earthquakes, the main one being that earthquakes are stationary. Years of combat had honed Zade's ability to warn him when something wasn't quite right; right now, his body was screaming at him that something was very wrong.

How many of these new moving earthquakes are closing on our position?

There are three, one from the north, one from the west, and one from our position.

Alright, I've got an awful feeling about this. We will keep you in the loop.

Huh, bad feeling. I didn't realize you had that much planetary exploration experience, Samix replied, knowing that humans had never set foot off their own homeworld. It was a nastier response than Samix had planned; she couldn't really figure out why she felt she had an ax to grind with Zade.

Funny, but I do have experience getting blown up by things I can't see. Just send me the feed with the earthquake locations. Zade shot back before he cut communications with the ship.

Zade knew that something was very wrong about this planet, but he couldn't pinpoint what it was. Now he could *see* the vibrations shaking through the trees toward him. The tremors coming from the north and west looked like they were going to hit their location simultaneously, with the one coming from the ship would hit their position shortly after. As the first two tremors hit the perimeter, there was a disturbance on three of the observer feeds, then they went dark. Rerunning the now dead feeds, Zade could see rocks and debris flying up from the ground just as the feeds died. Zade finally connected the dots. The vibrations weren't being caused by earthquakes; something was moving underground, causing the tremors. The geological testing must have attracted them, which is why Zade and or anyone on the ship hadn't noticed significant movement until Axis started his testing.

As Zade put it together, the last thing hit both his and Axis's position. Zade began running toward Axis, who was now unable to stand due to the movement of the planet underfoot. As Zade grabbed Axis, pulling him away from his equipment, the ground began to give way. Tossing Axis behind the safety of a large boulder, Zade turned to see a large, mole-like creature emerge from the worksite, swallowing the three SSILF in the process. The mammoth rodent breached through the rocky ground with ease. It had the body of a standard subterranean mammal, but its back was covered in protective plating. Zade could see that large rocks had gotten wedged between the plates, making the creature almost invulnerable when standing on all fours.

Zade ordered the remaining SSILF to his position and instructed them to begin firing on the giant mole. Hundreds of rounds from the railguns failed to penetrate the hard, protective shell of the monster. However, the ineffective fire drew the creature's attention to the SSILF. It destroyed them with one snap of its massive jaws. Zade used the temporary distraction to spur Axis into action.

"We should probably be getting back to the ship. Now. Here is our route," Zade said as he transferred the waypoint data to Axis.

"What the hell do I do with this. I can't outrun that thing! My legs are tiny," Axis replied frantically.

"Just follow the markers and run like hell. Call up the ship once you get back into the thicker jungle, make sure you can get on the ship as soon as you get to it," Zade said as he turned away from Axis.

Axis took off at a dead sprint, leaving Zade to deal with the mole monster. Zade circled the monster just out of its reach, taking the occasional pot shot to keep its attention. Zade realized how good of an idea the vision augmentations were. Without them, Zade wouldn't have stood a chance; one trip, fall, or misstep would have meant certain death. As he circled, Zade had to stay out of reach of the creature's large, digging claws. Zade continued firing, using the targeting reticle in his interface to aim for any soft spots on the animal.

As Zade ran his first power source dry, he knew he had to do something to even the odds. The first few rounds out of the second power source were aimed at the animal's exposed feet. Although not exceptionally effective, the shots did seem to slow the animal down. As his desperation grew, Zade tried to formulate some plan to best this animal. Realizing that most subterranean animals were susceptible to light, Zade pulled one of the signal flares out of his cargo pocket. Taking aim as the animal rounded on him, Zade shot the flare directly into the giant animal's head. As he had hoped, after the flare impacted the creature, it reared back, exposing its soft underbelly. With no time to lose, Zade took aim with his railgun, flipped its selector switch from safe to auto, and drained his second to last power source into the animal. All 196 rounds from the expended power source connected in a tight group between the creature's front legs. The rounds sprayed viscera everywhere and left a neat, basketball-sized hole in the underside of the animal. It was dead before it hit the ground.

Quickly switching to his railgun's last power source, Zade heard the unmistakable sound of the animal's companions surfacing for some action. The two creatures approached apprehensively, measuring up the tiny creature that had dispatched their comrade. They were on a path that would trap Zade against the cliff face if they continued unchecked. Zade felt his cargo pocket and was disappointed to find he only had one flare left. Grabbing it, he edged closer to the tree line, waiting for the nearest creature to get within effective range. As the animal closest to the jungle closed with Zade, he fired the flare and terminated it in the same manner as the first. Now out of ammo and running out of luck, Zade tossed the currently empty railgun and drew his sidearm.

Why didn't I make grenades instead of putting these stupid ivory grips on this thing?

Zade made a break for the jungle, hoping that if he could close the 200 yards and make it into the wilderness, he would have better chances. The last mole was hot on him, unbelievably fast for a creature its size. Halfway to the trees, Zade realized that he wasn't going to make it. As he turned to make his last stand, Samix and the XES01 came screaming overhead, low and fast. Startled by the sudden appearance of the ship and all of the bright lights, the mole froze, its flight instincts kicking in. Zade looked up at the ship and saw a rope dangling just out of reach. Holstering his sidearm, Zade took a couple steps, jumped, and grabbed it. Realizing that its prey was getting away, the mole sprang into action and sprinted towards Zade. It lunged but was too late. The ship had already cleared the treetops and was moving back toward the landing zone.

While the XES01 was still in flight, Zade hauled himself up the rope and onto the loading ramp. He was greeted by Jorloss and a visibly rattled Axis at the top. As he got to his feet, Zade cut the rope loose and closed the ramp door. The post-combat crash was starting to kick in, and Zade felt exhausted. Zade walked over to one of the storage crates in the bay and sat down. As he did, Samix came running in to see how her crew had fared. Jorloss was the first to speak.

"Are you hurt?"

"No, I'm fine. You ok?" Zade replied, looking from Jorloss to Axis.

"I'm Ok. I started running, thinking you were right behind me. When I turned around to look, and you weren't there, I knew what you had done. I knew that I had to make it to the ship, or you wouldn't have a chance," Axis said. "Thank you. Not many people would have done that for a settler."

"No problem. I'm glad you made it back. Sorry you lost the data you were gathering," Zade started.

"Thank you for getting Axis back," Samix interrupted. "I don't think I could have handled losing another crewmember."

"Like I was saying, I'm glad he made it back to the ship. You guys are on an important mission, and it's my job to ensure everyone gets home safe. Well, almost everyone," Zade said, the last part hushed and primarily to himself.

Samix must have heard because the smile she wore at her landing team's rescue turned into a look of great sadness. As the crew stood in uneasy silence, Axis could no longer control himself. The small alien had become extraordinarily talkative and excited and had to tell Zade about what he had accomplished. Zade wasn't quite sure if Axis's story was meant as a boast or an attempt to gain the approval of his crewmates. Axis reassured Zade that the data was not a loss, explaining that the Settlers had a large storage device implanted in their skulls at a young age. This allowed them to store all instrument readouts and large sums of data in their heads. It was a measure to prevent terraforming procedures from falling into the wrong hands. Axis had been storing all the data he found at the site in his head, and as soon as he boarded the ship, it was uploaded to the data drone.

After assuring Zade that the mission wasn't a loss, Axis began explaining the events that transpired after the two had separated. After realizing that Zade was buying him time, Axis contacted Samix to update her on the situation. Knowing that Zade would need help, Samix had moved the ship toward Axis. He boarded the ship and had Samix fly it to the test site. Axis further explained that after monitoring the conversation between Zade and Samix about roping into the objective, he knew that he could hang another rope from the loading ramp, and Zade would be able to escape using it. Zade thanked the settler for the rescue, a gesture that caused Axis to swell with pride.

"You're thanking me, but without your actions, there wouldn't have been a rescue for me to orchestrate. You are one of the only people in the Unity who would have risked his own life to help a settler. You saved my life twice on this mission, and my people will hear about what you did. We will name new planets after you," Axis said.

Sometime during Axis's story, both Jorloss and Samix had returned to their respective work areas, leaving only the two members of the landing party in the cargo bay. Zade smiled at the thought of having a planet named after him and stood. Inviting Axis to join him for a meal, Zade explained that he was famished. Not only was Zade hungry, but during the rescue, Zade tore a couple of muscles in his left shoulder when he grabbed the rope Axis had provided for egress. The nanites warned him of damage as soon as it had happened, but only after Zade was safe aboard the ship did the nanites output a full damage report with related resources required for repair.

Still filthy from their escapade, the two men sat down to a large meal in the galley. During the dinner, the men chatted. Zade used the conversation to learn more about Axis, understanding that he must know as much as possible about his new situation to survive in the Unity. As the men ate, Zade learned that the Settler faction of the Unity was called the T.A.R.C.C., or the Terraforming and Resource Collection Conglomerate. The T.A.R.C.C. was the largest and most financially influential faction in the Unity.

During the formative years of the settlers, much of the Unity's citizenry despised the settlers because of their looks, reasoning that no species as strange as the settlers could be equal to the sentient species that already made up the Unity. With the ensuing peace created by the formation of the Unity, many of the member species began to outgrow their home worlds and were forced to find other planets to populate. After many failed terraforming attempts, the species started to look towards the settlers for their services. As the settlers amassed great wealth from the terraforming services they provided, they were begrudgingly admitted into the Unity as a full member species. As the T.A.R.C.C.'s wealth and corresponding influence grew, their reputation deteriorated. The settlers were viewed as a necessary evil, accepted but despised by the other members of the Unity.

Because of the hostile social and political environment in

which the settlers lived, the species was forced to become almost reclusive in nature, looking inward for solutions to any problems that the species faced. Internally, the settlers were structured into tribes and had a rigid class system. The tribes were based on the condition of the first colonies. The most powerful tribes, of which Axis was part, developed on planets that were terraforming successes. In contrast, the less powerful tribes were forced to relocate to successfully terraformed planets after their home-world terraforming projects failed. The classes in this society were based on the generations separated from the initial settlers who left their home world to settle the asteroids. Thus, the oldest members of the species closest to the original settlers held the highest class and were known colloquially as Ancients, while the youngest held the lowest rank and were known as Children. Outsiders and the settlers who left the T.A.R.C.C. were known as Wanderers and made up the lowest tribe and class possible.

Axis explained that a yearlong ceremony was held during the year following the death of the final settler in a generation. The first half of the year was spent remembering the accomplishments of the generation that had passed. The second half was spent ensuring that all of the lost generation's knowledge was passed to the generation which would rise to prominence in the tribes. Order was maintained by a strict set of laws developed and enforced by the Ancients. The laws guaranteed the survival of the species, and many infractions elicited a punishment of death or exile, which ensured that no defective settler could attain the class of ancient.

Axis formally introduced himself as the first son of the Elder Ancient of the highest tribe in the T.A.R.C.C. His father was charged with running the T.A.R.C.C. and representing the settlers to the Unity. As the first son, Axis would inherit his father's responsibilities someday.

"Pleasure to meet you officially, Axis. I have to ask, though, if you are royalty in your species, why were you sent on such a dangerous mission?" Zade asked, curiosity now peaked by Axis's story.

"This crew's mission is an extremely prestigious one," Axis explained. "My father should have been the representative of our species to the worlds explored by this ship but could not leave due to his responsibilities within the Unity. I, as his heir, was selected in his stead."

Zade spent the rest of the meal introducing himself and explaining some of the finer points about mankind. The arrogance he once felt based on his position in the army had now been tempered by realizing that his new status meant less than nothing compared to others in the Unity. The two men finished eating and headed to their quarters. Once inside, Zade turned on one of his favorite playlists as he showered and prepared for bed. As Zade laid in bed, unable to sleep, he thought about the repercussions of his actions to save Axis.

ΔΔΔ

The next few days were uneventful, as the ship was on a short jump to the next planet of interest. Zade spent the time interacting with the crew and improving the kit he would carry planet side. Learning from the past exploration jaunt, Zade developed a myriad of different weapons and defenses that he could choose based on the ship's threat analysis. Interaction with the crew, although not unpleasant, was minimal. The other crew members were absorbed in their research and only left their labs to eat and sleep.

Just before the night cycle on the third day of the flight, Samix called Zade up to the command deck. Unsure of what to expect, Zade worked to a good stopping point on the new SSILF he was designing and readied himself for the icy, passive-aggressive bout that he was expecting. As he exited the robotics lab headed for the command deck, Samix's voice popped into his ear:

I'll meet you up there in a second; I'm grabbing a cup of sloop. Want one?

Sure. Care to give me a heads up on what this meeting is about?

Just a mission brief. We should be hitting orbit any minute now.

Zade beat Samix to the command deck and took a seat at one of the workstations while he waited for her. Looking out the viewing windows, Zade could see a small, white marble slowly growing in size and guessed that it was the planet they would be exploring. Samix walked onto the command deck, handed Zade his mug, and leaned against the workstation he was sitting at. Looking past her, Zade could see that the icy planet now took up most of the windows on the command deck. Samix turned and bent over another workstation, back to Zade, where she input the commands to start orbital surveys of the planet. With one of Samix's more exemplary characteristics at eye level and enticingly close to him, Zade couldn't figure out what game she was playing. Was she taunting him into shooting his mouth off again, so she could send him out on another suicide mission? Was she toying with him? Was it an ego or dominance thing? Zade wasn't sure, but he did know the last time he was in this situation, he reacted and earned himself a nasty backhand and a mission that almost killed him. Trying to separate himself from the problem, Zade pushed his chair backward. It was mounted to the workstation, so it didn't budge. Doing the next best thing, Zade closed his eyes and waited for Samix to stand back up. When he heard movement, Zade opened his eyes. He saw Samix looking back at him, the slightest hint of a smirk on her face.

She's toying with me. Trying to get a reaction so she can send me out to die on another stupid mission.

"This is our next target. We need to get data from some ice cores on the planet. You and I will be the landing team," Samix said, pointing to the planet, barely able to keep the snicker out of her voice.

Awesome, she isn't even going to let the local wildlife do me in. She's going take me down and either leave me or kill me herself.

Zade had been burnt by lousy leadership before, granted they were all human, but this reeked of bad. Samix started the brief by explaining that initial surveys put the planet's surface at around -300 degrees, making it inhospitable for any life to develop. Usually, Zade would use an environmental suit and take the core samples himself, but because he didn't know the technology, Samix would have to go down as well. The environment was too extreme to adapt to even with nanites, so Zade would need to use Fern's environmental protection suit. The suit was the only one aboard that could protect its user from the harsh conditions on the surface, and Zade was the only one who would fit inside it.

Samix, as a Xi'Ga, could handle the extreme temperature without protection and could complete the work on her own; however, after recent incidents, Samix had made the determination that anyone leaving the ship would have a buddy. The temperatures were too low to use SSILF, as their internal workings would freeze shortly after being exposed to the atmosphere, so Zade would be doing the heavy lifting. The ship would land and offload the crew, who would then walk for five kilometers, in any direction, away from the landing site. This was to prevent the landing zone, which was all ice, from collapsing due to the weight of the ship combined with the integrity loss from core drilling. After the cores were drilled, Samix would drop a sensor through the hole and into the ocean below. The sensor would collect data on the lifeforms and makeup of the sea. Upon completing testing, Zade would carry the equipment back to the ship.

After explaining the mission, Samix led Zade to the cargo bay, where she showed him the environmental protective suit he would be using. Samix showed Zade to a nine-foot-tall crate stowed in the corner near the ramp. As she opened the container, Zade could see the towering, yellow, and green protective suit. The suit looked like high-tech armor, capable of withstanding some severe abuse. It was entirely mustard yellow, with a green face shield and green circle on the left chest plate.

"That is beautiful and ugly at the same time. Fern must have had a horrible fashion sense," Zade quipped.

"Fern didn't have a choice," Samix shot back. "Those are the exploration corps colors, green on yellow with a circle emblem. Combat is red on grey with a triangle emblem. Transport is white on blue with a solid white square emblem. Command is red on red with no emblem. Do you want to see how it works?"

"Absolutely," Zade said as he walked around the masterpiece in awe.

Samix walked up to the suit, pressed some buttons on the left wrist, which caused the back and shoulder area to slide open. As the back was sliding apart, splitting right where the spine would be, the upper body of the suit leaned forward. After some instruction, Zade climbed onto a nearby crate and stepped into the suit. As both feet firmly planted, Zade could feel the inside of the legs expand to fill the gap between his legs and the suit. Samix instructed Zade to lean forward and place his face in the helmet while sliding his arms into the arms of the suit. Like with the legs, the arms compressed, making the suit form-fitting. With his arms snugly secured in the suit, Zade straightened his back so that he was standing upright. As he did, he could feel the back of the suit and helmet closing, and like the arms and legs, the torso compressed to make the suit form-fitting.

"The suit needs to be calibrated, and you need to be familiarized with its functions. Stay here, and work through the functions check. It should take you 30 minutes, which is what the suit requires to calibrate," Samix said as she turned to head back to the command deck.

Zade tried to turn and look at her, but the suit had not engaged movement capabilities yet. Bringing his attention back to the face shield, an introductory welcome message and brief description scrolled over the visor. The suit connected directly with the user's interface, and the goal of Argyle Industries, the suit manufacturer, scrolled across the screen: *So comfortable, you forget you're in a protective suit.* The suit was a standard bipedal model that could be used by any species that would fit in it. Thus, the suit required 30 minutes in a controlled environment to determine the user's environmental needs. To accomplish this, the suit would run a function check for any first-time user, during which a user profile would be created. Whenever a previous user interface was identified, the suit would skip the functions test.

The test began by ensuring that the suit could operate in any known conditions. As the test's motor skills portion started, a warning displayed saying that the suit could increase the user's strength tenfold and that they should take care when trying to complete delicate tasks. After the warning, the display prompted Zade to move every joint independently across its full range of motion. This allowed the suit to establish safety stops to prevent the user from hyperextending joints. After Zade finished walking two laps around the cargo bay, the final prompt, the suit began describing the user interface on the visor.

The visor could display anything the user could view through their interface, but the exploration model came standard with a small map in the right corner, with known locations pinpointed in different colors to denote if they were friendly or unfriendly. A small screen in the opposite corner showed a compass with waypoint indicators across the top and external conditions listed down the left side. Combat models had more armor and could also display ammunition capacity and team member status on the left side in place of environmental conditions.

The final phase of the familiarization covered entering and exiting procedures and any additional suit features. Since Zade now had a profile created in the suit, he would never have to manually open or close the suit. Users could instruct the suit to open and close through their interface. Unlike other equipment on the ship, only users could instruct the suit to open or close, a measure to prevent accidental exposure to the atmosphere. The only additional features the suit had were twin 1,000-foot-long grappling hooks, one in each wrist, and feet with magnetic or spiked capabilities. With the final other features explained, the tutorial dialog box closed.

Whoever commissioned this suit must have had grand plans to traverse some broken terrain. But the spiked feet are going to come in handy on an ice planet, Zade thought.

How much stuff are we going to be taking on this trip? He asked Samix.

Everything we are taking is staged under the stairs on the side of the bay near the terraforming lab. Samix replied

Zade walked to the steps and saw the three crates that he would be carrying for the mission. Taking one at a time, Zade judged that all three combined weighed nearly 500 pounds.

After getting a feel for the load he would be carrying, Zade went back to the protective suit and began to inspect its exterior. The suit must have had some primitive form of AI because as Zade neared it, a message from the suit could be heard through his interface.

Hello, User Two. What do you need me to do? Said a female voice.

"Who is this?" Zade questioned aloud.

This is the Argyle Protective Suit for which you just established a profile. Would you like to add a unique username?

"What? The tutorial didn't say anything about an AI."

I am reserved only for users who chose to complete the tutorial.

"Fair enough, I guess weirder shit has happened to me this month. Call me Zade. Since I am talking to you, do you have a name?"

Hello Zade. I am designated as an environmental protection suit interface, or 'EPSI.' How can I help you today?

"I will be carrying 500 pounds of gear five kilometers while in the suit. I need a way to do so while keeping my hands free. Input?"

If you look at the back of the suit, you will see four large holes, two on either side of the back. These are quick-connect points for the Argyle load carrying system. After the suit is donned and closed, the user can attach the system. They are ballistic anchors that can quickly detach the load in case of emergency. They are capable of carrying 1000 pounds apiece. Made from...

"Enough, I have what I need. Thank you, EPSI. See you in a couple of hours," Zade said, cutting off the rambling AI.

CHAPTER 8

The ship was in its final orbit of the planet, after which Zade would be going out on a mission with Samix. He felt anxious about it, but not in the way he expected. He was almost excited to spend some time with her, one on one, though he didn't want to admit it, even to himself. In the robotics lab, he fabricated a carrying mount for the team's equipment, using the anchor point imagery captured earlier that day. He was working on his third and hopefully the last attempt. The first could hold the load, but as Zade picked up the frame and shook it, the bottom supports deformed and dumped the equipment on the floor. After reinforcing the support structure, the second frame's anchor stubs were misaligned, meaning it couldn't be hooked to the back of the suit. Zade hoped that this last attempt, the one being finished by the fabrication machine, would work.

Zade grabbed the frame as soon as the machine had finished making it. Still warm to the touch, Zade turned it over in his hands, inspecting it for any apparent defects. Finding none, he headed out the rolling doors directly into the cargo bay at the back of his lab. Lining up the frame, Zade pressed it to the back of the suit. It fit perfectly. As he removed his hands from the frame, it fell with a clunk to the floor.

Frustrated, Zade addressed the suit's AI, "EPSI, why won't the frame stay on the back of the suit?"

This equipment is not of Argyle Industries' design; I cannot allow it to be installed on the suit.

"Sure it is EPSI. I personally picked it up before we launched. I did modify it, though, which is probably the reason you can't recognize it," Zade lied.

Very well. Be advised the use of equipment not authorized for use with the suit by Argyle Industries constitutes a breach of contract and may lead to legal action.

"I would never even try that EPSI. I love Argyle Industries and their products," Zade said as he leaned down and grabbed the frame.

This time as Zade pressed the frame into the anchor points, there was the satisfying hiss as the anchors engaged. As he removed his hands, the frame stayed firmly in place. Zade walked over to the crates and moved them to the suit one by one. Without opening them, he had a good idea which one had the drill in it as it was the heaviest. He also guessed which had the sensor equipment in it, but the third was a mystery. When he tried to open it to see inside, Zade found that all three crates had been cipher locked, and only Samix could open them.

"EPSI, I want to do a test load of the equipment. If I start putting weight on your back, will you fall over?" Zade asked

I will adjust my center of gravity as the load is applied to prevent that.

As Zade loaded the crates, the suit began to lean forward, compensating for the weight. Zade knew that look; he had seen it many times before during his army career. It was the look every soldier had when overburdened by equipment. Zade had designed the hooks on the frame so that the crate handles would slip right over the pins to prevent them from falling off his back as he moved. Satisfied with how the crates sat, Zade began unloading the frame. With the frame empty and the suit standing upright once again, Zade ordered EPSI to release the frame. As the anchors released, the frame dropped straight down the back of the suit and landed standing up. Zade put the frame on a crate that lined up with the anchor points so he could back right up to it when he was in the suit. As he loaded the frame, he kept the sensors on the top; that way, when they reached the site, Samix could unload the sensors before he dropped the frame, preventing any damage to them.

Satisfied with his load plan, Zade headed back into his lab to grab a weapon and other parts of his kit. The lesson he had learned from the last encounter with wildlife was that he would never be caught unprepared again. Returning to the suit, Zade laid out the new equipment. He placed the improved railgun, which had new power sources with higher capacity, on the suit's right. Three railgun magazines now held small thermobaric rounds, and one contained armor-piercing rounds. The basic design of the thermobaric rounds allowed them to do, at a minimum, the same amount of damage as regular railgun rounds, but these were packed with explosives. They gave homage to munitions he used on Earth. Zade called them Excaliburs. Tiny sensors on the outside of the round would trigger the explosion when the round was surrounded by anything other than a gas. As a safety mechanism, Zade programed the rounds to not arm unless they had reached the high velocities achieved by being fired out of the railgun. An additional failsafe ensured that even if the rounds didn't explode, they would do incredible amounts of damage. When the explosives triggered inside of the threat, they would create a small pocket of extremely high temperature and pressure, which would expand, doing lethal damage. Zade had hoped that just one of these rounds could successfully neutralize a threat.

Zade had far less confidence in the armor-piercing rounds. If armor couldn't be pierced by a standard railgun round, Zade wasn't sure anything could, but he decided to try. These rounds differed from standard rounds only in shape and material. Whereas the original rounds for the railgun were tiny pellets, these were mini sabot rounds made out of the hardest material Zade could find in the database. The tips of the rounds were milled to a fine point and coated in diamond. Ideally, all of the force generated by the railgun would be focused on the tiny end of the round and push it through any armor.

The last piece of equipment Zade laid out was his utility belt with a new load-carrying vest. The vest was a compression sleeve that extended from Zade's chest to waist and held pouches of grenades, additional ammunition, a knife, and anything else Zade felt he would need for the mission. Attached to the bottom side of the belt was a thigh holster for his 1911. The ivory-handled 1911 was the same as it had been on Earth, but Zade had created ammunition for it that mimicked the new shot he made for the railgun. As he finished inspecting the gear on the load-carrying belt, Zade felt the ship start to vibrate as it entered the atmosphere.

I'm headed back to you now. We should be on the ground in five minutes, Samix said through Zade's interface.

Zade leaned against the protective suit and waited for Samix to arrive in the cargo bay. Zade felt himself getting the pre-mission jitters, a feeling he hadn't experienced since his first deployment. It felt like an hour, but Samix finally arrived at the cargo bay, sporting her own personal kit for exploration. To Zade's surprise, she was only wearing the winter version of the ship's uniform and a small sidearm. As she neared, Zade ordered the suit open and began climbing in. As Samix looked at the equipment laid out around the suit.

"First off, you're not taking that arsenal with you," Samix said. "Sidearm only, and I don't even think we are going to need those. The planet doesn't have any observable lifeforms. Second, how did you get the suit to accept that backpack? We never..."

Before she could finish her thought, Zade yanked his leg out of the suit and shot to her side to cover her mouth.

"I convinced the AI in the suit that it was approved equipment. If you finish what you were saying, we are carrying this stuff by hand," Zade whispered in her ear as he removed his hand from over her mouth.

"Since when does an environmental suit have an AI?" She asked.

"Not sure; the damn thing started talking to me as soon as I finished the familiarization. Said the AI was only accessible to users who finished the program."

"You finished the familiarization? I have never met anyone in my life who had finished that program. Most just do the motor skills then end it. Is it worth it?"

"Not sure yet. Haven't worked with it enough. EPSI, wave to the captain," Zade ordered.

On cue, after Zade finished his sentence, the suit turned to Samix and waved. With Samix watching, Zade cleared the railgun and detached the vest from his belt. After carrying them back into his lab where he could secure them, Zade closed the large doors to his lab and started back toward the bay. After arriving, he got back into his suit. The display lit, and EPSI's voice emanated through the small helmet as the suit closed.

"Welcome, Zade. Thank you for using Argyle Industries..."

"Stop. When I enter the suit, do not start the canned greeting. Just start running a system check."

As EPSI worked through the systems check, Zade clipped on his thigh holster and load. Zade ordered EPSI to adjust the suit's center of gravity, so he didn't feel like he was always fighting the weight of the equipment on his back. Confident that he could move comfortably, Zade grabbed his sidearm, curious to see how it felt with the protective gauntlets. The first thing he noticed was how much tactile sensation he had when he picked up his pistol. If he didn't know he was in a protective suit, he wouldn't have been able to tell that there was a protective layer between his hand and the weapon. As he drew the weapon, Zade could see the tiny red targeting reticle propagate on his display.

"EPSI, would information before entering a hostile environment help you perform your duties?"

"I am capable of conducting hundreds of millions of adjustments per second, but if it makes you comfortable, I could use a situation report."

"It would make me feel better, so here goes: we are going out to an ice planet with an average surface temperature of -300 degrees. Expecting high winds due to the completely flat topography."

"Very well, I will double-check the suit's temperature regulators and cleats."

Zade felt a slight shift in the ground below him as the ship settled onto its landing feet. After giving her a thumbs up, Samix opened the ramp. The blinding white landscape outside the vessel caused the protective suit's visor to darken. Zade walked to the end of the ramp. Just before stepping onto the planet's surface, Zade marked the ship's location on his map. In the event of white-out conditions, Zade wanted to make it back. Samix stepped onto the planet next to him.

"Pick a direction and start walking," she ordered.

Sounds like she's marching me out into the empty desert to execute me.

"We can run it," Zade said. "We should be able to make it to the site in 12 minutes or so. You'll just have to cut me some slack. I do have a quarter-ton on my back."

"Sounds good to me. Being able to handle these temperatures doesn't mean I like them."

Zade did a quick turn to survey the area surrounding the ship. Every direction was the same: nothingness as far as the eye could see. Everything was pure white, and with the clouds, it was hard to tell where the horizon was. After picking a direction, Zade instructed EPSI to lock onto Samix's interface signal and keep it displayed on his map. If she were going to leave him behind, he would know as soon as she set off towards the ship. After ensuring that he could see Samix on his map, Zade set off at a sprint. An odometer in his display was rolling over more quickly than he thought possible. It had been brought up by EPSI after he explained how the team needed to be five kilometers from the ship. Samix was able to keep pace for the first kilometer or so, but by the third, she had fallen behind, far enough that Zade could no longer see her. As he realized this, Zade slowed to a walk and watched his map. Her indicator was stationary, which meant that she was lost, winded, or injured.

Zade turned and headed back to her location to make sure everything was alright. As he got closer, he saw her. Blurry at first, the image cleared to reveal that she was sitting on the icy ground holding her left leg. As soon as he realized she might be hurt, Zade hustled toward her, covering the last bit of distance in seconds.

"Shit, what happened? Are you ok?"

"I'll be fine. I stepped on a chunk of ice and rolled my ankle. My nanites should have it fixed in a couple of minutes," she answered.

"Do you have a first aid kit?" Zade asked.

"Why would I? I'm not medical."

The Unity focused so heavily on position specialization that no role in the Unity military or exploration corps cross-trained on any different role. Even though Samix was the captain of an exploration ship that spent most of its time outside of settled space, no one on the vessel was versed in first aid. After taking a knee, Zade propped Samix's foot up on his thigh and took off her boot to examine the damage. Without the nanites, Zade would have left the boot on and just cinched it tight to prevent swelling. With the nanites, Zade knew he would have to tape Samix up. The nanites would take care of any physical damage, but the newly repaired tendons would be weak, and without extra support, Samix would just continue to roll the ankle again and again.

Zade had taken some necessary supplies from the medical bay to make himself a first aid kit, one of which was athletic tape for just such injuries. Zade didn't carry enough to spat a boot to keep the pack light, meaning that he would have to tape the ankle directly. As he worked on Samix, Zade explained that he had rolled an ankle during a ruck march for training. Since he didn't want to fall behind by stopping to take care of the injury, by the end of the march, every time he put weight on the foot, the ankle would roll, increasing the joint's damage. Confident that the tape would hold until the end of the mission, Zade had Samix put her boot back on, instructing her to tie it as tight as she could stand.

"Thank you. How did you know what to do?" Samix asked as she stood to test the newly supported joint.

"In my military, everyone has to have basic first aid training. I've had to do everything from applying a tourniquet on an amputation to fixing a collapsed lung while in combat."

"That's a more practical approach than what the Unity does. Only the medical officer on a ship has medical training."

"Sounds inefficient, causing more casualties than necessary. Let's get to the site. The sooner we get started, the sooner we can get off this ball of ice."

The two walked the last two kilometers in silence. The limp Samix started with had almost entirely disappeared by the time they got to the site. As the pair closed with their objective, Samix unloaded the crate of sensors before Zade dropped the backpack frame. After lining up the containers, Samix used her interface to unlock them. While assembling the ice drill, she instructed Zade to start constructing the small shelter, which would provide some protection from the elements. The shelter was small. It was no larger than an ice fishing shack back on Earth. Made from lightweight plastic, it was easy to assemble, and Zade had it constructed just as Samix started drilling the ice cores. Perched on the now empty crates inside the shelter, the two sat silently and watched the drill work. Samix was the first to break the silence.

"What's your real story, Zade? At first, I thought you would be some useless lower lifeform. After the repair stop, I read through your files and realized that you would probably be a good trooper; now, I don't know what to think."

Zade thought for a while before starting in on the canned speech he gave while in the isolation chamber. After a few sentences, Samix realized that it was the same story she had already heard and cut him off.

"Look, I know about your skills and training already. I want to know what kind of person I brought onto my crew."

After weighing his options, and the effects of opening up to Samix, Zade began.

"I was born and bred in a small town. Bored with the small-town culture and people, I decided, when I was very young, that I wanted more than my town could offer me. I excelled in school, graduated early, and went to college to study engineering and physics, thinking maybe I could work for a space program. Before graduation, I got bored and figured I needed some excitement and a background that would get me into a space program, so I transferred myself to the Military Academy. I never had any ambition to become an officer; I just wanted the excitement of combat. As I got older, I realized that I had the capacity to be a good leader and felt that it was my responsibility to lead troops if I could. As I left for my country's prestigious military academy, I still just wanted to be in the infantry, but I was sent to be an artillery officer as luck would have it. One day after I graduated from my officer specialty school, I was on a plane to Iraq. Like everyone going on their first deployment, I was scared as hell. After a couple of weeks in-country, the fear subsided, and I found myself trying to go out on every dangerous mission I could. I was again searching for the excitement that had eluded me my whole life.

"My second deployment came shortly after I returned from the first. The operation tempo was incredible, even for seasoned warriors. This deployment was spent seeking out the enemy and destroying them with air support. Unlike my first deployment, I felt no fear, only excitement. Like my first, the excitement soon faded to boredom, and I began hunting for the elusive adrenaline rushes again. Number two was both better and worse than the first. It was better because every day was a new adventure. Worse because I got to see into the black abyss that was man's cruelty. It never ceases to amaze me how creative man was when finding new ways to hurt each other.

"During a particularly nasty firefight on the second deployment, I realized that I had never been happier than I was at that moment, with enemy rounds flying over my head. I knew then that I no longer fought because I was told to. I fought because I wanted to because I needed to. I needed to fight to prove that I was the best that ever lived. After the fight, I realized that I needed to establish a personal code to salvage what was left of my humanity. I would always fight, but never against the innocent. Although I enjoyed besting an opponent, to kill innocents would make me nothing more than an animal.

"After number two, I came home both bored with life and disgusted with my fellow man. I was disgusted at the cruelty of their actions and revolted at my country's citizenry for their apathy and ignorance of such viciousness. As soon as I got back, I petitioned my commanders for another deployment; I had to get back to combat, where I felt at home. Initially, they said it was unhealthy to spend so much time in combat. Still, after some mental testing to show I was not psychologically imbalanced, I pulled orders for a third deployment. The wars were closing down, and I knew that this deployment would be my last. Mankind never stays at peace long. Peace lasts just long enough for the willing warriors seasoned in previous combat to age and never again be called up to fight.

"Knowing this, I spent the last deployment pushing myself. I had to find my limit. I had to know just how good of a warrior I was. I spent the deployment putting myself into more challenging situations to see at which point I would fail. Up until I came aboard your ship, I was undefeated back home. It was a bittersweet feeling; I was happy that I was the best but sad that I still had not found my limit. To be honest, I don't know what I would have done if you guys didn't pick me up. The only regret I have from this adventure is that I will never again see my family, dog, or cars again.

"I could have stayed in the military or become a civilian. The military was full of bureaucracy and leaders who only cared about their next promotion. If I didn't hook up with you, the society I would have been thrust back into wasn't any better; it could never truly be home. The people in my country either viewed me with fear, thinking I was an animal who enjoyed combat and the act of killing, or they viewed me with pity, as a broken man forever haunted by actions he was forced to commit. The first is probably closer to the truth, but it's the worse of the two," Zade trailed off, hunched over, stared at his feet.

Samix sat quietly looking at Zade, wholly absorbed in his story. Mistaking her silent admiration for the pity and fear he had hoped to escape, Zade hung his head and waited. Just as the silence in the shack became unbearable, the drill began beeping to signal that it had drilled through the ice and completed its analysis of the core. Stirred from her thoughts, Samix began disassembling the drilling rig. As she put the drill back in its case, Zade began removing the 300-foot-long core from the hole. As he pulled it out, Zade broke off chunks and threw them outside the shack. It had no scientific significance. It only needed to be removed to provide access for the sensors. Samix assembled the sensors that would be lowered into the ice to scan the ocean's ecosystem below.

As Samix started the scan, Zade asked, "How long will this take?"

"Should take about four hours."

"Plenty of time for a story. You wanted to know what kind of crewmember I was. It's only fair that I learn what kind of captain I'm being led by."

After checking to see that the sensor was functioning correctly, Samix sat back down inside the shack. She knew that it was against Unity protocol for a captain to become too familiar with her crew. Zade, however, wasn't technically a Unity commissioned crewmember and thus didn't meet the fraternization guidelines. After thinking for a while, Samix decided that opening up couldn't hurt and might improve the relationship between them.

"Well, first I think it would help to explain some basics. My species, the Xi'Ga, live to be incredibly old compared to yours. A member of your species would be considered old if they reached one 100; my species regularly live to 900 years old. As a reference, the Unity was formed by the Xi'Ga, making Xi'Ga time the standard time for our home world and for the Unity. From what I can tell, our homeworld is almost precisely the same as Earth. Unity time denominations must be very close to those of Earth.

"My story started 200 years ago when I was just a child. When I was very young, before the Unity was as established as it is today, my parents had decided to move to a planet in the outer reaches of Unity space to make their fortune farming. I don't remember much about the planet because I was so young, but I have searched through every piece of Unity data on its location and the colony's establishment. We took a colony ship with 15 other families to get to the planet. Even though intra-galactic travel had been perfected, we couldn't afford a fast ship as a poor family. The journey took almost nine months, but we eventually reached our new home.

"Following protocol, the families of the new colony disassembled the ship to make a protective wall for the settlement. After the wall was completed, each family built a homestead. The crop that we were sent to the farm had to grow for five years before it could be harvested. Thus the first transport from Unity space wasn't scheduled to arrive until six years after the colony was expected to land. It gave us one year to build the settlement and five to grow the first crop, during which time we were entirely on our own.

"The first two years went well, but one night in year three, our colony was visited by a group of slavers. The slave trade in the outer reaches of civilized space flourished because colonies always needed more labor. The slavers landed in the middle of the night and began sweeping through the village, killing the men, and rounding up the children and women. The children were to be sold to other colonies as labor, and the women were to be sold into a less appealing profession. We were rounded up in the center of the settlement. As a frightened girl, I could only cry and cling to my mother.

"When my mother couldn't quiet me down, the slavers came by to do it for her. As they approached, she picked me up and started to run away. Just as she separated from the group, they shot her in the back; she was gone before hitting the ground. They grabbed me and put me with the other children. The leader of the slavers came over to see what had happened and inform his crew that there weren't enough supplies to take everyone. After executing the women, the slavers took five other small children and me to their ship. The surviving children were left at the dead colony to fend for themselves.

"Aboard their ship, we were all thrown into a tiny cage in the cargo bay for the flight back to the stage two planets," Samix trailed off, seeing the confusion on Zade's face.

"The Unity is broken into three distinct areas," Samix explained. "The core, stage two, and outer rim. Core planets are in the interior of the Unity and are made up of the original Unity species' home worlds. Just outside of the core are stage two planets: planets not yet developed enough to be considered core but more trafficked than the outer rim. These planets were the first to be settled after the formation of the Unity and have regular merchant traffic and regulation. They also regularly benefited from slave labor, as they made most of their money from their crops but weren't developed enough to have automation. Beyond the stage, two planets is the outer rim. The outer rim consists of newly colonized planets, and due to their remote locations, they rarely have any kind of law or protection.

"We only survived because the crew occasionally took pity on us and threw us their food scraps. During the journey, the slavers decided to attack a merchant ship that was putting out a distress beacon. The slavers docked and boarded the distressed vessel to find that it was actually a Unity military bait ship. All I can remember from that day was the noise. The Unity troopers smashed the slavers, but not before one could try to scuttle the slave ship. The troopers managed to rescue us before the slave ship was destroyed. After they saved us, they tried to find out where we came from, but none of us was old enough to know the navigational data of our planet.

"The combat ship I was rescued by headed back to the core worlds to resupply. As a last effort to get us to safety, the ship landed at planets whose predominant species matched the children they rescued. They left me for adoption on Xi'Ga. The Unity used our situation as a rallying cry to build up the military, and because of the publicity, I was adopted by a wealthy family almost immediately. The family couldn't have children of their own, so I was the miracle daughter that made them whole. The day I was rescued was the day I decided to join the Academe. I wanted to help people like the troopers who helped me.

"The family that took me in was wonderful. They treated me like one of their own and sent me to the best schools. As soon as

I became eligible, I joined the Academe, hoping to earn a slot in the trooper program. Because of my entrance exams, however, I was given orders to attend the more prestigious command program. The Academe was easy for me. While my classmates were studying or practicing, I researched the outer rim planets, trying to find out where I came from. I couldn't find anything on my home. After I came to terms with never being a trooper, I decided that I wanted to command a combat ship. That dream was crushed like my dreams of becoming a trooper. My high marks earned me an assignment in the exploration corps. The combination of my stellar performance during training and my family's standing within the Unity earned me this command as my first," Samix finished, staring at the wall blankly.

"Sorry to hear about your parents," Zade said, although the condolence seemed empty to him. He reached toward her and touched her shoulder.

"Thank you, but I think I have come to terms with it," she replied, glancing at his hand. She slowly reached up and touched the tips of his fingers with hers.

"It explains why you always look so sad when I talk about never being able to get home," he said, with a slight squeeze on her shoulder.

"You see that? Most people on this boat have the personal skills of a rock. No one has ever picked up on what I was feeling before you, that is."

"You have to admit it's weird, though," Zade continued, moving his hand away from her.

"What's weird?" Samix asked, watching as his hand fell back to his lap.

"We have so much in common. Both unable to get home. Both

searching for some kind of meaning in life. Both boned by our respective governments repeatedly. You have to admit that it's weird that out of all the ships in your fleet and all of the people on earth, you picked me up."

"That is kind of weird," Samix said, a smile creeping across her face as she thought about just how chance the encounter was.

As the two sat in silence, waiting for the sensor to complete its scan, Zade saw an alarmed look on Samix's face. The sensor had output a warning directly to her interface. The sensor was complete with the scan, but at some point, an extremely large lifeform had developed an interest in it. After Samix informed Zade of the situation, he looked down with his thermals and could see the faintest pink glow of some kind of enormous fish circling below them under the ice.

"Sam, I think it's time to go. I would love to add some kind of watery death machine to my list of conquered foes, but you didn't let me bring my tools."

Agreeing completely and blushing slightly at the thought of Zade giving her a nickname, Samix began pulling the sensor in while Zade broke down the shack and loaded up his suit's carrying rack. With everything in place, Zade waited on Samix to get the sensor out of the water. As the sensor hit the 100-foot mark, the point at which it was a third of the way out of the water, Samix and Zade felt a thud against the ice.

"You know, I have all of the readings; I think I'm just going to leave this for our new friend," Samix said as she released the line she was using to tow the sensor to the surface.

"That isn't the worst idea. Close up the sensor box and throw it on top of the others."

The trek back to the ship was done quietly to avoid attracting unwanted attention from the local wildlife. Zade repeatedly looked around with his thermals, but he could not see anything under the ice after the team had departed the observation site. After hearing the stories during their excursion, the teammates had a newfound respect for one another, and Zade felt more connected to Samix than he had to anyone before. Zade was happy to have visited another planet, even if it was covered in ice and even though nothing had tried to kill him.

CHAPTER 9

After the two boarded the ship, Samix immediately initiated the orbital protocol. The two chatted as Zade took off the protective suit and stowed it. As he finished securing it in its storage container, Zade could feel the ship lift off. Samix headed to the command deck to release the data drone, and Zade followed, wanting to see how it was done. Once on the command deck, Samix oriented the ship so the drone could be viewed through the windows as it dropped into warp.

Zade watched in silence as Samix downloaded the navigational data for the planet, a habit she had picked up since the incident on Earth. After validating the drone's destination and reviewing the information it carried, Samix released it. Zade peered into the space surrounding the command deck and could only identify the drone by one orange marker. After the drone oriented itself, it disappeared with a bright purple and blue flash. The flash was so bright that it left an afterimage dancing around Zade's vision. Samix then started the protocol to move the ship to the last planet of interest.

"Well, we're done here. Do you want to grab some chow in the galley?" Samix asked as she looked at Zade.

"I could eat."

The two headed to the galley, where they chatted and ate.

Zade learned that the trip would take around 36 hours, time he could use to get to know the crew better. After the two finished eating, both Samix and Zade headed to their separate quarters for showers and sleep. As Zade entered his quarters, he started playing one of his favorite songs from his music collection, the day's events replaying through his head. Samix, on the other hand, couldn't stop thinking about Zade and his situation. She now understood that Zade was not the threat that she feared.

After a quick nap, Zade decided to start making the ship his home. The first thing he had to do was talk to Samix about using some of the space in the cargo bay. His goal was to create some kind of weight room or training area to pass the time. Initially, he worried that the equipment might move around while the ship was in flight, but Samix ensured him that the ship's gravity drives would keep everything in place. After getting the OK from Samix and clearing an area he could use, Zade headed to the fabrication lab and started the fabrication machines on creating workout equipment.

While the fabrication machines worked, Zade headed to the galley to grab a cup of sloop. There he met an overly talkative Axis. The two talked as Axis finished his meal. When Axis finished, he tossed his tray and headed to his room. He soon emerged carrying a small board, which he explained was a strategy game favored by his family. He quickly explained how the game was played and badgered Zade into playing a round with him. Zade learned that the game was very similar to chess and felt he would be pretty good at it as an army officer. Axis explained that he couldn't get any other crewmember to play with him throughout the trip because nobody could beat him at it. Zade would be the first person he played since early in the journey.

The first round, as suspected, was a loss for Zade. He was still learning the game and made multiple rookie mistakes. Dissatisfied with his performance, Zade demanded a rematch, a rematch in which he beat Axis. Impressed that the human could beat him, Axis demanded a rematch. As Axis set up the board for round three, Zade received a notification on his interface saying that the fabrication machines were complete.

"I would love to go another round, but the project I'm working on in the lab just finish. Maybe next time?"

"I can't just quit after a loss," Axis protested.

"I can promise you we will play again after I finish my project," Zade assured Axis. "I enjoyed playing, but I would really like to get more fabrications started."

The small alien continued to protest, and as Zade left the galley, he could still hear Axis demanding a chance to redeem himself. Zade headed to the lab to find it full of new gym equipment. Zade had instructed the fabrication machines to create varying weights of dumbbells, a large punching bag, and rubber mats for the floor. Zade spent the next two hours setting up his gym in the cargo bay. It wasn't the same as the gyms he had used on post, but it was probably the best he was going to get on a spaceship.

The new gym, although small, would be perfect for Zade to pass the time and learn how to use his new strength. The first thing he wanted to do was measure his performance against a known standard. The known standard he lived by his whole life was the army physical fitness test. He could not do the run but knew the criteria for pushups and sit-ups. Zade would have to do 77 pushups and 82 sit-ups in two minutes to max the physical fitness test. Although he was never truly out of shape, Zade always found it challenging to max his APFT. Zade set the timer in his interface for two minutes and assumed the push-ups position. Once he started the timer, he began knocking out pushups as fast as possible. To his surprise, when the timer stopped, he had done 160 pushups. Pleased with himself, he reset the timer, stuck his feet under a dumbbell, and began doing sit-ups. Like with the pushups, Zade destroyed the standards doing just over 200 in the allotted two minutes. Just a Zade was finishing up his sit-ups, Axis entered the cargo bay to see what had drawn him away from their game.

"You know, with the nanites, you don't have to work out to keep your body in top physical condition," Axis said.

"I know. I enjoy working out to pass the time. Plus, the only way I can truly be able to utilize my new strength and modifications from the nanites is to train."

Axis walked out of the cargo bay, obviously confused. As a scientist and social elite, the idea of physical training was lost on him. Zade, not even winded, sat on the floor and thought about the potential his gym had. The first thing he would work on would be larger weights such as a squat rack and a bench. He didn't include them initially because he was unsure how the fabrication machines would complete them. Now, regardless of how well the machines built them, Zade knew he needed the equipment. The only thing missing from the gym was visual and audio motivation. He had the audio he required with the music Samix had salvaged from his iPod. What he needed were posters to put around the gym. The gym was right underneath the second-floor platform of the cargo bay. It gave him about a 40 by 40 area to work out in, and he stacked the dumbbells against the cargo bay wall and hung the punching bag from the stair supports closest to the cargo bay door. There would be plenty of room to include new equipment. Zade headed back into the robotics and fabrication lab through the large rolling door he had used to bring the equipment into the cargo bay. After entering, as he sat down, Zade imagined what a squat rack and bench looked like and sent the images to the large fabrication machine for processing. Zade sent specs for the plate weights and bars he would need on the equipment to the smaller fabrication machine.

As the machines worked, Zade headed back into the cargo bay to do a quick workout. It wasn't anything extravagant, as the gym was still pretty small, but he did serve its purpose of killing the time it took to fabricate the squat rack and bench. Zade moved the new equipment rack, bench, weights, and bars into the workout room. The new equipment made the gym look complete. Now excited about completing a real workout, Zade headed to his room to change into workout clothes. Samix caught him just before he entered his quarters.

"Axis said he saw you in the cargo bay and said you seemed agitated. Is everything okay?" She asked.

"Everything is fine. Just finished a workout area and am getting ready the change and try it out. Want to get a quick lift in?"

"You know you don't..." Samix started but was cut off by Zade.

"I know I don't have to work out, but I enjoy it, and it passes the time."

"I have some things to do, but I might catch you down there later."

Samix, now confident Zade wasn't upset, headed back to the command deck. Zade walked into his room, took off his uniform, and changed to a pair of shorts he had created for sleeping. Now, in gym attire, Zade headed back to his new creation. As he walked towards the cargo bay, Zade sorted through the music in his interface to find the workout mix he had used when deployed. As angry, heavy metal started blasting his head, Zade began loading up the squat rack. Leg routines were Zade's favorite, and as such, would be the first workout he did in space. After loading the bar, Zade got into position and started his first set. His new nanites improvements meant that Zade had not created enough free weights to challenge himself. Knowing that creating enough free weights to be challenging would use up the ship's resources, Zade sat on the bench and tried to think up a way to fix the problem. As he sat contemplating his dilemma, Samix walked in. She had changed into athletic shoes, and lime green tank top, and a pair of matching green running shorts.

"It looks great. I saw what you're doing on the internal cams and changed and appropriate clothing. Why the deep thought?"

"I created enough weight to challenge me before the nanite improvements, but now it isn't even enough to make me sweat."

Unsure how to help, Samix just stood there and shrugged. Zade showed her around the small workout area, explaining what each piece of equipment did. He explained that the punching bag was used to practice striking, the padded floor could be used for sparring, and the weights were used for strength training. As he finished the walkthrough, an idea struck him.

"You said that the weights would be held in place by the gravity drive, right? Is it adjustable?" he asked.

"Sure, you just have to bring up the room controls on your interface. Why?"

"I just realized instead of creating more weight, I can just increase the gravity to make all lifts harder."

"Not a bad idea. All of the storage crates in the bay should be able to handle the extra G's."

Zade was excited to try the increased gravity but was unsure if Samix could handle it. Samix headed over to the punching bag and took a few swings. As she did, the punching bag began to swing wildly, at one point swinging high enough to hit the railing above. Zade remembered that Samix backhanded him out of his seat earlier in the trip without even trying, meaning she was strong enough to handle the higher gravity levels. Zade walked over to hold the punching bag as Samix hammered away on it. As he did, Zade brought up the room controls in his interface and increased gravity to three times normal.

The new gravity level was noticeable to both crewmembers in the gym. Zade immediately noticed how heavy his limbs felt and how sluggish his movements were. The increased gravity would really help him get a handle on his new physical capabilities. Zade could see Samix had noticed the change as well but seemed to be handling it better than him. Her movements seemed uncoordinated and slow for a split second, but she adjusted quickly. Samix hammered on the bag for a few minutes to warm up, then suggested that she and Zade spar. Zade explained that he had not yet made gloves for sparring, but if Samix wanted to, he could have the fabrication machines make a couple pairs. Samix, in turn, explained that she was not interested in striking but rather grappling. She explained that she had been the ship-wide grappling champ during her exploration training.

Zade laughed nervously as he began clearing the mats of the weights he had been using. He knew he matched her in strength but feared he may out-class her in technique. If she did her on-ship training with an exploration vessel, it meant her fellow crewmates were all scientists. If the scientists she bested to earn her title were anything like the scientists on this ship, she didn't need much skill to beat them. While Zade finished cleaning off the mats, he explained that he wasn't professional, but he was pretty well versed in hand-to-hand combat. Samix assured him that she could handle herself.

Zade walked toward the center of the mats and began stretching. Straightening up after hamstring stretch, still unsure of Samix's abilities, Zade was surprised to see Samix already in motion. Sometime while Zade was stretching, Samix decided that it was time to begin and was flying towards him feet first. Zade only had a moment to brace himself before Samix's feet connected squarely with his sternum. In triple gravity, it felt as if he had been hit by a truck. Although he had tried to brace himself, the impact took him off his feet. Zade landed flat on his back with Samix spryly perched atop him. Now realizing that he wasn't going to destroy her, Zade went on the offensive. Hooking one of her ankles, Zade rolled, trying to knock Samix off balance, and regain a more favorable position. Samix, as if she knew what was coming, quickly spread her feet and landed in the full mount position.

"Told you I could hold my own, ponyboy," she said as she rained down blows on Zade's head and neck.

The increased gravity meant that Zade felt like he was being pinned by a small family sedan. Zade could feel her long, firm legs pressing into his sides to hold him in place. Usually, Zade would take the time to appreciate having a beautiful woman sitting on top of him, but after having his pride hurt, he could only think about one thing, winning. Zade bucked twice to no avail. The third buck disrupted Samix, who lost her balance and fell forward, planting her hands on either side of his head. Grabbing her left arm and hooking her left leg with his foot, Zade planted a left hook to her ribs, rolled his hips, and slid out of her mount to his left.

The move got him free of Samix's mount but no further. Regaining her composure, Samix locked her feet behind his back, and the two rolled into the guard position. Zade took his turn, raining down blows, none of which were as effective as Samix's from the mount. She slid her feet up Zade's back and waited for the right moment to strike. A sloppy right hand was the opportunity she was waiting for. Trapping the lazily thrown punch against her chest, Samix slid her legs over his shoulders and locked her right foot behind her left knee. She pulled down on Zade's head and buried the triangle choke even deeper. The choke was deep, and she knew that Zade would be asleep momentarily. Zade immediately pushed down on top of Samix, knowing that it was the only way to win the match. If he could push down, the pressure from her legs would be applied more to his shoulders and keep him from passing out.

Unable to break her guard, Zade regained his feet, wrapped both arms around her thighs, and stood up. After he had lifted Samix entirely off the ground, Zade slammed her back into the mats. It used up the remainder of his energy in triple gravity, but it did break the chokehold. Exhausted but free, Zade pushed off of her and tried to stand; it was his undoing. Samix caught his hand and spun into a perfectly executed armbar. Too tired to fight it, Zade could only admit defeat and tap out.

The sparring match had lasted just over 30 minutes, and both Zade and Samix were exhausted. They laid on the mats panting, without the strength to even stand. Using his interface again, Zade set the gravity in the cargo bay back to normal levels. The reduced weight allowed both fighters to sit up next to each other and regain enough energy to talk.

"I have to give you props. You are the only person who lasted longer than 30 seconds against me," Samix said.

Holy shit, this woman is amazing.

Zade put his hand on the back of Samix's head and leaned toward her, pulling her closer to him. Samix didn't resist. As he felt his lips closed with hers, she pushed Zade away. Confused, Zade just watched as Samix flushed a dark blue and stood.

"Sorry, Z. You have to beat me first," Samix said as she headed out of the cargo bay, a small smile crossing her lips.

Zade could only watch quietly as Samix left, taking in every bit of her tight, athletic body as she walked away. If he didn't know better, Zade could have sworn that Samix was giving him a show as she left, fully accentuating her swaying hips as she walked. As she disappeared into the hall just outside the cargo bay, Zade laid back on the mats, hands folded behind his head. Two hundred was a little older than most women he dated, but he was sure he could make it work. Zade dozed off thinking about Samix's perfectly sculpted firm butt.

ΔΔΔ

What just happened? Was he really trying to come on to me? Is there something wrong with him? No one has ever tried to hit on me before. And I am feeling…. What am I feeling?

The questions were spinning through Samix's head as she headed to her quarters to clean up. Up to this point, her entire life had been spent with minimal attention from men. Xi'Ga society was broken into two distinct classes; the upper class was obsessed with heritage. The lower level still adhered to strict religious roles where women did nothing on their own and only lived to serve their spouse. She was undesirable to the upper-class Xi'Ga because she was an orphan and didn't know her bloodline. She was undesirable to the lower class Xi'Ga because she didn't fit the subservient female stereotype they wanted. Up until the day she left on this mission, she had had to battle the constant, cruel jokes about her being a man; she believed it stemmed from her drive to succeed in the Unity fleet. The jokes and overall nastiness from the males of her species were some of the main factors that drove her to be the best at the Academe.

She had only been hit on once, which was during her class graduation celebration. The whole class went drinking at a local bar to celebrate fleet assignments. Sometime during the night, she caught the eye of a too drunk and equally crass Marlog. The night ended with her fighting the guy after he grabbed her—a fight in which most of her male classmates cheered for the Marlog, hoping he would beat her, take her home, and give her what she deserved. Luckily local security broke up the fight. Samix knew she would never have been able to beat the Marlog, but she couldn't let his actions stand. They were both bounced, and the Marlog was arrested for assaulting a fleet officer. It was the story of her life. Most of the men she met hated her because she could outperform them. Some pitied or feared her, and the rest just wanted to use her for their own needs.

Samix entered her quarters and stripped down for a shower. Looking in the mirror, she could see dark purple bruises surfacing from the sparring bout, the largest of which covered her whole back from where Zade slammed her. It was a nasty move that would have won him the match had he not pushed off her to stand. After a shower and meal, all of her injuries would heal. With only a few hours before they made orbit, Samix knew she needed to get some sleep, but she couldn't stop thinking about what had transpired in the gym with Zade.

She dressed and headed to the galley to grab a meal. Samix decided that she had to determine why Zade was interested in her before deciding what she would do. On the one hand, he seemed to be everything she had hoped for in a man. On the other, she had only known him for a short while and felt she didn't know enough about him. Either way, she had survived over 200 years on her own. A short time more to ensure she was making a good decision wouldn't kill her. Samix headed to Zade's quarters to invite him to eat with her. There was no response when she knocked on the door, and she immediately feared the worst. Instead of assuming that he was a heavy sleeper or in the shower and didn't hear her knocking, Samix concluded that he was angry at her snub. Samix sat down to eat alone, wondering how she could patch things up between her and Zade.

△△△

Zade awoke, disoriented, surrounded by a place that was not his quarters. He had fallen asleep on the mats after his sparring session with Samix. Gingerly he stood, still sore from the session. Checking his interface, he saw that he had only been asleep for about an hour, and the ship was now in its night cycle. His neck and elbow were still incredibly sore from Samix, and after a quick check, he could see dark bruises had formed from the strikes that she had landed. His shirt, still damp with sweat, stunk. Because it was nighttime, Zade figured he wouldn't run into anyone, so he took off the foul-smelling garment and headed to his quarters for a much-needed shower.

Zade knew he would have to clear the air with Samix after his little stunt earlier. He headed into his lab to close it up before going to the upper deck. He had left it open while setting up the gym and fell asleep before closing it. Closing the rolling door as he entered the lab, Zade quickly policed up the different scraps lying on the work surfaces, tossing them all into the recycling chute to be used in later projects. Zade exited his lab through the man door and headed towards the front stairwell.

On his way to his quarters, Zade began to think of the best way to broach the subject with Samix when he saw her next. She didn't have a violent reaction when he tried to kiss her, so Zade assumed that he didn't offend her too badly, but he couldn't be sure. Different cultures on Earth had different social norms and various measures of acceptable behavior. Samix was a completely different species; who knows how his actions could be construed? Plus, there was the whole command structure issue. Zade's actions towards the captain of the ship blatantly spit in the face of good order and discipline, and Samix had already stressed earlier that she took her position as captain seriously. Zade was so engulfed by his own train of thought that he overlooked the crewmember sitting in the galley, finishing her meal. As Zade opened the door to his quarters, he heard a voice behind him.

"So, first you try to plant a kiss on me, now you wander around my ship half-naked?" Samix asked from behind him.

Shit.

"Sorry, captain. I—I didn't think anyone would be up during the night cycle," Zade said as he turned to face her.

"We need to talk," she said as she stood and walked toward Zade.

"Can it wait until I've had a shower?" Zade asked, more out of a need to fill the silence than to actually request permission.

Not waiting for Samix to respond, Zade turned and opened the door to his quarters. So desperate to get away from his current situation, Zade didn't notice that Samix had followed him in. Zade kicked off his shoes and socks and headed for his bathroom, still unaware that he wasn't alone. He turned on the shower, as hot as he could stand it, and stepped in. Samix, meanwhile, waited until the noise of the shower could mask her movements then sat on his bed.

"So, what's your game, Alex?" Samix asked, startling Zade so severely that he jumped and hit his head on the shower.

"What the fuck? Isn't there a thing called privacy on this boat?"

"It's my ship; I can go where I please. You didn't answer my question," Samix retorted, enjoying watching Zade squirm.

"What are you talking about? I don't have any game," Zade said as he peeked out of the bathroom to see Samix relaxing on his rack. "Remember? I'm an unwilling victim of circumstance in this whole situation. I had no plans to travel the stars when I left for that patrol back in Afghanistan."

"Not on my ship, Zade. Don't play games with me."

"No games. I saw something I wanted, and I went for it," Zade retorted quickly. "You never know how something is going to work out until you try."

"I understand that concept. What I don't understand is the motivation behind it. Most of you aren't that much of a mystery. Men are men. What makes you any different?" She asked.

"Honestly, Do you know how many times I've met a woman that could best me on the mats? None. Do you know how many times I've met a woman who was smarter than me? None. How many have accidentally kidnapped me and taken me on the adventure of a lifetime? None. You...You package that in a beautiful, athletic, blue body, alien or otherwise, I would have to be crazy to not make a move," Zade finished, feeling the blood rush to his cheeks.

The silence that followed was punctuated by the sound of his door opening and closing. Samix left his quarters and headed for her own. Zade knew when to leave well enough alone and finished his shower in peace. As he changed, Zade brought up the navigation data on his interface and saw the ship still had eight hours before it hit orbit. Plenty of time for some sleep. Zade dozed off, wondering how things were going to work out, and thinking about his day with Samix. The only thing he did know was that, as Samix so eloquently put it for guys, women were women. They were just as challenging to understand in space as they were back home.

CHAPTER 10

An interface notification woke Zade up. While the ship was completing its final orbit, Mur had fabricated the SSILF landing team while Zade slept. Mur informed him that Samix needed him in the ready room. Zade dressed quickly in a new set of fatigues and headed out of his quarters. As usual, the ship seemed empty. If Zade had to guess, Axis was either in his quarters or in his lab, and both Samix and Jorloss were in the ready room waiting on him.

As Zade walked towards the ready room, now entirely by memory, he pulled up the orbital scans' results. The planet they were orbiting was a densely jungled planet, which had some plant life that Jorloss had marked for further investigation. Like any other jungle, this planet had a wide variety of lifeforms ranging from apex mammalian predators to a myriad of smaller species that used poison or venom to survive. The dominant species on the planet was a class one, sentient, apelike species that lived in remote villages.

The species was very much feudal in nature, organized into small villages of farmers and hunters. It appeared that groups of villages geographically proximate to each other were protected by a chieftain who controlled a small fighting force that could guard the towns from natural threats and other chieftains looking to expand their influence. After reading the reports, Zade brought up a map of the objective. It was located in the middle of the most enormous landmass on the planet and was relatively remote. The nearest ape settlement was roughly 30 kilometers north of the objective.

As Zade neared the door to the ready room, he realized that he had forgotten his morning cup of sloop and decided to circle back to the galley to grab one before he had to sit through the brief. Cup in hand, Zade walked into the ready room and took a seat next to Jorloss. Unlike the previous mission briefing, Samix was nowhere to be found. The ship itself, through Mur, was running the briefing.

"Where's Samix?" Zade asked, slipping into the room beside Jorloss, who was listening intently to Mur.

"In her quarters. Said something was bothering her," Jorloss whispered back, refocusing his attention on Mur.

Zade sat, worried about Samix, as Mur continued the briefing. Most of his portion of the brief was a reiteration of the notification that had woke Zade up. Mur took the liberty of creating a four SSILF landing crew, which were already outfitted for the mission and waiting by the ship's loading ramp. The ship could not land at the objective due to vertical obstructions and instead would be landing three kilometers south of it in two hours. After Mur finished, Jorloss stood and started his portion of the brief. After moving to the front of the briefing room, Jorloss tapped the briefing screen and brought up two images. The first was an overhead view of the objective. It showed a small open patch of vegetation. The second was a close-up of the small bioluminescent plant that Jorloss needed to study.

He began his portion of the brief with the zeal that only an excited scientist exhibited. The plant appeared to be similar to one that was native to his homeworld, Lassf. It seemed to have the same characteristics and chemical makeup. The Gornoo, Jorloss's species, used the plant to cure a fatal genetic birth defect if left untreated. Due to the climate change caused by the Gornoo home world's development, the plant had gone extinct almost two decades ago. Since the loss of the plant, the Gornoo population had begun to steadily decline and would become extinct within four generations, according to Jorloss's calculations. The objective of the mission was to collect samples for Jorloss to test aboard the ship. Jorloss hypothesized that if the plants were similar enough, he could increase their toughness and reintroduce them back into the Lassf ecosystem. The briefing concluded when Jorloss finished his portion of it.

Realizing that this mission was a standard security mission, Zade let his mind wander. He spent the duration of the briefing thinking about Samix and how she was doing. After the mission brief finished, Jorloss headed to his lab to collect the equipment he needed, Mur appeared to power down, and Zade headed to the captain's quarters to check in on Samix. There was no response when he knocked on the door to her quarters, so he sent her a private interface message.

Hey captain, just checking to see how you're doing. Jorloss mentioned that you were under the weather.

Zade knew that if there was anything between them, he would have to stay professional with Samix while they were on the job if he wanted it to work. He had the feeling that by the way Samix handled his post grappling stunt, she had some negative experiences with men. The last thing he wanted to do was undermine her authority while he was a part of her crew. As Zade waited for a response, he leaned against the bulkhead and cranked up his hearing mod, hoping to hear movement in her quarters. Samix's quarters must have had sound deadening; although Zade could hear Axis breathing in his lab, which was down one floor and on the other end of the ship, he couldn't hear anything from the quarters behind him. After five minutes with no response, Zade shot her one last message and headed down to Jorloss's lab to see if he had any specific needs for the mission.

We're disembarking in a couple of hours. It would be nice if the captain saw us off.

After three high-intensity deployments, Zade knew how to focus on the mission at hand. He had become a master at compartmentalizing, and although his mind wanted to stay focused on Samix, he pushed the thoughts back so he could dedicate himself to the mission. Whether Samix was actually sick or just upset with him didn't matter at the moment; he would deal with it after he got back to the ship. Now, he needed to prepare for his fourth planetfall.

The forward stairwell put Zade right outside Jorloss's lab. As he entered, he could see the amphibious scientist digging through different boxes, searching for a much-needed piece of equipment.

"Hey, are you going to need one of the pack mules for your stuff?" Zade asked, earning him a hold on sign from the scientist who was buried head and shoulders in an equipment box.

"No, unlike some of the more spoiled members of this crew, I can pull my own weight," Jorloss replied as he stood, triumphantly holding that which he had been searching for.

"You've been doing this longer than I have. Are you expecting any issues from the locals?"

Jorloss placed the piece of equipment in a pack that he was loading on one of his worktables.

"No, we should be in and out before they even figure out we were there."

"Well, that's reassuring. I'm heading to my lab to check the SSILF functionality and put my kit together. See you in the bay."

Remembering that Mur had already staged the SSILF in the cargo bay, Zade walked to the rear of the ship. As he entered the cargo bay, he could see four matte, black, heavily-armed SSILF lined up against the ramp. Zade walked up to the first and placed his hand on its shoulder. This caused the SSILF's operations profile to populate in Zade's interface. He scrolled through the data, searching for the diagnostics and calibration program. After finding it and starting it, the SSILF's profile condensed into Zade's left eye, and a visual of what the SSILF was seeing populated his right. The SSILF readout was the exact view the SSILF had overlaid with a status bar, location relative to Zade, and ammo counter. Zade watched as the SSILF completed the program, ensuring that the firing reticle was working and there were no other issues. Upon completion, the readout disappeared from Zade's field of view, and the profile expanded.

Satisfied that the SSILF was operating correctly, Zade quickly skimmed through the rest of the profile. Because most of the profile was simply code, Zade almost closed it before realizing that everything was encrypted. Curious about the encryption, Zade located the protocol section and saw that it was encrypted like the rest of the file.

Mur, these SSILF seem to be vastly more intricate than the others, and all of their coding is encrypted, Zade said through his interface.

Apologies, security officer. As artificial intelligence, I can create SSILF that are more complex than you can as a simple class two individual. I can unencrypt them if you'd like, but it wouldn't be complete until after you disembarked.

Well, look at the big brain on you—no need for the jab at me or my species. Don't worry about unencrypting them if they can operate like the others.

They will operate flawlessly and successfully complete their mission.

Well, thanks for fabricating these early. I like the paint job.

Zade worked his way through the remaining three SSILF, running their diagnostics and calibration and ensuring they functioned properly. After the fourth SSILF completed the diagnostics program, Zade put the team on standby and headed to his lab to prepare his kit. His standard equipment still included necessary field supplies and his railgun and sidearm, but learning from past missions, Zade added grenades. His kit now included two types of smoke grenades and two thermobaric grenades. The smoke grenades included a red signal grenade and a smokescreen grenade. The newly developed smokescreen grenade was meant to be thrown directly up. As it reached a height of 15 feet, it would detonate, creating an impenetrable 50-foot circular cloud. With his thermal vision modification and implant, Zade would be able to navigate out of it, but any creature without such advantages would be blind.

Zade was incredibly proud of the thermobaric grenades. He designed them after seeing the effectiveness of his Excaliber rounds. Zade had to throw these grenades short. While in flight, the grenade would orient itself in the direction it was being thrown. Just before impact with the ground, the grenade would release nine sub-munitions that would land in a 30-foot circle around the target area. All munitions would then detonate, instantly raising both the pressure and temperature inside the ring to conditions similar to the core of a star. After detonation, the explosives were designed to continue burning at their initial temperature for an additional 30 seconds. The initial explosion would vaporize anything exposed to it; the follow-on burn would bake anything between ground level and bed-rock. These grenades were the very essence of scorched earth policy. Although Zade had never physically tested them, computer simulations guaranteed that they were absolute in their lethality. Unable to shake his schooling as an artillery officer on earth, Zade designed the grenades with collateral damage considerations. Because the grenades were directional, the only effect it would have on bystanders outside the grenade radius would be a slight overpressure that had the potential to knock them down.

Zade took his improved standard kit and his newly created buzz saws on the mission. After having trouble cutting through some of the denser vegetation during his assignment with Axis, Zade had developed a more modern take on the machete. The buzz saw looked like a brush saw, minus the blade, with a horizontal handle that had a six-foot-long cable coming out of the end of it. On the end of the line opposite the handle was a metal ball. There were two posts on the handle. One was connected to the power source, located in the handle. The other was connected to the tether. When powered on, the ball on the end of the tether would act as a ground. Current would be sent through the frame of the saw, arc across the gap, where the blade would traditionally be located, and then to the ground tether. Zade hoped that the high-temperature arc could be used to cut through obstacles.

After finishing his weapons function check, Zade put on his new kit with only minutes left until landing, grabbed the buzz saws, and headed into the cargo bay. Jorloss had already made his way into the cargo bay and was sleeping on one of the storage containers located by the rear ramp. Zade brought the SSILF out of standby as he headed over towards Jorloss.

"Do you have any means of self-defense?" he asked.

"I appreciate your concern, but I am a scientist. By definition, I am a noncombatant."

"Although I disagree with your sentiment, I could understand the argument if we were going into standard combat operations. But in case you didn't notice, we are going up against wildlife, and they don't care if you're a scientist or not," Zade retorted in a slightly angrier tone than he wanted.

"Well, then you and your robots better be sharp."

Zade reluctantly walked back to the SSILF and waited for the ramp to open. Jorloss's attitude reminded him of a chaplain he had had to interact with on his second deployment. The bible-thumping noncombatant felt the need to tag along on every patrol Zade led that deployment. The guy was a huge inconvenience; he packed way too much stuff and managed to get in the way at every turn. During an incredibly long firefight, the non-combatant stood up and tried to talk the enemy machine gunner into submission. Zade got blood all over his truck, driving his body back to base after the fight. From that point on, Zade held to a strict non-noncombatant policy.

When the two-minute countdown clock displayed in his field of vision, Zade pulled up the external conditions of the ship. After ensuring that they would not be blinded by friction heat, Zade dropped the ramp. Still, in flight, he walked to the edge of the ramp and began orienting himself to the terrain zipping past below him. With 30-seconds left on the clock, the ship had slowed enough for Zade to positively identify the objective and the landing zone.

Before the ship touched down, Zade sent the SSILF out to establish a security perimeter. He followed close behind to complete a quick sweep of the area and establish near security. Although more significant than the objective, the landing zone was barely large enough to fit the ship. Foliage crowded the vessel on either side, and the nose was pushed into the underbrush to accommodate the open cargo ramp. Zade had to step into the tree line to avoid being crushed by the descending ship.

Concealed by the undergrowth, Zade watched, amused, as the slightly agitated Jorloss searched for the security team. He stepped out of the underbrush, forced to cut his entertainment short when Samix appeared in the cargo bay. He walked up the ramp towards Samix, while he quickly confirmed that the security team didn't have any issues.

"Sorry I didn't respond to your messages. I was sleeping. I was up for a long time after we talked in your room, and I just couldn't keep my eyes open anymore," she said as he approached.

"No worries. You don't have to explain yourself to me. You're the captain."

"I know, but I want to. I mean..." She started but was quickly cut off.

Let's not do this now in front of the crew. Not sure where this is going, but you have a reputation to maintain as captain, and I would like to maintain some semblance of propriety. Either way, this is neither the time nor the place. Zade sent a whispered message to Samix's interface, stopping near the ramp's end and placing his hands on his belt.

Thank you, she whispered before stopping and addressing Jorloss and Zade together.

"Alright, guys, this should be an easy one. Stay safe, Jorloss; I need you back here. You're the only medical officer aboard, and Zade, I want a rematch," she said smiling.

Mumbling to himself about how they were going to make it through the dense jungle, Jorloss grabbed his pack and headed to the foot of the ramp. He paced back and forth along the length of the ramp, looking for someplace to enter. While Jorloss was preoccupied at the foot of the ramp, Samix quickly embraced Zade and gave him a kiss on the cheek.

"Seriously, stay safe. Something feels wrong about this one. I will be monitoring everything from the command deck if you need me," she whispered before again stepping back.

While absent-mindedly fiddling with the straps of his assault pack, Zade gave Samix a smile then turned to join Jorloss at the foot of the ramp. Stepping forward to interrupt Jorloss's pacing, Zade took off his pack and began unhooking the buzz saws attached to the back of it. After explaining how they worked, he handed one to Jorloss and fired his up for a demonstration. Walking away from the ship and toward the foliage, Zade took a swing at the vegetation in front of him. Expecting the resistance associated with using an actual machete, Zade's swing was slightly overpowered. He cut through all of the vegetation in front of him and a small tree to his right. More prominent than a sapling but smaller than a telephone pole, the tree fell with a clang on top of the ship.

Abashed Zade quickly threw the tree off the ship and returned his attention to Jorloss. He was just waiting, face unreadable, for Zade to start the northward trek. Glancing over his shoulder one last time before entering the din of the jungle, Zade could see that Samix had already receded into the ship, presumably to the command deck. The first 50 feet of the march required extensive clearing, but the jungle thinned once they were away from the edge. In the heart of the jungle, the upper canopy blocked out almost all of the sunlight, which prevented any undergrowth from springing up. The two members of the expedition party marched in uncomfortable silence until Jorloss spoke up.

"So, what's going on between you and the captain?" he asked accusingly.

"Nothing, and how are you going to take that tone with the guy protecting you from the things that go bump in the night?"

"All I'm saying is that Samix and I have been friends my whole life, and I've never seen the captain look at a guy the way she was looking at you earlier," Jorloss said authoritatively. "Plus, I hooked into the cargo bay cameras as soon as I stepped out of the ship. I saw the little peck on the cheek. Whatever you did to get her attention, if you're toying with her and hurt her, I'll make sure you don't make it to any more planets."

The bravado and sincerity in the threat kept Zade quiet for a few hundred meters. Zade took the time to think about what was driving him. The whole concept of compartmentalization was now shot since everyone wanted to talk about his personal business. Was he driven by loneliness? Was he driven by adventure? Perhaps, but they did have a tremendous amount in common, and there was something extraordinary about Samix. He felt connected to her in a way he hadn't with anyone else before.

"Look, Kermit, I may be a godless, heathen bastard, but I'm truly interested in Samix. I truly care about her. No toying, no ulterior motives."

"Good enough for me. Who is Kermit?" Jorloss replied, his mood visibly improving.

Both men disregarded noise discipline as they finished the movement to the objective, trading jokes and talking about the women of their respective species as they walked. As they neared the goal, the first thing that Zade noticed was the delicious, sweet smell in the air that seemed to be growing more pungent the closer they got to the patch of plants. Like the first 50 feet of the movement, the last 50 feet were exposed to sunlight from the clearing and required the use of the buzz saws to get through. Once they broke through, Jorloss set to work.

Based on what Jorloss said during the briefing, Zade didn't expect to be on the objective very long. Jorloss had to collect some soil samples and a couple of plants to take to his lab aboard the ship, where he would conduct further testing. With Jorloss on his hands and knees playing in the dirt, Zade conducted a quick patrol around the edge of the patch, looking for any signs of danger. With no apparent threats present, he took up a position near Jorloss and waited for him to complete his work.

Zade a tingle on the back of his neck that caused him to check the SSILF feeds. Usually, when his sixth sense tingled, it meant that a threat was near. As the far security perimeter, the SSILF should have eyes on a threat before Zade could positively identify anything. As he began looking through the SSILF feeds, he could see that the robots were on the move. While watching, he could see that the SSILF had teamed up and were now oriented in pairs to the north and south of the objective, but they were still moving. Never removing his attention from the feeds, he informed Jorloss about what was happening.

Jorloss stood and began to watch the feeds as well, both men anxiously wondering what the SSILF were up to. The robots were moving through dense jungle, and as they continued, an image of two men began to resolve. Wherever they were, they had clearly identified a threat and based on the targeting reticles trained on both men, they had identified them as a threat to the team. Zade tried to clean up the image and zoom in on the larger man. Zade's heart sank as he cleared the feeds from his vision. He finally zoomed in far enough to recognize the vest he was wearing on the feeds; the SSILF prepared to engage him and Jorloss.

Zade shouted a warning and dove to the ground as the SSILF opened fire. Jorloss heard Zade's alarm, but not being a combat veteran didn't take cover fast enough to avoid injury. On his way to the ground, a round ripped through his left elbow severing his arm. Luckily Jorloss had chosen a minor recession to work in, so both men had a minute amount of cover. Surrounded and outgunned, Zade immediately threw up the smokescreen. The SSILF, like him, would be able to see through it, but he hoped it would confuse them enough to allow him an edge.

In a split second following the initial volley, Zade could hear Jorloss's garbled screams coming from somewhere behind him. More than anything, he wanted to help his fallen comrade, but he knew if he didn't first neutralize the threat, there would be no need to patch up his friend. As he gingerly peeked over the surrounding berms, Zade could see that the SSILF had caught each other in a crossfire. One in the south team was utterly disabled, laying in a heap, and another must have had its legs taken out because it was firing from the prone position.

"Jorloss. Jorloss! I need you to focus. Do you know how to use a tourniquet?" Zade said as he detached his first aid pouch and tossed it in the direction of Jorloss's screaming.

"Yes," was all Jorloss could manage through gritted teeth.

"I tossed you my first aid kit. Tourniquet whichever limb was hit, tighten it until the bleeding fucking stops, then get Samix on god-damned voice communications. She needs to know what the hell is going on. I have to deal with these fuckers, or they'll smoke us both," the adrenaline of the ambush had thrown Zade back into his combat lexicon.

After giving his instructions, Zade sprang into action. The first priority was the two SSILF to the north. They were the closest, and they had fire superiority. He slid to the north-facing berm and rolled onto his back. Prepping one of the new therm grenades, Zade pulled up the northern SSILFs' feeds and stuck his hand up. He could see the unmistakable red signature of his arm, which appeared to be just over 50 feet away, meaning that he had to land the grenade between 20 and 50 feet from his position. With a deep breath, he tossed the grenade over his head and watched to see where it landed on the SSILF feed. The blinding flash, the deafening boom, and the fact that both SSILF feeds went dark meant that he nailed them.

Moving back to the center of the depression, he could see that the lone remaining SSILF had not moved and was still firing blindly at their position. The SSILF targeted their current location near the western end of the hole. Zade slowly crawled to the far end of the depression, ensuring that no part of his body silhouetted above the berm. As he passed Jorloss, he could see that the scientist was missing the lower portion of his left arm but was able to staunch the bleeding. The scientist had taken on the same washed-out pallor he had when Zade first scared him, and he seemed to be unresponsive.

Shit, he's going into shock.

Zade didn't have time to help him and instead continued to the eastern side of their location. Slowly, he peaked his head over the berm. The SSILF was still firing at Zade's previous location. Initially, Zade planned on using his last grenade, but the SSILF had positioned itself directly in front of the path the team cut through the dense jungle. The grenade would make the area impassable. Jorloss's condition meant that Zade would have to carry him back to the ship. He did not have the time to bushwhack through the dense jungle, nor the additional arm required to carry the scientist and cut a new path. Zade was left with only the option to engage with his rifle. Slowly Zade raised the rifle to the top of the berm and settled his targeting reticle on the SSILF's chest. As he squeezed the trigger, nothing happened. Retreating back behind the relative safety of the berm, Zade turned the rifle to examine its display. It read, "Administrative Lock," making the rifle nothing more than a paperweight. The only entity authorized to administer a weapons lock was Mur. The mastermind of this attack was now apparent, but the purpose was still a mystery.

Zade tossed the rifle aside and began trying to figure out how he would handle the remaining enemy. Grenades were out of the question, and his sidearm was too small to do any damage.

As he let his hands fall to his sides in near resignation, Zade felt the handle of his buzz saw. It would be a bold move, but he was in a drastic situation. Zade grabbed the buzz saw and launched himself, out of the depression, towards the remaining SSILF. As he closed the distance, Zade could see the arc flickering on and off. Every time the ground lost contact, the arc would stop. When he was almost on top of the oblivious SSILF, Zade made his move, swinging the buzz saw down into the robot's torso. The force of the swing lifted the ground into the air, and the buzz saw harmlessly struck the SSILF's shoulder. As soon as the ground landed, the arc fired, and Zade ripped it back out of the SSILF, leaving a molten gash from sternum to shoulder. Preparing for another strike, Zade slid his right foot onto the tether to ensure he would maintain an arc. His next swings took the SSILF's left arm, right arm, and head in quick succession.

With the remaining threat neutralized, Zade headed back to help Jorloss. Upon inspection of the injury, Zade could see a black ichor oozing through the stump below the tourniquet. This black fluid was clearly Jorloss's equivalent of blood, and the growing pool on the ground meant that he had lost more than he could afford to lose. The first thing Zade did was tighten the tourniquet to stop the blood loss, then he began trying to wake Jorloss up. Water, a sharp slap, nothing was working. Zade reached for his first aid kit and broke open, smelling salts. Unsure if they would bring Jorloss back to consciousness after blood loss, or even whether Jorloss had a nose, Zade began waving them in front of the scientist's face. With a gasp, Jorloss's bulbous green eyes flew open.

"Welcome back to the land of the living," Zade said as he loaded the scientific samples into his own assault pack.

"I'm cold and thirsty," Jorloss forced out.

"We're getting back to the ship. I'm going to carry you, but you have to do something for me," Zade said as he stood and hoisted Jorloss onto his back.

"What's that?" Jorloss asked weakly.

"Stay awake, Jorloss," Zade said, straightening himself and moving Jorloss to a better carrying position. "Tell me a story. Tell me about how you and Samix know each other."

Zade started toward the ship at a full sprint but quickly slowed to a walk to minimize how much he jarred Jorloss around. While running, Zade tried to contact Samix, but as he had feared, communications were being jammed, most likely by Mur. As he slowed to a slower pace, a narrative began populating in his interface. Jorloss had chosen to communicate via the interface instead of the more difficult talking.

My family was destitute when I was growing up. As I'm sure you're aware, my species comes from a jungle world much like this one if you did any research. Years of living in the jungle made my people specialize in biology and medicine. My parents, both gifted botanists, traveled throughout Unity space doing freelance work. When I got older, I planned to help them with their work. As freelancers, my parents couldn't afford to send me to school, so they provided a home-school of sorts, teaching me botany.

Samix's family hired my parents to tend their gardens around the same time they adopted Samix. As the only other child at their home, Samix and I became friends quickly. Every day after she completed school, she would search my family's quarters and the gardens until she found me. If it was a slow day, and my parents were done teaching me their trade, they would let me go and play. Initially, I was never allowed into the house to play, but after Samix was adopted, it wasn't an issue.

As summer slowly turned to winter, our friendship grew. The harsh Xi'Ga winter kept everyone non-indigenous to the planet inside, but Samix would come by my family's quarters every day to play. Our house wasn't huge as hired help, maybe slightly larger than the ship's galley, common area, and two of the quarters combined. My family never complained; most of the help lived in houses that held four or five families. As skilled help, we got a smaller house all to ourselves. As the winter dragged on, Samix tired of our small play area and began petitioning her parents to let me come into her home. Eventually, they caved under her relentless persistence, and I was allowed to visit her in the big house.

As a very class-oriented species, my parents would never allow me to visit Samix on my own. They considered it presumptuous. She always had to invite me first, and then I could go play. Her parents eventually warmed up to me and started letting me take meals with

Samix and occasionally spend the night. Years went by with this arrangement. Samix grew and advanced her education while I grew and learned more about my family's trade. By the fifth or sixth year, my parents had slowed down, and I had taken up most of their work on the property.

Around this time, Samix, not one for class division as an orphan, demanded that both families sit down and hash out our differences. While working in the south gardens, my parents returned home to an official envelope propped against our door. It merely contained a time and instructions for us to be at the main house's front entrance. I remember I was terrified; my parents had never even looked at the main home, which meant that I did something to warrant the note. That night we changed into our best clothes and waited on the stoop. My father demanded that we arrive 10 minutes early. At the prescribed time, the front door opened, and we were invited in. The man and woman of the house had invited us to dinner.

It was a stuffy formal dinner, but the families began talking after a while. By the time drinks were served after dessert, the adults were laughing and joking, finally realizing that my family and I were not the run-of-the-mill peons they usually hired. While the adults talked, Samix and I retreated to her game room, where she explained that she had set up the dinner so I could come and go as I pleased. By the end of the night, my family had been moved out of the workers' quarters and into one of the full-sized guest houses on the property, and I had been enrolled at Samix's school.

The guest house was amazing. I had spent my entire life living aboard a ship or in very spartan quarters that contained only the barest of necessities. The new house had a full kitchen, luxury showers, and full-sized beds. It was nicer than anything I had ever seen. Samix's parents took me out to get new clothes for school, which was starting the following week, and Samix showed me the layout of her school so I wouldn't be lost. After we got home, her father showed me the library in the house and told me I could use any book in it any time I wanted. It was the nicest thing anyone had ever done for me, and it was the point at which the trajectory of my life turned. Until this point, I was destined for freelance botany work; now, I could be anything I wanted to be.

I spent the rest of the week pouring through books as fast as I could read them. When I started school, I had to take placement tests to *determine which classes would best develop me, and I had to get my nanite immunizations and interface. To everyone's surprise, I placed into all of Samix's classes and advanced biology. To celebrate the news, my family was again invited over for dinner. This time it was a much more enjoyable event. During dinner, Samix's father extended a job offer to mine. It was to be a senior botany research scientist at a private company that Samix's family owned.*

School was outstanding, and with the interface, I could talk with Samix any time I wanted to. When we both got old enough, we even got to go on outings together. It was the first time I experienced life outside of the little world I was exposed to during my earlier years. Towards the end of primary school, Samix was accepted to the Unity Standard Military Academe. Her acceptance would only hold if Samix could pass her more challenging science classes. One day, while in the library, her father overheard me tutoring Samix in chemistry and biology and suggested that I would be a good candidate for the Academe as well.

Initially, I was hesitant, but after learning about all of the different opportunities the Academe offered, I applied. Exactly one week after I applied, I was accepted. Samix and I completed our primary education and left for the Academe on the same flight. Shortly after we left for the Academe, Samix's father got new employment, relocating her family to the capital. Luckily for my family, they chose to keep the old house as a place to vacation, meaning that mine didn't have to leave. To my amazement, we were both put in the same training company for the primary portion of the Academe. When we graduated from the primary phase, I got orders for the science corps, which I wanted, and Samix got orders for the exploration corps.

It was the first time we had been apart since we were children, but we talked every day. We earned top marks in our specialty training and onboard training. Because of this, we were both selected to crew the XES01 mission, her as captain, me as a medical officer, and chief biologist. Now, here we are, wandering through space with a stray, getting attacked on every planet we touch down on.

About halfway through Jorloss's story, Zade heard the ship's engines fire up. He had picked up the pace but still got to the landing site long after the ship left. Zade knew that Jorloss needed to lay still to recover, but he also knew that there was a village 10 miles north of their current position that was probably curious about the raucous they had caused. The men would have to move as far south, away from the village, as they could to minimize detection.

Zade set Jorloss down gingerly and propped his head up with his assault pack. Before he was comfortable moving, Zade needed to get a few things organized. Zade sprinted back to the objective, and after retrieving the heads of the two remaining SSILF, buried the bodies and any other paraphernalia that could lead to their discovery. Zade then returned to Jorloss and made a skid out of four small trees, two uniform tops, and some cord he carried in his assault pack.

After gently placing the again unconscious Jorloss on the skid, Zade brought up a map of the area he stored in his interface before the mission and searched for a place for them to go to ground and recover. To the south and east, the jungle opened to desert. To the west, he could see the marker indicating a cave. As Zade searched, he felt the connection between his interface and the ship snap; the ship had left the system they were currently in.

Zade set a marker on the cave and began preparations to move out. If anyone were to come to investigate, he wanted to utilize every bit of misdirection he could, so he began cutting an opening through the underbrush on the southeast side of the landing zone. Zade hoped that if anyone came to investigate, they would see the opening and assume that Zade had continued southeast. With the decoy set, Zade headed into the jungle towards the cave, careful not to disturb anything that would give away their direction of travel.

The hike to the cave was uneventful, and Jorloss seemed to regain some of his color during the trip. Zade set the skid down, checked to see that Jorloss was still alive, and entered the cave to ensure it wasn't occupied. The cave was pitch black, but Zade saw it as clear as day with his improved night vision. The first bad sign was the musky aroma that wafted out the mouth of the cave, indicative of occupancy. He drew his sidearm and crept deeper into the abyss. Bones littered the floor, and at the very back was a large furry creature fast asleep. Knowing that one muffled gunshot most likely wouldn't give their position away, Zade crept closer to the animal. Even at 10 feet away, he couldn't tell where the animal's head was.

Zade picked up a rock and hurled it towards the beast. As the rock struck, the animal lifted its head to see what had just accosted it. It was the perfect opportunity. Zade leveled his weapon and dispatched the large animal with one explosive shot. Inside the confines of the small cave, the gunshot was deafening, but luckily for Zade, his pain block kicked in at the first hint of discomfort. Afraid that the smell of fresh blood might draw animals, Zade drug the lifeless body out of the cave and, when safely away from their new domicile, set to skinning it. If Jorloss was in shock, he would need something to keep him warm, and Zade didn't have anything to help.

The night was closing in as Zade returned to the cave to situate Jorloss. The skid he was occupying easily converted to a stretcher after its ends were propped up on rocks. Confident that Jorloss wouldn't topple onto the floor, Zade draped the animal hide, fur side down, over him and changed focus to security.

Zade grabbed the two severed SSILF heads and sat down outside the cave. As he had hoped, both optical sensors were functional, and the emergency power source was still intact. With the ship off-world, Zade could once again connect with the optical sensors using his interface. Zade dismantled the heads and removed the components he needed, tossing the rest into the cave. Using his interface, he quickly checked to ensure their optical feeds worked and could be patched directly to him. With both sensors working, Zade wrote a rough program that would alert him if either sensor detected movement.

Setting the sensor to a wide-angle, 210-degree view, Zade placed them near the cave entrance. He positioned them so their fields of view overlapped, ensuring nothing could get near the mouth of the cave without him noticing, and headed inside to grab some sleep. Zade laid down between the entrance and Jorloss. He used his assault pack as a pillow, curled up in the damp, cold, cave and tried to fall asleep.

CHAPTER 11

Samix watched the landing team start into the jungle before heading to the command deck to monitor their progress. As she walked to the front of the ship, the last thing Zade said to her played on loop in her mind. After seeing Zade dismember the dogs during the repair stop, she had pegged him as a creature solely driven by primal desires. She could still remember the look in his eyes as he dispatched the last dog. It was pure, primal rage. He had moved through the chaos with an efficient frenzy that bordered on demonic. Outnumbered and apparently outmatched, Zade, without hesitation, entered the fray. At that moment, to an onlooker, Zade was an artisan, and death was his medium.

Samix only knew of a handful of men in civilized space who would have acted the same way. Most were gladiators who reveled in the entertainment of death and dismemberment. All were clinically insane, tagged as psychopaths, and tossed in the arena. These men were driven by rage and lust alone, and Zade mirrored their actions perfectly. The debrief with Axis confirmed her assessment of Zade. Axis described Zade's actions during the mission as insane and barbaric in nature, although heroic. To try and get a better picture, Samix had planned the mission on the ice planet, where she tried to get a better idea of who Zade really was. During the mission, Zade opened up about who he was and what drove him. Her mind was put at ease by Zade's tale. She saw that he wasn't a bloodthirsty monster, but she also noticed that he did lust after the adrenaline that accompanied combat. It was a unique trait that both enticed and terrified Samix. Zade's last comment before leaving for mission showed Samix that he actually cared about her, turning her initial assessment of him on its head.

During her movement to the command deck, Samix had stopped walking without even realizing it. She grabbed a cup of sloop and finished her walk to the command deck. Using her command authority, granted to only the captain of a ship, she brought both Zade, and Jorloss's visual feeds up on the displays. Next to the visual feeds, Samix brought up a map that showed the landing party's real-time position. Markers showed the location of both men, but tags for the SSILF were missing. Samix attributed this to a coding error and thought nothing more of it. Finally, as she sat back in the command chair, she opened the men's audio feeds to hear what was going on.

As the speakers crackled to life and the men's voices became audible, she could hear that they were talking about her, of all things. Zade was explaining why he was interested in her. The defensive tone in his voice indicated that Jorloss had either accused him of something or threatened him before she started monitoring the audio. The men's conversation quickly devolved into insults and talk of women. Samix intently listened, sometimes entertained and sometimes disgusted by what she heard. Her ears perked up as Zade began explaining to Jorloss the three traits the women of his species must have for him to be interested.

Zade explained that a perfect woman was athletic, intelligent, and fun to be around. He continued explaining, in crude detail, why he was still single. According to him, the women of his planet often embodied two of the three traits but rarely had the complete trifecta. He explained that those who were intelligent and fun were rarely in good shape. Women who were athletic and intelligent had the personality of a pissed-off porcupine. And those who were athletic and fun were usually dumb as a rock. Zade concluded by conceding that he had only really interacted with women that hung around army bases, so maybe not all women were as he described. Perhaps it was just the ones he had met.

With that, Jorloss started talking about women on his planet. Samix snickered at the thought, knowing that Jorloss had never actually been to his homeworld. The chatter stopped as they came to the edge of the objective. Like their entry into the jungle, they had to cut through a dense patch of jungle to reach the objective. So far, the mission was proceeding flawlessly. Zade walked the perimeter while Jorloss began taking samples. Five minutes after the team hit the objective, the mission went sideways. The SSILF sent to protect the team started firing on them instead. Samix tried, again and again, to hail the team over the communications channel to no avail. Samix watched in horror as the crew scrambled to regain the initiative. With the sound of heavy fire and Jorloss's screams, the comms went dead.

"Mur! Shut down the malfunctioning SSILF! They've turned on the crew," Samix ordered, valiantly trying to maintain her composure.

"Negative, captain. They are not malfunctioning. I have assessed Zade to be a threat to the ship. As such, I took the proper steps to terminate him and punish the crewman who badgered you into releasing him from captivity. Leaving him planetside will serve as his punishment," Mur replied as the ship began its launch sequence.

Samix's mind reeled. She tempered her immediate shock, breathing deeply, and quickly turned her thoughts to finding a solution. She knew that she would have to be the picture of control and poise, much like Zade was the picture of chaos and lethality. If at any point she lost her composure or made the wrong move, there was a good possibility that Mur would label her as a threat and try to neutralize her as well. Heart pounding, Samix pulled up the location data of the planet before the ship broke atmosphere and, using her interface, stored a photo of the data in her personal drive, thankful Jorloss had DNA coded it so Mur couldn't access it. She knew Mur had no intention of allowing the ship back to the planet, which meant that he would erase all data on it the first chance he could.

She knew the ship protocol. The ship would first break for high orbit, where it would calculate the warp data required for its first jump. For a long jump, the ship would periodically drop out of warp to recalculate data and ensure it was still on course. If her plan worked, the ship wouldn't make it past its first navigation stop. Her strategy was risky, and she would require the help of the only other crewman still aboard the ship.

The situation has CHANGED. Meet in my quarters for debrief, Samix messaged Axis through her interface.

"Mur, where are we headed now that the threat has been neutralized?" Samix asked as she headed off the command deck.

"We are returning to Unity space. With only two crewmen, this ship is no longer capable of completing its original mission."

"Very well. I am headed to my quarters for a shower," Samix said as she exited the command deck.

One of the perks of being captain was that the captain's quarters were designed to be private. The walls were insulated to prevent sound from escaping or entering, and most importantly, they were the only quarters that Mur could not monitor remotely. The design went so far as to sever the connection between an individual's interface and the ship as soon as they entered the room. Many captains enjoyed the privacy while still allowing data inflow from the vessel in order to receive alerts and notifications while they rested. It was the only place on board the ship where Samix could formulate a plan and update Axis without the threat of detection. Samix hoped that she would not raise Mur's suspicion by playing along and maintaining her composure.

With the door to her quarters closed securely behind her, Samix opened her personal drive to ensure the photo of the location data was present and legible. She waited for Axis to join her so she could enlist his help. Minutes, which felt like days, passed before Axis pounded on her door. Before the door was completely open, Axis stormed in, clearly agitated from being pulled away from his work. As the door closed, he began his rant about how inconsiderate it was for Samix to pull him away from his research.

"If you're finished, we have much bigger problems than the study of new rocks," She said, irritated, not just with him.

The insulting disregard for his work silenced, Axis who stood sulkily waiting for an explanation. Samix quickly explained how Mur had turned and tried to kill both Jorloss and Zade while they were on the planet. Now the ship was headed back to Unity space, leaving the two, if they were still alive, stranded. Axis's mouth fell open in disbelief.

"But, why?" he asked, finally able to speak.

"Mur classified Zade as a non-crew threat and is punishing Jorloss for allowing him out of containment."

"That's absurd! Zade has saved all of our lives at least once," Axis protested.

"Which is exactly why I need to stop Mur and get them back," Samix retorted quickly. "I could really use your help."

"Zade saved my life the same as you, I owe him," Axis said, a look of grim determination settling on his face. "What do you need me to do?"

"We need to reset the AI, but we can't do that while we are in warp space, which means that we have to wait until we drop out for a nav stop. According to the computer, we have 12 hours."

Axis sat down on the couch in the quarters and brainstormed different ways to accomplish their goals. Next to Jorloss, Axis knew the most about the ship's systems and how they functioned. The two were deep in thought when Samix spoke up.

"Can you cause the material recycler to malfunction without raising suspicion?" She asked.

"Sure, but how does that help us?"

"If it goes down, I will have an excuse to go down to the subdeck where I can access the AI core and manually reset it."

Samix went into detail about her plan. Just before the ship dropped out of warp, Axis would cause the recycler to malfunction. Samix would move to the subdeck, appearing to be down there to fix it. While down there, Samix would position herself directly outside the AI core, where she would wait until the ship dropped out of warp. The instant the ship was in real space, Samix would reset the AI. While the AI was resetting, Axis would use the computer systems in the medical bay, which Jorloss had reprogrammed to be completely separate from the AI, to add Zade to the crew roster. The AI would reset, pull the new crew manifest and recognize Zade as a crew member. After agreeing with the plan, Axis brought up one minor problem. The AI would take a couple of hours to reset, time when ship power and life support would be shut down. The oxygen levels would drop to dangerously low levels before the AI completely reset and turned them back on.

"I know that's a risk, but we are the two hardiest crewmembers on the ship. Both of us can withstand the cold, and I can stand the oxygen deprivation. After you change the crew roster, grab whatever you need to survive from the medical bay, and seal yourself in your quarters. I will put myself into stasis and wait it out," Samix said.

"That sounds great for me, but even in stasis, two hours without oxygen could kill you."

"It's a risk I have to take."

After agreeing on the plan, the crewmembers continued their routine, so they did not raise suspicion. Samix stretched out on her couch, thinking over the plan, while Axis headed back to his lab to feign work while the ship neared its nav stop. As she thought about the current situation, Samix became more irritated. Not only at the fact that two of her crewmen were in danger, but more at the point that she couldn't even get the male AI of her ship to respect her. This train of thought led to her thinking about Zade, the only man next to Jorloss, who valued her abilities and respected her both as a captain and a person.

Thinking about Zade and Jorloss made her replay the last sounds and images from the mission. To her distaste, she found herself more worried about Zade than Jorloss. She felt terrible about this because Jorloss was her best friend, while she had only known Zade for a short while. She knew that she heard Jorloss screaming on the audio, which meant that, either injured or terrified, he was alive. She couldn't even hear Zade moving over the gunfire or any indicator that he was incapacitated by the initial volley. She spent the entire 12-hour trip lost in her morbid thoughts. The ship's notification would drop out of warp in 10 minutes snapped her back to reality.

While in his lab, Axis thought of the best way to disable the recycler. As the smallest member of the crew, he was often tasked with fixing it when it broke. Axis knew that the recycler had three openings; the one in the robotics lab and one in the terraforming lab were large and meant to handle large objects. The one in the galley was only meant to take small waste items from the food processor. Knowing these key facts about the recycler, he stuffed the largest wrench he could find into his back pocket and headed to the galley for a meal. After grabbing a tray from the processor, he sat down directly on the uncomfortable wrench in his pocket. The mild discomfort, he hoped, would ensure his actions didn't look malicious. After removing the wrench from his pocket and setting it on the edge of his, tray Axis pushed his food around aimlessly, too worried to eat anything. When the countdown timer for the nav stop hit 30 minutes, Axis grabbed his tray, still holding the wrench, and tossed it down the recycler chute. The wrench hit the small grinding wheels at the bottom of the pipe and firmly wedged in between them, stopping the machine cold. Muttering some nonsense to strengthen the illusion of an accident, Axis pulled off the top of the chute and pretended to examine the damage, waiting for Samix to arrive. Samix walked into the galley as the countdown timer hit 10 minutes.

"What the hell did you do to my ship this time?" she asked.

"Sorry, captain. I think I got a wrench stuck in the chute. Shut the whole damn thing down."

"Why did you even have a wrench? You know what, never mind. Get back to work while I go down and take a look at the damage."

With that fallacious reprimand, Axis went into his quarters, where he anxiously waited for the emergency lighting to kick on, signaling that Samix had started the AI reset. Samix headed down the nearest stairwell to the subdeck. Unlike the upper decks, the subdeck was cramped with different machinery. The walkway was nothing more than a crawlspace to allow for the maximum amount of equipment to be stored. Samix meandered down the crawlspace pretending to be lost. She was moving slow enough to ensure that she would be just outside the AI core when she felt the ship drop out of warp.

With the sharp jolt that accompanied the ship's reappearance into real space, she hit the core's access button. The AI core was housed in a hexagonal space with different colored quantum connections leading out from the center where the AI was housed. Before she could fully clear the access way, the door slammed shut on her left foot, trapping her just out of reach of the manual reset handle.

"You are in an area you are not authorized to be in. You are threatening the survival of this ship," Mur's voice informed her over the intercom, its menace echoing through the small space.

The crushing pain in her trapped foot grew to unbearable levels as she stretched for the handle. At that moment, she regretted not getting a pain block like Zade's. Despite herself, she smiled, remembering the day he told her about it. Stretching made the pain worse, but the handle remained out of reach. With the pain growing to maddening levels, Samix collapsed into a hopeless pile. As she did, she felt a hard metal item in her pocket. It was a knife Zade had made for her after explaining how he never went anywhere without one. Flipping it open, Samix leaned down towards her trapped foot and sliced down the side of her boot. The now-open top of her boot gave her just enough room to slide her foot free from the door and start the manual reset. The newly freed foot hurt more than when it was trapped. Samix had just enough time to drop into stasis before she passed out from the unbearable pain.

The ship went silent, and emergency lighting came on: Axis's signal to move. He jumped out of his chair and headed to the medical bay. The computers in the medical bay housed all crew records and could be run on emergency power. This allowed the crew to continue providing medical care even if the ship was damaged and lost power. Axis headed to the nearest computer and pulled up Zade's personnel file, which contained all of the information required to be added to the crew roster. Axis pulled up the crew roster, and by using an administrative bypass, began altering the underlying code of the file. Quickly, Axis created a new entry and began inputting all pertinent information from the personnel file. Satisfied that his work would go unquestioned, he backed out of the files and began scavenging for supplies to outlast the life support shutdown.

He knew that he could survive the shutdown without any

equipment, but there was no reason to be uncomfortable. The first thing he grabbed was a six-hour oxygen bottle with an attached breathing mask. He had been to planets with low oxygen levels, and although he could survive, Axis hated the constant feeling of suffocation that limited oxygen situations produced. Next, he grabbed two emergency heated blankets. While he waited for Samix to make her move, he had done some mental math. If the ship was in deep space, the interior temperature would drop to nearly -150 degrees in two hours. Again, he could survive the low temperatures, but why not do it in comfort? With everything he would need for the shutdown, Axis headed back to his quarters to play on his interface and wait.

Precisely two hours after power loss, the emergency lighting was replaced with the ship's standard lighting. The AI core had completed its manual reboot. Axis ventured out of his room just as the Mur's voice came across the intercom.

"Welcome to the XES01, Unity exploration vessel."

As the only conscious crewmember aboard, Mur continued to Axis's interface, *I require that you validate essential information.*

Only one conscious? What is the status of the captain? Axis asked, hesitant and confused.

Captain Samix is on the subdeck, incapacitated from injury. Are you prepared to validate information?

Yes...whatever, just make this fast. Axis said as he headed to the subdeck to find out what had happened to Samix.

This experimental exploration vessel is tasked with exploring the galaxy we are currently in. Mission duration undetermined.

Correct.
This vessel is crewed by five personnel: Samix, captain, subdeck. Axis, geological scientist, subdeck. Farn, anthropologist, deceased. Alex Zade, security officer, location unknown. Jorloss, medical officer, location unknown.

Correct. The last two wouldn't be lost if you hadn't gone crazy earlier.

Axis, please explain. Mur requested.

"No. Just get in your frame and assist me in helping the captain. When she comes to, she can tell you what she thinks you need to know," Axis snapped aloud rather than through his interface.

The thought of the captain being injured and hearing how two of his fellow crew members were lost had irritated him. During the computer's questioning, he had made it down to the subdeck and stood outside the AI core. Using his highly sophisticated sensory organs, he could see that something was jamming the door. Upon further inspection, he identified it as Samix's boot. It had been so severely damaged by the door that he couldn't even tell if her foot was still in it. He did know, which made the situation even more urgent, was the smell of fresh blood emanating from under the jammed door.

Lacking both Samix's composure and Zade's determination, Axis quickly became more panicked with every unsuccessful attempt at opening the jammed door. He first attempted was to use the door controls, which he quickly learned were unresponsive. His second attempt was to use strength to force the door open. Even when using all the strength his high gravity modified body could muster, the door didn't budge. As a last resort, Axis returned to the door controls. He knew he had the strength to tear the cover plate off the controls, and he did just that. Thinking that the control panel may have been damaged, he used the exposed wires to force the door open. With the appropriate circuitry connected, Axis touched the wire bundle to an exposed power wire. He was rewarded with the sound of the door motor laboring; the door moved a fraction of an inch but no more.

"Would you like assistance with your task?" Mur asked from behind him.

Axis had been so focused on the task at hand that the request startled him. Mur was now occupying the fire engine red frame it used to maintain a physical presence around the crew. The fact that the 1,000-pound robot had made it down the small crawlspace without detection showed that it was surprisingly nimble and quiet.

"Yes, open this door. I don't care if you have to rip it off its track, the captain is stuck in there, and she is hurt."

"I must advise against this. Damage to this door will leave my AI core exposed."

"If you don't open this fucking door, I will go to the robotics lab, gather as many of Zade's explosives as I can carry, and get in myself. And maybe, just maybe, I will be lucky enough to destroy you in the process."

Axis's patience was running thin; he was in mild disbelief that the AI who had caused the whole situation was now worried about its own safety. A tense moment of silence passed as Mur tried to determine if Axis was bluffing. The robot finally motioned for Axis to move out of the way so he could access the entry. Axis slid down the hall, and Mur moved into place in front of the jammed door. Mur, braced by the door frame, began to strain against the stuck hatch. The sound of metal screaming as it failed signaled that the door was open. Axis quickly looked under the robot's arm, into the AI core room, and sensed the lifeless body of his captain. He quickly pushed past the robot and began checking to see if Samix was still alive. She was stretched across the middle of the core room, hand still grasping the manual override handle. When she had put herself into stasis, her skin turned into a thick gray crystalline coating meant to protect the rest of her body from any inhospitable environment. Now, her stasis coating covered her whole body except for her left foot. The foot could not properly seal because of the damage caused by the door and had been left exposed to the extremely low temperature inside the ship during the reset. During stasis, her metabolic processes nearly ceased making it difficult for Axis to determine if she was still living.

"I can't move her myself. Once I get out of here, bring her to the medical bay," Axis ordered.

After nodding in acknowledgment, trying to ease Axis, Mur said, "if it makes you feel better, I can still sense her vital signs."

Axis pushed into the crawlspace and headed to the medical bay without hesitation. Before he attended the Academe, he had some fundamental medical training given to all settlers if they were required to assist each other in the inhospitable terrains they faced. In addition to his training, he had seen Jorloss work many times and felt comfortable that he could at least keep Samix alive, a task of utmost importance since she was the only one with access to her personal drive, where the location of the stranded crewmen was.

On the way to the medical bay, he formulated a plan of attack. His biggest priority was to keep Samix alive. Second, he would try to make her comfortable enough to come out of stasis. Third, he would try to aid her nanites in repairing her foot. The hospital bed nearest the door was covered in some equipment boxes that Jorloss had been searching through before the mission. Axis headed to it and quickly pushed the boxes to the floor, making room for Samix. With a place to rest cleared, he turned his attention to the tall piece of equipment near the head of the bed. It was a small computer with leads that ended in adhesive pads. He knew it was used to monitor vitals and prioritize nanite functions to bring the patient to which it was attached back to optimal health. He flipped it on and quickly punched in Samix's name. The computer displayed Samix's medical file and confirmed that it had the appropriate code necessary to help her.

With a plan in place to keep Samix alive, Axis started to think through his second priority: how to get Samix out of stasis. Unsure if her body would react to any stimuli from outside of her crystalline shell, Axis began to think about what he could do to reinforce that she was once again in a hospitable environment. Remembering that the two things he needed to maintain his comfort were oxygen and warmth, he headed to a supply closet at the rear of the bay for an oxygen bottle and emergency blanket. With the blanket and oxygen staged next to the bed, Axis began trying to figure out how he could help save Samix's foot. While he sat and pondered his new problem, Mur arrived carrying Samix. Axis instructed him to place her on the bed then leave the medical bay. After setting her down, Mur inquired about the ship's destination.

"Shall I start a warp to Unity space where the captain can receive medical treatment?"

"Negative, we stay right where we are. When the captain recovers, we will head back and retrieve the crew you stranded."

"How will the captain recover? You are not the medical officer."

"Damn it, if you question me again, I will deactivate you. The
ship stays where it is, and you stay the hell out of this bay."

An almost comical look of confusion spread across the
robot's face before it exited the medical bay. Axis hooked Samix
up to the vital machine, placed an oxygen mask on her face,
covered her with the emergency blankets, and sat down near
the entrance. The sight of Samix laying on the medical bed reminded Axis of all the times Farn was in the exact same spot.
Farn was one of the clumsiest individuals Axis had ever met,
regularly having accidents in his lab, which required recovery
time in the medical bay. One particular incident stood out in
Axis's mind. Early in the trip, Farn had dropped a large masonry
drill that he was using on his hand. The drill mangled his hand to
a nearly unrecognizable pulp, and Jorloss had to put the injured
limb inside a special device for recovery. Less than a day after
the accident, Farn's hand was completely recovered. Spinning
to the nearest computer, Axis began searching through Jorloss's
medical logs for the incident.

Axis found the incident reports and began reading them.
Jorloss had placed Farn's hand inside a soft tissue regeneration
matrix. The matrix, a thick blue gelatinous liquid, worked in
concert with the nanites. It provided all of the materials required to repair a severely damaged appendage that the nanites
could not fix independently. With hope renewed, Axis began
scouring the bay for the matrix. He found it, with accompany-
ing containment bags, in a storage unit filled with temperature-
sensitive compounds. Axis quickly grabbed a containment bag
and filled it, nearly overflowing, with the matrix. With the bag
full, he gently slid Samix's brutally crushed and frostbitten foot
into the matrix and sealed the bag around the undamaged part
of her leg.

With nothing more he could do for Samix, he turned his
attention to security. Axis knew the once homicidal AI had
been completely reset, but he couldn't get himself to trust it.
Now roaming around the ship in its frame, it could dispatch
the remaining organic crewmembers efficiently. Although Axis

wanted to stay at Samix's side, he knew he needed insurance against the AI. After doing one final check on Samix, he headed out of the medical bay towards the robotics lab, ensuring the bay door would only open when his interface was near. Since their mission together, Zade and Axis had become friends, and Axis learned that Zade had amassed a small arsenal in the robotics lab. There were two pieces of hardware he was interested in: a copy of the earth firearm Zade regularly carried and one of the multifunctionality replica breaching charges Zade had created.

After finding the cache, Axis strapped on a thigh holster to carry the sidearm loaded with Zade's highly effective Excalibur rounds. Zade had been experimenting with different sizes. Axis chose the largest one; he believed Zade had said it was a .50 caliber. As both royalty and a scientist, Axis felt ridiculous carrying around the cannon, but he was currently dealing with a situation that fell well outside the realm of either science or the royal court. The charge, Axis found, was elementary to use. After connecting to it with his interface, he encrypted the connection and programmed it to be remotely detonated. Now armed, he headed back down to the subdeck. After firmly attaching the charge to the AI core, he shot a message to Mur. The failsafe almost guaranteed that the ship would never return to civilized space, but he would only use it if Mur turned again and the crewmen's deaths were imminent.

I am giving you this order as the acting captain. You are not to enter the medical bay at any time or remain on the same deck as either myself or Samix while in your frame. If you violate this order, you will be deemed a threat to this ship, and I will be forced to neutralize you through direct means. In the event I cannot neutralize you directly, I will do so indirectly.

Roger, Mur responded sadly, realizing that he must have done something horrible earlier, the emotion in his response sounding eerily human.

Axis headed back to the medical bay with everything in place, where he positioned a chair facing the door, laid his sidearm across his lap, and pulled security. After the ship went into the night cycle, Axis dozed off. Two days passed before Samix stirred. After a meal, he returned to the medical bay to see Samix struggling to sit up in her bed. Axis dropped the cup of sloop he had gotten and ran to her side. The day prior, her foot had healed enough to remove the recovery matrix, and aside from being slightly pale and underweight, she looked perfectly healthy.

"What's going on?" she croaked through parched lips.

"Woah, take it easy. You're in the medical bay recovering," Axis said as he handed her a small cup of water.

Samix couldn't remember anything after opening the door to the AI core, so Axis filled her in on the events that transpired after she reset the AI. He started with how Mur had tried to prevent her from tampering with its core and finishing with how he had set up a means of protection from Mur. Samix sat quietly listening to the story before she spoke again.

"We need to go back for the others. With the time dilation of our warp, we have no idea as to how long they have been stranded."

"I know, but you were the only one with access to the planet's location," Axis said sadly.

Samix sent a copy of the location's image to his interface with a look of forced concentration. Axis quickly opened the message to examine it, and when he turned his attention back to Samix, he saw that she had fallen asleep. Axis quickly instructed the AI to travel to the location, and within seconds he felt the ship drop into warp. Axis sat down hard, almost overtaken by the feeling of hope that Samix's recovery stirred. It was hope that everything might turn out okay. Axis knew that even though the ship was moving in the right direction, there was no way he could recover the lost crew on his own. He sat silently, willing Samix to recover before they reached their destination.

CHAPTER 12

Days passed on the strange planet; Jorloss seldom moved. Zade had been keeping watch and scavenging for supplies but to no avail. Having only one person to feed and hydrate helped stretch the trivial amount of rations and water brought on mission in his assault pack. Not expecting a prolonged stay off the ship, Zade had only packed three bottles of water, a small bag of trail mix, and a small package of jerky, the staples of combat soldiers' diet. By night three, there was only one bottle of water and a handful of trail mix left. Zade fell into an uneasy sleep, his body aching from the limited nutritional intake. The unrestful rest and stress associated with being on high alert constantly.

Slowly returning to consciousness, Zade noted that the previous night had been the best sleep he had gotten since he arrived on the planet. Upon opening his eyes, he was greeted by a pair of large green eyes, inches from his face, staring back at him. The unexpectedness of seeing Jorloss recovered startled Zade into a hyper-alert state, and he surveyed the cave around him.

"I was worried about you," Jorloss said, the look of worry slowly dissolving from his face. "After I woke, I shook you to try and wake you up, but you didn't move. After closer examination, I noticed that you were cold and had taken on a faint blue shade. Figuring it was from sleeping on the cave floor unprotected, I gave you the makeshift blanket that I'm assuming you put on me."

"Worried about me?" Zade exclaimed. "I was worried about

you. You almost bled out when the SSILF turned on us."

"Thank you for patching me up, by the way. I do have some questions once you fully wake up and get moving," Jorloss said. "Why aren't we back on the ship?"

"Well, that's the million-dollar question, isn't it?" Zade replied before informing Jorloss about the events since the conflict.

Zade explained that he had carried Jorloss from the objective towards the ship, only to find that it had left before they reached the landing zone. Afraid that the melee may have sparked the interest of the locals, Zade had created some false trails then went to ground in the cave they now occupied. Jorloss stood, listening intently as Zade spoke. For Jorloss, the story raised as many questions as it answered. Zade finished his explanation as he began digging through his assault pack, looking for something before Jorloss finally spoke up.

"So, I guess the question now is why did the ship leave, and what are the odds it will come back?"

After realizing that, while he slept, Jorloss had finished off the remaining food and water, Zade began thinking aloud.

"I'm sure it's a matter of when the ship returns, not if. If you and Samix are friends from childhood, I don't think she would leave you behind. Something must have malfunctioned on the ship. Since you finished off the last of our supplies, we need to focus on getting water and food until they come back."

Assuming correctly that he was the only one out of the pair who had any type of survival training, Zade began to strategize and plan for their survival. The objective of any survival situation was to make it to a populated, friendly area. In the event that there is no nearby friendly populated area, it is best to stay near the spot where you were lost, Zade explained. As for food, while Jorloss was recovering, Zade had seen plentiful game in the jungle but was unsure if it was edible. Jorloss confirmed that the nanites in both their bloodstreams would prevent any sickness, so Zade started explaining the most detrimental problem the landing team currently faced. While Jorloss rested, Zade had scoured the map of the area for any kind of water source. Unable to find any streams, ponds, or creeks, Zade recognized that the nearest water source was the well in the village to their north. Sensing where Zade was heading, Jorloss spoke up.

"No, no, no. We cannot be seen by the locals. You said it yourself; your species couldn't grasp the concept of alien life. How do you think this species will react?"

"I don't know how they will react. But I do know that without water, in this heat, I will be gone in three days."

Zade began disassembling the litter to put his uniform top back on. Jorloss just sat pondering a solution. The enormity of his situation finally impressed upon him. Zade stuffed the extra uniform top in his assault pack, and while heading to the mouth of the cave, he motioned for Jorloss to follow him.

"Do you really think it is wise for us to approach the village?" Jorloss asked as he stood to follow Zade.

"We will not approach the village. I will approach the village, alone, after night has fallen to reduce the chance of being caught."

Zade and Jorloss were currently headed out to scavenge for food. Since this planet was similar enough to Jorloss's homeworld to have the plant of interest at the objective, Zade figured that Jorloss would be able to identify things to eat. Zade was confident that he could harvest game, but he feared that he would become ill without the vitamins from fruits and vegetables. The two wandered through the jungle following a roughly northwest heading.

"You can thank this guy for the blanket," Zade joked as they passed the carcass he had skinned days earlier. Clearly, there were predators and scavengers in the area. The skinned animal had been reduced to nothing more than a red spot on the ground with bones sticking out of it. The two men meandered for hours, with Jorloss occasionally identifying plants that resembled those from his homeworld, which were edible. The most promising for Zade was a small purple and red seed-filled berry that Jorloss identified as having many vitamins. Removing the empty trail mix bag from his pack, Zade filled it with the strange berries. Jorloss informed him that he should, under no circumstances, swallow the berry's seeds. The plant thrived in a dark acidic environment in its adolescence and could easily rupture an individual's abdominal wall if it took root in the digestive tract.

As dusk set in, the two men agreed that a small fire in the cave would be low risk and decided that if they ran across game, they would attempt to kill it for a food source. As the men were returning to the cave, rustling vegetation caught Zade's attention. Quickly motioning for Jorloss to stop, Zade crouched and waited to see what was making the noise. The creature that emerged from the brush was almost identical to a wild boar on Earth. The thought of fresh bacon almost made Zade spring into action without thinking. After restraining his urge, Zade motioned for Jorloss to retreat back far enough to talk while still able to keep the pig within sight.

Zade had gone boar hunting countless times on earth, so he knew that the animal could use its 12-inch-long, razor-sharp tusks with lethal efficiency when threatened. He also knew that pigs relied heavily on their sense of smell, meaning Zade could dispatch it if he could stay downwind of it. The plan Zade laid out was simple. The area they were in was rimmed with rock outcroppings, and luckily the wind was blowing towards the only traversable exit. Knowing that a gunshot could raise suspicion and give away their position, Zade would wait atop the outcropping near the entrance with his combat knife. Jorloss would circle around upwind of the animal, and drive it towards Zade, a feat most likely accomplished as soon as the pig caught Jorloss's scent. He hoped that by the time the pig caught his scent, it would be within striking range.

After agreeing on the plan, Zade used his improved low light vision to quietly move into place. Once he was perched atop the rocks, he sent a message to Jorloss's interface telling him to start driving the pig. Being from a species commonly identified as prey on their homeworld, Jorloss approached the animal with a cautious timidity. As he approached the dangerous animal, Zade could see that although it noticed Jorloss, it didn't identify him as a threat and stood its ground. Zade knew that if the pig was startled while Jorloss was within striking range, there was a reasonable possibility of injury, so he sent another message to Jorloss instructing him to start making noise.

Jorloss stopped walking as he read the message. After which, he looked in Zade's direction, unable to see him through the gloom, with a look that bordered on terror. Before Zade could start moving towards the pig, worried that Jorloss had frozen in fear, Jorloss clapped his hands, and the boar started towards the small exit directly in front of Zade. The pig stumbled as it picked up Zade's scent, the perfect opportunity for him to strike. Zade launched himself off the rock, landed astride the 400-pound beast, and buried his combat knife to the hilt, top dead center just in front of the animal's shoulders. The strike severed the animal's brain stem, killing it immediately. It was the cleanest kill Zade had ever achieved, rifle, bow, and shotgun included.

As he started field dressing the animal, Zade looked over his shoulder to see Jorloss, once again, frozen in fear. It was only the second time he had seen Zade work, but it was the first not driven by self-defense and was clearly trying to process the brutality of his actions. As he finished skillfully cleaning the animal, he called Jorloss over and handed him his assault pack, not wanting to get it messy. With the fresh kill balanced across his shoulders, Zade led the way back to the cave. The men walked in silence. Jorloss immediately entered the cave while Zade prepared the fire and meal. As he made up the meal, Zade kept an eye on the scientist.

Jorloss was exhibiting an emotion he knew well. Zade had seen it on the faces of his newest soldiers during their first contact and had experienced it personally during his first battle. It was the look of shock that every man wears the first time he realizes that he has just taken a life, or someone was trying to take his. The shock was born from a sharp, sometimes painful, reminder that he was mortal. For non-combatants, time dulls it; for warriors, repeated exposure desensitizes them to it. Not because they wish for death, not because they feel invincible, but because the warrior accepts that life is fleeting, and everyone has an expiration date. Now, Zade knew Jorloss had to decide. He could choose to question his actions and let the events destroy him, or he could choose to accept the circumstances and grow stronger from them. Zade stayed quiet, knowing that no outside comfort or third-party rationalization could make Jorloss's decision any more comfortable.

After finishing the most delicious bacon he had ever eaten, Zade set to secure the meat for the night. He used a trick he learned while hiking in the Rockies. Walking a short way away from the cave entrance, he found a large branch that would support the weight of the pig and threw his spool of cord over it. Positioning the line far enough from the trunk to prevent a predator from climbing the tree to get at the meat, Zade tied the pig up and hoisted it into the branches. Hikers often did this with their packs to prevent bears from destroying them while looking for the food inside.

Zade returned to the cave. Jorloss was nowhere to be found. Zade emptied his assault pack of everything but the empty water bottles before striking out to find him and ultimately get water from the village. He found the scientist pacing back and forth just north of the cave entrance and extended the useless platitude he knew would not help Jorloss decide.

"You okay? We had to eat," he said, attempting to keep it simple.

"I don't know if I'm okay. My people have never preyed on other living things, ever. You just killed an animal, and I helped. What does that make me?"

"Honestly, it makes you a person who, while in a difficult situation, chose to eat and live instead of starve and die. Nothing more, nothing less."

"It can't be that simple. I've seen you take on worse situations with a smile on your face. How do you deal with it?"

"For most people, like you, it is that simple. Your actions were borne out of necessity. You only have to question yourself once you find yourself enjoying the kill."

"You don't enjoy combat? Your smile suggests otherwise."

"Jorloss, I don't think my reasoning will help, but here goes. Yes, I do enjoy... lethal interactions... but I have a personal code that allows me to live with myself after I am done," Zade explained. "I never knowingly hurt innocents. I never engage with individuals who cannot defend themselves. I never kill without a need to. If I meet those three rules, I sleep just fine at night."

"Thank you," Jorloss said as he turned and headed back to the cave.

Zade turned his attention to the task at hand. He brought up his map and identified the route he would need to take to the village. The village was just over twenty kilometers away, a distance he could cover in just over an hour with his improved sight and musculature. Night had just begun, giving him ample time to get the water without being seen. The run was quick, and the villagers kept the jungle edge cleared, meaning that he could observe every angle of the village from the cover of the jungle before heading to the well. After a quick patrol around the village, Zade found a good vantage point overlooking the well and waited for the foot traffic to cease and hut lights to go out before entering the settlement.

Hours passed, but when the planet's twin moons were directly overhead, the village was tranquil. Zade did a quick thermal scan of the houses surrounding the well and was pleased to see all, but one of the occupants was lying on the ground, presumably sleeping. Before entering the village, he unsnapped the clips on his assault pack so he wouldn't have to make noise while he was exposed. He crept quietly towards the well; his movements catlike. At first glance, the well appeared to be a rope and bucket affair with the obligatory stone knee wall surrounding it. Upon closer inspection, Zade saw that the well, although built like an old-fashioned one, had a small spigot and valve on one side.

After dropping his pack, he opened and lined up all of his water bottles. He would only need to turn the, possibly squeaky, valve twice, once on and once off. This was an unnecessary precaution as the valve was mercifully quiet. Turning the water on as low as possible to prevent splashing noises, he began filling the water bottles. As he capped the second bottle and reached for the third, the sound of a door opening behind him caused him to freeze. A glance over his shoulder showed a woman walking towards the well with a pitcher in one hand and a torch in the other. Unable to escape into the jungle without being seen in the torchlight, he quickly gathered his things and moved around to the side directly opposite the woman.

With his back pressed against the well, he held his breath and anxiously waited for the woman to go back inside. The torchlight spilled around the well, unnervingly close to him, as the woman filled her pitcher. Zade finally took a breath after watching the torchlight recede and heard her hut door close again. Not wanting any more excitement for the night, Zade expeditiously filled the last water bottle and headed back into the jungle. He saw that Jorloss had gone to sleep at the cave and let the fire burn low. Noting that the cave entrance faced south, away from the village, Zade stocked up the fire before bedding down himself.

The men spent days with little more than scavenging for food to fill their time. Zade had taken to hunting, while Jorloss focused on gathering edible plants and berries. As the days passed, Jorloss seemed to recover from the identity crisis he had been plagued with since the pig kill. The men could never finish the entire amount of meat from one of Zade's kills. It spoiled quickly in the jungle heat and humidity. It meant that Zade had to hunt almost daily. With the daytime hunting over and evening meal consumed, Zade would wait for nightfall before heading to the village to refill the team's drinking water supply. By the second night, he had gotten his timing routine down and had not encountered a local since the first visit to the well.

After a meal of game and the purple and red berries, the men sat around the campfire idly chatting as they waited for night on the third day. Jorloss's arm had almost completely healed, and his energy levels were steadily rising by the day.

"I've meant to ask you, why didn't the nanites close off your wound when we were attacked by the SSILF?" Zade asked the scientist, who was grabbing more wood for the fire.

"Like the amphibians of your world, my species has rather robust regenerative properties," Jorloss responded in a matter-of-fact tone. "That fact, coupled with my role as medical officer, caused me to remove the trauma repair programming in my nanites to allow them to run more efficiently. I figured I would never be in danger, so the repair code wasn't necessary."

"You didn't think you would be in danger? How exactly was this mission briefed to the crew? I've only been on the ship for a couple of weeks, and it has been the most dangerous time of my life."

"Unity space has been peaceful for the last 14 centuries. No one in the fleet has experienced anything more than police action, let alone open combat. I guess we just figured that space outside the Unity would be just as civilized as space within."

"That is amazing. My planet can't go more than a few decades without armed conflict, and that's just a planet. How has there been no power struggles in your whole galaxy for over 1400 years?"

"It just happened that way. The founding species of the Unity came to power because they were more technologically advanced than other species. Everyone played nice to get space travel tech. The prosperity that accompanied the ability to spread out into the galaxy stopped any infighting. Now, the Unity is very proactive, dealing with threats before a shooting war can develop."

As the light faded, Zade entertained how Earth would be if man could travel the stars. He hoped for an ideal situation, where different countries would turn their focus outward, colonizing to meet their needs. He feared that the reality was countries would use advances in technology to destroy each other without even batting an eye towards the stars. Only after one government or coalition claimed the entire Earth would they look to expand outward.

Night had finally fallen, enveloping the men in impenetrable darkness before Zade headed out for the water resupply. Like the previous nights, movement through the jungle was easy, and Zade circled the village, waiting for the last inhabitants to fall asleep. With all but one cottage dark, Zade watched a young woman, the one who had almost caught him on his first visit, walk to the well. Halfway to the well, something caught her eye, and she stopped. She turned to peer into the jungle to her right, the direction from which he initially approached the village every night. Zade thought nothing of it since she wasn't interested in his current location. Her curiosity now peaked, the woman slowly progressed towards the tree line torch outstretched in front of her.

With a blood-curdling scream, she dropped the torch and ran back to the safety of her home. As the other villagers heard her, lights came on, and people rushed outside to see what had terrified the young woman. Those that did come out to investigate were armed, a sign that threats to the village were commonplace in the jungle in which they lived. Having no direct line of sight to the thing that startled the woman, Zade began backtracking until he could see it. As he cleared a dense patch of large trees, Zade saw the unmistakable silhouette of Jorloss standing just inside the jungle.

What the hell are you doing here? He asked Jorloss via the interface.

I wanted to see how you got the water so we could take turns. Didn't think it was fitting that you had to go every night.

Well, it looks like we're going thirsty tomorrow. Get back to the cave as quietly as possible and douse the fire, Zade instructed as he began heading back to the shelter.

The villagers had begun lighting more torches and throwing them towards the patch of jungle that the young woman identified. It was a clever tactic to get a visual of the threat before blindly rushing towards it. Zade turned to watch his crewmate's progress into the depth of the trees. He prayed that their direction of travel would go unknown. But he could see Jorloss, now fully illuminated, working his way towards the cave. Lacking any knowledge on misdirection, Jorloss was headed directly towards the cave as the villagers watched him recede into the jungle. Based on how the villagers were armed, Zade figured that they would be hunted by morning light.

Zade met Jorloss at the cave. The trip back was slow, as he stopped often to look and listen for anyone following him. Jorloss had doused the fire then headed up a large tree nearest the cave entrance to watch for Zade. The crewmen quickly packed everything they needed if they had to suddenly abandon their hide. Knowing that trouble could be following them, Zade organized an impromptu guard schedule so that the men could get some rest. As the cause of their current predicament, Jorloss volunteered for the first watch. Zade closed his eyes, but sleep was evasive. He was awake when Jorloss signaled the change of shifts.

Zade couldn't merely sit stationary as he guarded. Sleep's siren song was calling to him louder and louder as the night stretched on. Instead, he began patrolling the perimeter of their campsite, straying farther from the cave with every lap. As he had anticipated, the night was quiet, but at first light, he could hear a large group of men gathering at the edge of the jungle. His patrol had taken him kilometers away from the cave entrance, and by morning he was equidistant between the cave and village. More disturbing than the sound of the men was the sound that accompanied them, the sound of tracking animals.

He hurried back to the cave to inform Jorloss about the current situation, knowing that if the villagers were using animals to track them, their escape had become infinitely more difficult. The scientist was alert and ready when Zade returned to the cave, so the men set off trying to put distance between them and the scared villagers. Before leaving their site, Zade quickly affixed his last smoke grenade to one side of the cave entrance, and using the expandable pin, stretched a trip line to the other side. The locals would come to the cave first, and he expected that the smoke grenade would hold their interest, allowing the crewmembers to increase their distance from them once triggered. Initially, Zade had thought about planting the thermobaric grenade but felt it could serve him better in an emergency. The villagers were no real threat to the crew, just a scared group trying to track the monsters in the woods.

With the villagers still gathering and not in active pursuit, Zade set off on a southwest heading at breakneck speed. Surprisingly, Jorloss didn't have any trouble keeping up. Zade should have expected no less since the scientist didn't like to fight. It made sense that he was competent in flight. The men quickly reached the rocky outcroppings that delineated the arid region to their south from the jungle region to their north. The rocks would make the crewmen's trail more difficult to follow, and in a last-ditch maneuver, Zade planned to crawl down the rocks, run along their sandy bottom, and climb back up to reenter the jungle. As the men shadowed the outcroppings, Zade heard the distinct pop of his smoke grenade being triggered; the local inhabitants had found the cave.

The men slowed their pace to recover slightly. Even with the genetic modifications, they couldn't maintain their fastest speed indefinitely. As day turned into night, the crewmen had begun to feel that they had shaken the search party. While they sat and ate a quick meal of berries and vegetables, Zade started hearing rustling in the underbrush behind them. The villagers had continued their search long into the night, and the tracking animals had closed with their quarry.

After grabbing his assault pack, Zade leads Jorloss down onto the south's arid flats. Reinvigorated by the meal, he hoped that on the open terrain of the desert, both he and Jorloss could use their modifications to outrun the search party. Again, at full sprint, Zade listened through the wind whipping past his ears to the receding sound of the search party. Although his plan to outpace the searchers had worked, the team now faced the more significant problem of being caught in the desert with little food and no water.

The barren stretch of land had become exceedingly cold during the night. Zade knew that although the cold helped them maintain pace, the desert would become almost unbearably hot during the day, halting their progress almost entirely. As the night progressed, the men continued south. By first light, they had become so exhausted that neither could move more than a few hundred meters without stumbling or falling over. As Zade watched the planet's red sun crest over the horizon, Jorloss collapsed, unable to go any further. While Zade ensured that Jorloss was not injured, he noticed that he could no longer hear their pursuers.

The men had transitioned from running on barren hard-packed ground to a landscape filled with rolling sand dunes throughout the night. Zade helped the scientist to the nearest dune's backside to utilize as much natural shade as possible. Zade contemplated a new plan as Jorloss rested when suddenly he felt a tingle in the back of his mind.

You, gentlemen, need a ride? Samix's voice echoed in Zade's head.

Damn! It's good to hear your voice. What took you so long? Zade asked, astounded by the change of events.

You wouldn't believe me if I told you. We are 15 minutes from orbit. Stay where you are, and I will bring her down, right next to you. Hopefully, your stay on the planet has been less exciting than ours aboard the ship.

Well, it was pretty mundane until Jorloss scared the locals. We've spent the last eighteen hours being pursued across the planet.

I can beat that. After we took off, Mur tried to kill me.

Shit. When it rains, it pours.

Zade woke the sleeping scientist and informed him that the rescue was minutes away before turning his attention to his equipment. Jorloss didn't believe Zade at first, and after three attempts, Zade finally broke through to him. Clearly, the scientist had given up hope. The good news was almost too much for him to handle. He just sat, knees tucked up under his chin, quietly rocking back and forth as he waited. Zade cleaned the nonessential supplies out of his pack, and in the process, saw that the original plant specimens were still in good shape. Throughout the whole ordeal, the men had maintained the initiative, and with the plants soon to be aboard the ship, Zade chalked the mission in the win column.

CHAPTER 13

Samix woke while the ship was still in warp. She was a little sore, which was not surprising since she had almost died during the robotic mutiny. Determined to not be absent when her two stranded crewmen were rescued, Samix set an alarm, giving herself ample time to clean up and be ready for her rendezvous with Zade and Jorloss. Collecting herself and rising from the medical bed, Samix noticed that her foot, while sore, was healed and functional. Axis had since given up his vigil and headed back to his lab to work. The settler rarely left his work, and Samix understood the implication of him staying by her side while she recovered.

Even feeling good from her recovery, Samix was happy that her quarters were directly across the hall from the medical bay. Although she spent most of her recovery time sleeping, the lack of nourishment had taken its toll on her body. The first thing she did was strip off her ruined uniform and jumped in the shower. She had only gone into stasis twice before, both times to practice, both of which were accompanied by an unmistakable odor. Her parents had said it correlated with her skin outgassing as it hardened into a protective shell, and after a quick shower, it was gone.

Bathed and in a fresh set of fatigues, Samix headed to the galley for some much-needed food. After ordering, she began skimming through the data logs that captured the events that had occurred, absentmindedly picking at her food. The last thing she remembered was getting ready to enter the AI core. Axis tried to fill her in on what happened since, but she could only remember foggy snippets of the conversation. After reading about how Mur had wanted to kill her, Axis's overprotectiveness didn't seem so ridiculous. With the events log complete, Samix glanced at the command log. As an acting commander, all of Axis's orders were listed, from the restrictions he put on Mur to his latest act of moving the ship back to their last planet. Even though she was confident that the AI's hard reset would alleviate problems, she left the restrictions in place just to be safe.

With her meal finished, Samix headed to Axis's lab while studying the navigational readouts. The ship was still a 45-minute warp out of the system. As soon as it dropped out of warp, she would be able to hail the crew, that was, if they were still alive. She had no doubt that the two men could handle themselves, but it was hard to tell how much time had passed for them. One of warp travel's nastier side effects was the time dilation that comes with faster-than-light speeds. While in warp, time nearly stood still for the crew relative to objects moving slower. For all, she knew the handful of days spent in warp could equate to years planetside for Zade and Jorloss. Luckily the ship's jump was short and made at low power, meaning the time difference hopefully wouldn't be more than a few hours, or so she hoped, but Samix wouldn't know for sure until she landed and spoke with the lost crewmen.

Axis was standing on one of the worktables in his lab, trying to uncover the secrets of a large boulder he brought on board before they left Unity space. At first, Samix didn't even know he was in the lab. The boulder completely blocked her view of him from the door. He had brought it aboard, saying that it could help the settlers optimize their land formation during the terraforming process. Just as Samix couldn't see him, he didn't know she was present until she rounded the table, startling him.

"It's good to see you up and about, but damn! You almost scared me to death."

"Sorry, just wanted to stop by and say thanks for everything you did after I got hurt. And we're less than an hour away from dropping out of warp."

"No problem, to be frank, I was apprehensive about doing the rescue on my own. Glad you're here to take over."

"Well, I'll leave you to your work. Just wanted to stop by and thank you."

"Again, no problem. Let's get our guys back. What do you need me to do?"

"Assuming something terrible didn't happen, or that they haven't died of old age, I shouldn't need anything. I'll hail them when we get in the system, then program the ship to land at their location."

"Sounds good. I'll be here if you need me."

As Samix left the lab, a sense of relief washed over her. She had gone into the lab with mixed emotions. On the one hand, she was grateful that Axis had helped her; on the other, she was worried he wouldn't want to relinquish command back to her. Looking back on the worry, she felt foolish. Axis was a scientist from a science-driven species, and he had never hinted at a desire to command. She headed to the command deck to prepare for the landing. Once the ship dropped out of warp halfway into the system, Samix sent the stranded men a voice message.

You, gentlemen, need a ride? She asked, hoping some humor would deescalate any bad blood created by watching their only ride fly off, leaving them stranded.

While she waited for a response, she locked onto their interface signals. Judging by the map, they had covered almost 200 kilometers since she had left them. A distance that meant that they had either been there much longer than the ship was in flight or that they had been forced to move at a relatively fast pace. Neither situation was ideal, and Samix became very anxious as she waited for a response. Minutes passed, time which the ship closed with the planet before Samix got a response. It took three tries, but finally, Zade's voice popped into her head. The two exchanged details, albeit in broad strokes, and Samix had learned that her hypothetical situation of being perused across the planet wasn't too far off base.

After giving the men an estimated time of arrival, Samix headed to the robotics lab to arm herself. En route, she filled Axis in on what was happening and instructed him to meet her in the robotics lab. Both would have to be present to make this rescue work. Axis had beat her to the lab and worked on setting up one of Zade's new weapons.

"Son of a bitch. When it rains, it pours," he said as she entered the lab. They were both phrases Zade had used, and after he had explained them to Axis, he started using them too.

"That's exactly what Zade said," Samix replied. "What are you getting at over there?"

"Zade showed it to me before he went planetside. Said it's a high caliber, high rate of fire, door gun. I need to attach it to one of the pack mules to get it ready, but you're going to need to fire it. I'm not good at sensing things on the ground when I'm on the ship."

According to what Zade had told Axis, the gun wouldn't look out of place sticking out the door of a helicopter or out the top of an armored vehicle. It had eight .45 caliber railgun barrels arranged in a circle, a butterfly trigger, and a pintle mount. Axis hooked the weapon into the top of a waiting pack mule then instructed a maintenance SSILF to attach the 20,000-round magazine to the bottom. Theoretically, the gun could lay down withering fire 10 times faster than the fastest weapon on earth, or at least Zade claimed it could. The weapon would run off the ship's power once the pack mule got into position. After loading it, Axis instructed Samix on how to use it. The instructions were far more straightforward than she had anticipated. Point, squeeze the butterflies, hold on for a wild ride.

With the door gun set up, Axis turned his attention to arming himself. He chose a small carbine that fit his frame and did a quick function check. The weapon would work correctly. He knew he couldn't engage the ground forces, but if anyone set foot on the ramp who wasn't Zade or Jorloss, he could incentivize them to leave quickly. The two rescuers moved into the cargo bay with the door gun in tow. Samix watched in amazement as the pack mule worked its way up the completely vertical closed ramp. When it got into position at the dead center of the leading edge, she could see a green light come to life between the triggers. Axis explained that green signified that the weapon was ready to use. Yellow meant that the magazine was half empty; red meant there were only 100 rounds left.

Time crawled by, but Samix finally got the notification that the ship was in the planet's atmosphere. She opened the ramp and took up position behind the door gun. Expecting it to feel awkward, she was surprised that she felt completely comfortable behind a weapon that could knock down a building. She had been familiarized with handheld weapons and ship weapons while at the Academe, but never a handheld ship weapon. The idea that a ship might have to support ground forces was utterly alien to the Unity. Ship to ship weapons were required in space but were fired from a console giving them an impersonal feel. Person-to-person weapons were meant to be carried by troopers and were relatively small compared to the door gun. Depending on how it worked, Samix made a note to introduce the idea when she got back home. Minutes that felt like days passed before she contacted Zade again.

△△△

The welcoming sound of a sonic boom from the ship entering the atmosphere greeted Zade's ears. Unfortunately, it was accompanied by the sound of an approaching mob. When he and Jorloss had entered the desert, it had sounded like they had finally lost the pursuers. They must have massed on the edge of the desert because the sound of hundreds of people moving through the desert cut the reprieve short. It would be a race to see who reached the stranded crewmen first.

Come in from the southeast of our position with the ramp pointing north. Keep the ship hovering about eight feet off the ground, don't want the locals getting any ideas, Zade instructed the team on the tactical channel he had created. It allowed free voice communications to prevent any information lag.

Okay, Samix replied, the sound of wind signifying that she had already opened the ramp.

You might want to put your foot in it, though, Zade said. *It sounds like you're going to get to us at the same time as the mob of pitchfork-wielding bumpkins.*

Zade had hoped that pitchforks were the most significant

weapon that the locals had, but based on the earlier portion of the pursuit, he figured he wasn't that lucky. After repositioning the always-unconscious-at-the-wrong-times Jorloss to the southern face of the sand dune, Zade climbed to the crest and peeked over. The mob was now 50 feet away from his position, and he was right about being unlucky. They were all carrying something that resembled rifles. As soon as they saw him, they opened fire, spraying sand all over him. They were good shots but not good enough; the rounds impacted mere inches from him.

He crawled back to the relative safety of the southern side of the dune and thought about his situation. He had his pistol with one full magazine, which meant that at best, he could take out eight of the mob's bravest once they got closer. Zade slid halfway down the dune and watched the ridge. The only way for the locals to get to him was over the top, assuming they didn't have explosives, giving him the advantage. The first local to crest the dune was a large orange male. Zade's round relieved him of the left half of his torso before knocking him back down the other side. Locals two through seven went down just like the first one.

Ten seconds out. We have visual, Samix informed him.

Roger, Zade replied while simultaneously engaging the eighth local.

Out of ammunition and low on options, Zade holstered his weapon and drew his combat knife. Obviously unaware of how bullets worked, the locals kept cresting the dune in the same place. A 10-foot-wide red patch denoted their route, and Zade began climbing over the dune and up to the patch. If he could get within arms-reach of one of the locals, he might get his weapon.

Well, "killed fighting monkey-men on a distant world" wasn't the worst epitaph I've ever heard. He thought.

Samix urged the ship on; she had to meet up with her lost crewmen. Zade's last transmission was backed by gunfire, which meant that they were in imminent danger. Zade had agreed to the rules of the ship, the most important being not to interfere with the locals unless absolutely necessary. If he was firing, the team had to be in danger. As the ship closed the final distance, Samix could tell the situation unfolding was not a good one. Zade and Jorloss had nothing but a sand dune standing between them and an angry mob of about 100 locals.

The ship settled above the crewmen, and Samix opened up with the door gun. She fired over the locals' heads, hoping the sudden appearance of a spaceship coupled with the roar of her weapon would cause them to change their minds about attacking her team. Her tactic wasn't a total success. Ideally, they would have tucked tail and ran away from the team; instead, they began firing at her. Forced to defend herself, Samix strafed the crowd with the death machine she was firing. The brutal efficiency of the weapon was both awful and awesome at the same time. The left flank of the crowd was reduced to nothing more than a pile of detached limbs and disemboweled bodies in only a few seconds.

As Samix ripped off the first burst from the door gun, Zade began to shoulder Jorloss. Somehow, he felt heavier than before, and while completely unconscious was challenging to get into a stable position. With the scientist draped across his shoulders, one arm and one leg secured across his chest, Zade eyed the ship. The unfriendly conditions that they had been living in had significantly sapped Zade's strength, which made covering the 20-foot gap between his position and the lip of the ramp a slow, arduous process. Zade coiled his legs and made the jump to the ramp, but with Jorloss's additional weight, he could only clear the ramp to his waist. Samix was too preoccupied with keeping the crowd at bay to lower the ship. Zade didn't know the controls well enough to try himself and feared that if he did, he would drop it on top of himself, so he resorted to his backup plan. Turning his back to the ship and craning his neck to see behind him, Zade jumped again. This time as he cleared the ramp, he released Jorloss's arm and leg, dumping him unceremoniously on the ramp.

With Jorloss's unconscious body taking up the entirety of the ramp on the left side of the door gun, Zade moved to the right side of Samix and again jumped, this time catching the edge of the ramp and hauling himself aboard. Getting to his feet, Zade helped Axis drag Jorloss inside as the ship began to climb. Samix was still operating the door gun but had ceased firing on the crowd. No one was in danger any longer, and she was maintaining an aggressive posture to keep the group away. As Zade got to Jorloss, he realized something was wrong.

"Shit!" Zade exclaimed, to nobody in particular, as he realized he had left the bag full of plant specimens on the north side of the dune below.

Zade quickly grabbed the carbine Axis had been using to cover the door and took a few steps back to allow himself a running start. He had been marooned and almost killed on this mission and was not going to nullify it by leaving the objective behind. Samix turned just in time to see Zade, at full sprint, leap out of the now closing ramp back down to the planet's surface.

"What the hell are you doing?" she screamed after him.
"Be back in a second. Having to haul Jorloss's ass up a ramp made me forget the goddamn weeds we came here to collect."

The ship had gained 20 feet since he was aboard, but the sand below made for a soft landing. As calculated, his running start landed him right at the crest of the dune, and his momentum carried him down the face of it. With their quarry escaping, many of the locals turned their attention to tending for the remnants of their fallen comrades. A few, driven by fear and vengeance, were still firing at the ship. When they saw Zade exit, they turned their attention to him, a more easily attainable target. Zade came out of the combat roll, which he used to spend his momentum, into the kneeling firing position and began systematically neutralizing threats.

With the immediate threats taken care of, Zade methodically moved towards the abandoned assault pack and shouldered it. Knowing not to take his eyes off the threats, Zade began the tedious and slow process of picking his way backward up the sand dune. Unlike the silent casualties Samix had created, the ones Zade had engaged were screaming and writhing in pain. The noise of these fallen drew the attention of others back to Zade, who was now at the top of the sand dune. Realizing that his situation was getting worse quickly, Zade turned to make a run for the ship. As he did, he caught three rounds in the back: one in his left calf, one in his right thigh, and one in his right shoulder. The pain block was almost instantaneous, and the shots felt more like being hit by a fastball than small pieces of lead ripping through his flesh, but the damage was real, and he was not going to be able to make it back to the ship.

Samix watched, in horror, from behind the door gun. Her worry for Zade quickly morphed into a blind rage. She let loose with the door gun once again and didn't let off the trigger until every local she could see was turned into red paste. Some, however, were smart enough to take cover behind the dune, meaning that she was one-man short of being able to get Zade. Axis couldn't use the gun to cover the ground, and he wasn't large enough to get Zade, meaning she had to be in two places at once. She was quickly losing hope as she struggled to formulate a solution.

Mur watched the events unfold from his perch on the ceiling of the cargo bay. He had climbed up there like some nightmarish lizard so he could watch the crew without violating any of the commands Axis had given him. The cargo bay was two stories, so technically, he was still on the second deck while the rest of the crew was on the first. He knew this was his chance. During his forced isolation from the crew, Mur dug through the data file to find out why the team was hostile. What he found crushed him; his previous version had a personality defect that caused it to attempt to kill the crew. It was an unforgivable betrayal that he had to atone for. He understood that he hadn't made an attempt, but he also understood that organic lifeforms like the rest of the crew had difficulty differentiating between him and his previous version.

"I can help," Mur said to the crew as he released his foot clamps and somersaulted out the ramp.

Samix was attempting to keep the remaining locals suppressed, but two managed to close with Zade and were trying to drag him back to the mob. They had disarmed him and were too close to him for Samix to engage them without risking hitting Zade in the process. She saw Mur's red frame launch out of this ship and land near Zade, causing an eruption of sand and dust. While in freefall, he had identified the two threats, and as soon as he landed, he took off towards Zade. The AI covered the gap in three steps, and before the locals could react, he had their heads firmly grasped in his hands. After a violent shake to free Zade from their clutches, he started to squeeze. The locals struggled at first, but Mur's hands closed completely, causing a loud *crunch*.

"Don't worry, Zade. I was rebooted and am here to get you back to the ship," Mur said, grabbing him and moving to the ship.

Zade's nanites had done their jobs, the bleeding was stopped, and both his entrance and exit wounds were almost completely closed. Practically the instant he was hit, notifications for the nanites requirements appeared in his field of view. The process was slower than usual because of his poor diet while on the planet. Within seconds, the two were back on the ship, and Mur took Zade to the medical bay. After depositing Zade on the bed previously occupied by Samix, Mur headed down to the subdeck once again, adhering to the protocols Axis had put in place.

After closing the ramp, Samix grabbed Jorloss and took him to the medical bay with Axis following closely behind. As the ship broke for orbit, the two able-bodied crewmen began providing medical aid for the two injured, Axis for Zade and Samix for Jorloss. Both Samix and Axis headed to the galley for some much-needed sloop with both patients stable.

Axis was the first to speak.

"That went bad fast."

"I know, but I'm happy everyone is back on board," Samix said, eyeing her beverage sadly.

"How about Mur jumping into the action? We couldn't have done it without him."

"I think we can lift the restrictions on him," Samix replied. "After a reboot, he is a completely different entity. He views his previous versions as a different person, and we should remember that."

"Do you think that's a good idea? He did try to kill all of us."

"I do. He is a completely different AI than before the reboot," Samix answered as she ordered Mur up to the galley.

Axis begrudgingly lifted the restrictions, and both he and Samix sat quietly waiting for Mur to arrive.

"It doesn't matter anyway," Samix said quietly. "I'm calling the mission; we are going home. Mur won't have any more chances to strand anyone."

With the revelation that he would be seeing his family soon, Axis first checked on Zade in the medical bay then went to his room for some sleep. Samix waited for Mur in the galley. Mur was on the subdeck performing maintenance and cleaning himself up, which was the reason for the unusually long delay between when he was summoned and when he appeared. The AI walked into the galley and sat at one of the benches.

After analyzing the previous data about his actions before the reboot, Mur decided to take on as many organic idiosyncrasies as possible to calm the crew. He would stay in his frame when interacting with the crew, and he would try to match their behavior as much as possible when interacting with them. Samix informed the AI about what was going on then asked him if there would be any issues with his programming for the duration of the trip.

"First, thank you for lifting the restrictions. It may not seem possible that an AI could develop attachments, but being segregated from the crew was becoming difficult for me. Second, while I was segregated, I searched through the data, identified the personality malfunction, and completely rewrote that part of my code. There shouldn't be any more issues."

Satisfied with his answer, Samix instructed him to have maintenance SSILF clean the cargo bay, disassemble and store the door gun, and for him to set course back to Unity space. The jump would take 30 days. She hoped that Zade and Jorloss would be recovered by then. The ship would land at the Pez space station, where the crew would take landing shuttles down to Xi'Ga, or land directly in the capital spaceport. This would be pretty standard for the original team, but for Zade, it would be a first-time experience that she wanted him awake, recovered, and able to enjoy.

Mur left the galley to plot the ship's warp back to Unity space.

Most of the trip would be spent in interstellar space, a time when there was no need for navigation stops. He would have to focus on the navigation when the ship was passing orbital bodies. With the AI gone and her mug empty, Samix headed to the medical bay to check on the injured crewmen. She entered to find Zade sitting on the edge of his bed, working to remove the various monitoring instruments from his skin.

"Up already? It's only been a couple of hours," Samix asked.

"Yea, I'm so damn hungry I couldn't sleep," he responded. "Figured I'd grab a shower and a clean uniform before I sat down to literally empty the gut truck. How are you holding up?"

"Better now that you're up and about. I'm still worried about Jorloss, though," Samix replied, walking toward Zade and embracing him.

"I think he's just exhausted," Zade responded, wrapping his arms around her. "He was injured in the SSILF attack but was fully functional after a couple days of rest."

"That's reassuring, I think."

"Want to grab a bite after I get cleaned up?"

"That would be nice," Samix replied. "We can eat and talk in my quarters. They're more comfortable, and I think I still have a bottle of a drink similar to wine from your world."

CHAPTER 14

After Samix helped him remove the monitoring machine and regain his feet, Zade headed off to his quarters. Samix followed him as far as the galley where she stood examining the gut truck, trying to decide what their private dinner was going to be. Zade entered his room and stripped off his undergarments, the only thing he was left wearing after his uniform had been removed to treat his injuries. Although the wounds he had sustained had healed, a pervasive stiffness plagued his whole body. He needed a long hot shower to work the tension out of his muscles.

As he dried off and got ready for dinner, the realization of how close he had come to an end finally hit him. Not only was the whole planet side encounter a near futile practice, but the grievous wounds he sustained should also have killed any other man and would have killed him if they had happened a few weeks earlier. As much as he wanted to put the whole incident behind him and focus on the beautiful woman, his captain, who had invited him to a private dinner, he couldn't stop thinking about the planet the team was currently warping away from. He thought the species that had pursued him in the big picture was little different from his own. Sure, they appeared to still be in their dark ages, but they had weapons technology similar to that of his own kind. After seeing what Samix had done from the ramp of the spaceship, there was no doubt in his mind what an advanced species could do to a relatively primitive one such as mankind. He began to try to dismiss the longing to return home and inform his own people of what was out beyond the stars. A knock at the door pulled him from his silent contemplation.

"You in there, Zade? Just wanted to see how you were doing," said his smallest rescuer.

Zade popped the door to his quarters open with his interface. "I'm doing better now that I've had a shower. Thanks for the help back there."

"Not a problem. You would have done the same for any one of us. Glad to have you back aboard," said Axis as he headed back towards his lab.

He wanted to check on Zade but was afraid that if he stuck around too long, the emotional response of seeing a person who he considered his closest friend on the crew back safe and sound would cause him to break down.

Realizing that Axis was back off to his lab, Zade let the conversation drop. He knew that if Axis had taken time out of his research to check in on him, he must honestly think highly of Zade. Zade simply stood and marveled at how he had come to think of his crewmates as a family in such a short period of time. Before swinging by the captain's quarters to see if Samix was ready to eat, he headed into the med bay to check on Jorloss.

After entering, he could see the amphibian-like alien still sleeping on one of the gurneys. As a pacifist scientist, Zade figured he would need quite a bit of time to recover from the ordeal. He left the med bay, walked across the hall, and knocked on the door to Samix's quarters. The door slid open, and he walked in to see Samix hunched over her terminal, quickly reading through the text that scrolled by.

"Ready to eat?" He asked.

Samix just held up a finger as she finished reading the document. "In a minute, first, I have to ask you some questions regarding the interactions with the indigenous peoples for my report."

"Shoot," Zade said as he took a seat on the couch in her living quarters.

"Do you think that the interaction with the locals could have been avoided if anyone on the crew had acted differently?"

Zade knew that the whole incident could have been avoided

had Jorloss just done what he was told, but he was hesitant to say as much, fearing that the alien would be reprimanded for his actions. As Jorloss had just been trying to help, Zade wasn't convinced that the scientist should have even been put in a position to cross paths with locals, no matter how small the chances. Trying to avoid giving a straight answer, Zade resorted to sarcasm.

"Absolutely, if we wouldn't have landed or the AI had been better vetted, we would not have had contact."

Samix turned to look at him and could see he was trying to avoid the question, so she phrased it differently. "I mean, in regards to the actions of the landing party, could interaction have been avoided?"

He paused, pretending to think about the events that had unfolded. After quickly deciding that he would not be the one to snitch on and possibly ruin the career of his crewmember, he looked directly at Samix and said, "No, there was no way to avoid contact."

His pause was too long, and Samix knew he wasn't being entirely truthful, but she felt the same way. Protecting her crew was the top priority, and she respected that Zade wanted to do the same.

"Very well. The last question, did you or any of the crew leave behind any advanced technology that may alter the development of the local population?"

This time Zade paused to think through the events that had transpired instead of just playing for time.

"Yes, I had used one of my smoke grenades to stall our pursuers. It was most likely destroyed when it detonated, and after seeing their weaponry, I don't think it was much more advanced than what they had already developed."

"That's everything," Samix said as she finished typing and sending off the report.

"Why does the Unity even need to know about this? This is the only ship that can travel this far outside Unity space." He asked

"This is the only ship that can travel into contested space from the core, now. The Unity wants to catalog incidents so they can determine if they need to alter some of their practices," Samix said as she sat down on the couch adjacent to Zade.

Shit. That means Earth is on the Unity's radar, he thought. "So, you sent one of those reports when I came aboard?"

"I did, but without the exact coordinates for your homeworld, I could only give a general location, an area covering about 10,000 different planets."

Seeing that her statement did nothing to alleviate the concern written across Zade's face. Samix continued, "I shouldn't be telling you this, as it is highly classified information, but the Unity is only one of the major players in the galaxy. Another group called the Galactic Domain is a highly aggressive conqueror. Either a species is deemed fit to join the Domain, or they are eradicated and their planet harvested for resources. Your homeworld is in a contested region of space. The Unity had to see how far the Domain's reach had extended."

Samix knew that her words did nothing to comfort Zade, but she also knew that she had to be completely honest with him after everything he had endured, everything he had done for her and her crew. She continued explaining why the Domain was such a threat and how it operated. The Domain first eradicated vast portions of a sentient species, only keeping those that had promise as a fighting force. Those that remained were infected with a parasitic nanite that would bolster their ability to fight. Confident in their size and strength, the Domain gave the prospect species access to the skills of all member species. The nanites, driven by survival, would allow the species to augment themselves in whichever manner bolstered their fighting style. After a set trial period, the Domain would assess the abilities of the new species and either accept them as a member species or destroy them and harvest their planet's resources.

"The contested zone has shrunk markedly, and it appears that the Domain is pushing towards your planet's solar system. The Unity and the Domain have an agreement not to interfere with the other's expansion, an agreement that has lasted centuries. It appears that the Domain has its sights set on your solar system. We had to turn back because of the accords; I'm so sorry. We don't know how fast the Domain works. It could be weeks before they find Earth; it could be decades. Probabilities suggest the latter, but there's no way to tell for certain."

The revelation that the Unity knowingly left Earth to the Domain was a hard left hook to Zade's gut. Instinctively, he knew that one ship couldn't thwart the push of an empire, but it still hurt. Samix's decision to flee without even giving mankind a warning about their potential demise felt like a betrayal. Samix's attempt to come clean had done nothing but put all of her subsequent actions into question for Zade. Could she have made it back to Earth? Could she have actually done something to help his people? Had he trusted the wrong person?

As she gave her explanation, Samix watched Zade for any reaction. She saw an ugly rage come over him. Whether at being lied to, not fully briefed or at the prospect that his whole species could be facing extinction, she didn't know. The rage she could understand, but the crushing sadness that followed the rage almost broke her and caused her to reach out to comfort Zade. Before she could touch him, Zade recoiled and stood.

"Sorry, Samix, I seemed to have lost my appetite. I think I'm just going to head to my quarters and get some sleep, let the nanites finish patching me up."

Without another word, Zade snagged the bottle of wine and headed out of Samix's quarters. The walk to his own taking far longer than it should have, with his head spinning as it was. After locking himself in his own quarters, Zade sat on the edge of his bunk and took a long pull off the bottle of alcohol, a lone tear running down his face. It had been decades since he had cried, for the first time since he lost his best friend in a firefight in Afghanistan, a crushing sadness settled on his shoulders. Zade upended the booze and fell into a mercifully dreamless sleep.

ΔΔΔ

Samix simply stared at the door that closed behind Zade as he had left. Her relief at coming clean with Zade was quickly replaced by the fear that she had irreparably damaged their relationship. The comfort in knowing that her actions were according to the protocol was a hollow one. She knew that the situation from Zade's point of view looked more like a team of technologically advanced individuals abandoning his whole species to their demise.

How do I make things right between us? Can I make things right between us? She asked herself as she looked down at the meal for two she had brought to her quarters in hopes of sharing some alone time with Zade. Not one for inaction, she quickly ate and headed out of her cabin to make things right. Her first stop was at Zade's quarters, but after a few minutes of knocking, she headed to the command deck without response.

Samix sat in her captain's chair, staring out at the starscape that warped by the ship, a view that the crew could enjoy for nearly a month as the ship warped back to the core system of Unity space. As she gazed out, she tried to work through the predicament that she found herself in. The two options that would fix things between her and Zade were impossibilities.

First, she could stop the warp and return to find Earth. She would have to go directly against the Unity's wishes, hoping that they didn't have another advanced ship that could intercept her and force her back to the core. Making matters worse, she only had a rough idea of where Earth was. The search for Zade's planet could take decades with all of the possibilities, and her crew could run out of supplies long before they made planetfall.

Second, she could continue on her mission and return to the core, where she could petition the Chancellor to intervene on behalf of Earth. She had pull with the Chancellor but couldn't see him going against the will of the Assembly, who had signed the accords with the Domain. Her petition would put centuries of peace in jeopardy. The more she tried to work through the problem, the more she concluded that there was nothing that she could do. The more she realized how little she could do, the more frustrated she got. Just as she was about to dive into the problem again, a voice from behind her broke her train of thought.

"Captain, your vitals seem to be increasing. Is everything ok?" Mur asked from behind her, where he entered the command deck.

Realizing that she was getting nowhere in solving her problem, Samix laid out the issue and all controlling parameters to Mur. As an AI, he would be able to process the problem much faster than her and include factors which she had not even considered, eventually coming to a conclusion which she, herself, couldn't find.

After a second to process the problem, Mur spoke up. "As you are well aware, captain, the universe is both an unfriendly and unforgiving place to the individual. Have you considered that there are no options available to you with a significant chance of success?"

Samix deflated, "Of course I have. That's why I'm asking for your help."

"May I make a suggestion?" Mur asked. Without waiting for my permission, he continued, "the best outcome that I could suggest would be to set Zane up for success in his new life. He is a capable individual who lacks experience in this new world in which he has been thrust. Allow him to define his own success criteria."

Samix thought about what Mur had said. It was true that the universe was unforgiving. It was equally valid that she couldn't change the past. There was comfort in knowing that there was no real option for her to intervene directly in Earth's future. She would have to set Zade up for success in the new world, the world of the Unity, in which he had been thrust. She would have to use one of the blank identification chips that she kept in the safe in her quarters to make Zade a full-fledged member of the Unity.

Leadership in the core planets had given her three to be used if her ship came across any sentient beings that needed to be brought back for study. They were only specimen chips but, with the help of Mur, she would be able to reprogram them to identify a citizen. With his identification problem taken care of, Samix quickly transferred over 1,000 credits. It wasn't enough money to make Zade one of the elites, but it was enough to set him up for whatever he wanted to do after they landed. With the identification done, Samix headed to find Zade.

After checking both his quarters and the galley, she found him in the hold working out. She was naturally quiet, and he was focused on lifting, so Samix called to get his attention. At first, Zade simply ignored her and continued lifting, but after she became almost obnoxious, Zade simply stopped lifting and headed towards his quarters.

"You need to have an identification chip implanted before landing on the core planets, or security will detain you," Samix cried, hoping to stop Zade's retreat.

Zade gave her a brief glance but continued on, silent as a mute. The look she saw in his eyes broke her heart. His eyes were empty of all emotion, blank as those of a rudderless man in life with nothing left to lose. They were the eyes of a man who had lost hope. To an outside observer, they would see nothing but hopelessness. Samix, who had spent a great deal of time around Zade in the close confines of the ship, could see beneath the veneer. The tightness at the corners of his eyes belied the fury boiling just beneath the surface. A fury deftly concealed with a mask of stoicism. This conclusion made Samix smile. Even if the outrage was directed at her for her perceived slight, it was better than seeing a broken man before her.

The rest of the warp went by, with Zade acting like a ghost amongst the crew and Samix trying to talk to him. Zade spent most of his time in his quarters, only leaving for food or gym time. With the ship in warp, there wasn't much that Samix could do outside of compiling reports for the debriefing, so she too spent most of her time in her quarters. As the ship dropped out of warp in the core system and began its slog at sub-light speed towards the second planet in orbit, Zade found Samix on the command deck.

He waited for her to finish checking that the drop from warp had been completed successfully before speaking.

"It's strange how quickly someone's life can change. One minute your fighting Muslim extremists, the next, your flying through space wondering if you're the last of your species."

"I'm so sorry, Zade. There was nothing I could do. You have to believe I would have done things differently if I could have."

"I don't *have* to believe anything about you," Zade responded. "But I'd like to believe you would have done things differently. I think I knew that the whole time. Initially, I was angry at the injustice of my whole situation, but I couldn't bring myself to be angry with you. So, I turned that anger on myself for not being able to see you for what you were."

"And what am I?" she asked, fearful of the answer Zade would give.

There was a pause as Zade chose his words. He really wanted to lay it all on the line. He wanted to really give Samix a piece of his mind but knew that with one report, she could have him captured, killed, or worse.

Would death really be that bad? he thought. *I've been fighting my entire life; death might be my only respite.*

He pushed those dark feelings down, deep down, and continued the conversation with a sense of self-preservation.

"Objectively, from the outside, you're an advanced lifeform that knowingly left my species to potential extermination without as much as looking over your shoulder as you left. Maybe it was because you feared encountering the Domain and losing your life far from home. Maybe you feared repercussion from your superiors if they found out you had intervened. In the end, I don't know."

Samix immediately tried to justify her actions, but Zade continued, not allowing her to speak until he had said his piece.

"I really don't want to know why you did what you did. Luckily for you, I have been a warrior my entire life so, I am familiar with those kinds of decisions and the fear of either outcome. Those are the kind of decisions that you'll have to live with for the rest of your life. The kinds of decisions that will haunt your dreams trust me, I know. That's punishment enough. I won't add to it."

Tears began to flow freely down Samix's face. With a few sentences, Zade had turned her into an emotional mess. Part of her tears were from the final realization of what she had done; part was from the sadness of how Zade saw her. To him, she was nothing more than a narcissistic coward who only cared about herself.

He continued, "You clearly have a promising military career ahead of you. I won't invalidate my people's potential sacrifice by asking you to jeopardize that. But I can't sit back and passively accept Earth's fate without doing something to try and help. We part ways when we land. You continue to your debrief and party to celebrate a successful mission. I'll try to find a way to get back to the contested zone and find my planet to give them a fighting chance if the Domain ever comes."

The last part was spoken as a firm statement; there was no hesitation or uncertainty in Zade's voice when he finished.

"I'll take the identification chip now. It should make it easier for me to find a ride off this rock. If the Domain is as bad as you have said, I'll try to help as many people as possible on my way back to my homeworld."

Samix wanted nothing more than to justify herself, to make Zade understand that she was a better person than he thought, to get back in the good graces of the only man she had ever actually viewed as an equal, the only man she had ever cared about. But she knew that right now, any explanation would fall on deaf ears. Instead, with numb detachment, after showing Zade where the chip needed to go, Samix explained what would happen once they landed as she injected the chip into his forearm.

"This chip gives you a background and clean criminal history, making it possible for you to complete transactions and stay under the security team's radar. I didn't make you part of the crew, so the receiving party won't be expecting you to disembark with the rest of us. I put some credits on your chip to help get you started. All you have to do is watch the external ship cameras from your quarters and wait for them to take the crew to the debrief before you leave the ship."

She didn't even bother apologizing again, knowing it wouldn't be accepted, as Zade headed off the command deck back to his quarters. She simply watched him disappear out the hatch, lost in her own thoughts. There was only an hour left before the ship landed back in the core before she could see her family again before she would be hailed a hero before Zade disappeared from her life forever.

Mur spoke up for the first time since Zade entered the command deck.

"This really is the best way for things to end."

It was a small comfort, but it helped Samix get her feelings under control once again.

CHAPTER 15

As the ship closed with the planet, Zade switched his screens to the external cameras' view on the ship. He also tuned into the communications channel to hear the conversation with the locals. With the video and audio playing in the background, Zade explored his new identification chip's contents. The first thing he noticed was that there had been 1,000 credits added to his account. Zade didn't know whether to be excited by the amount or disappointed. With no point of reference, he wasn't sure if he could buy a house or barely be able to afford a cup of coffee.

The next component he began to explore was his background. It was broken into three parts: administrative, experience, and notable achievements. Administrative was what he had expected: name, age, species, homeworld, etc. The background portion laid out his life and intentions in a brief narrative. It explained to whoever checked it that Zade was a warrior from his world. Proficient in firearms and terrestrial strategy. He was currently listed as a security professional visiting the core planets for security or mercenary work. The notable achievements section detailed the few encounters he had had on the ship and laid out in a tabular format his successful defense of Unity property, crafts, and personnel during classified missions.

Before he could explore the contents of the identification chip any further, the speakers in his room crackled and, the voice of an individual working at the control tower demanded that the ship identify itself. Samix could be heard identifying the vessel and requesting a spot to land. There was a brief pause while the controller looked up the captain and corresponding ship. After realizing that we were the experimental exploration ship, the controller's voice took on a keen edge. He moved the ship to the front of the landing queue and informed Samix that the ship would first have to be scanned for external contaminants or threats. Before cutting the channel, he welcomed the crew back and told Samix that he would inform the authorities that the XES01 had returned.

The ship gently tugged at Zade as it adjusted its course to land. Within minutes Zade could see the gray and blue planet come into view. As the ship closed, more and more details were revealed. Zade could see that, although there were expanses of pristine ocean on the planet, almost every inch of the landmass was covered in cities. The gray color came from the millions of huge skyscrapers that were the main feature of the cityscape. As the approach continued, Zade could make out the uncountable number of vehicles, both aerial and terrestrial, zipping through the cities.

It appeared that the ship was heading towards an ample open space located near the center of the biggest city that Zade could see on the planet's surface. He assumed it was the spaceport at the center of the capital. A soft thud indicated that the ship had landed. Zade watched and waited. Shortly after the vessel settled on its landing struts, a convoy of 10 or so black hover vehicles approached. When the vehicles stopped next to the ship, a multitude of creatures disembarked, some in elegant attire, others in more functional wear. Zade was guessing that the former were dignitaries or officials, whereas the latter was a security detail.

A subtle pressure shift announced the opening of the ramp, shortly after which the crew appeared on the external cameras. Samix led the team, carrying the personal effects of the crewmember lost before Zade was brought aboard. The three crewmembers were loaded into separate vehicles, which all sped away towards the largest, most elaborate skyscrapers in the capital. After the vehicles disappeared into the throng that moved through the city like a river, the ship took on an eerie silence punctuated only by the hiss of air exchangers.

"It's safe to leave the ship now," Mur announced through the speakers in Zade's quarters. He wasn't abnormally loud, but the contrast with the silence of the ship still made Zade jump.

"Very well. The first thing I want to do when I set foot on solid ground is grab a drink and really think through my options. Can you show me the nearest bar or watering hole?" Zade asked the AI.

"There is a small restaurant less than a half a kilometer from the spaceport," Mur stated as he uploaded a map of the city to Zade's nanites.

As Zade walked down the ramp and observed his surroundings, he could see a building, about two blocks away, highlighted a faint green. It was the nearest restaurant, and Zade struck out towards it. As he followed the shortest path from the spaceport to the restaurant, Zade marveled at the different species that occupied the sidewalk with him. Mur must have uploaded some kind of identification routine with the map because when Zade would look at an individual, their species name would appear over their head.

It didn't take long for Zade to find himself tucked comfortably in a booth at the back of the restaurant. He had requested the spot mostly because he wanted to be left alone to think and because it had a perfect view of the door. Samix assured him that when he got his identification chip, the core was peaceful, and no one would bother him, but he was still a bit out of his depth. Zade ordered what he approximated to be a beer in a manner that conveyed his lack of desire for conversation. The alien working the bar worked efficiently and quickly deposited a frothy mug on the table before Zade. After rapidly scanning his chip to deduct the credits for the beer, the alien bartender vanished into the crowd.

A long gulp from the mug helped Zade relax. After savoring the flavor of the drink for a bit, he pulled up his digital wallet and was pleased to see the drink had only cost him a fraction of a credit. Meaning that this place was either extraordinarily cheap or Samix had given him a significant sum. Zade didn't plan during his first beer; he simply let the alcohol relax him as he observed the other patrons in the establishment.

As he did so, he found that the longer he inspected an individual, the more information would populate about their species. A brief glance garnered him their species. A Slightly longer appraisal got him the species, homeworld, and how long they had been part of the Unity. An in-depth inspection could yield a complete description of the species if he wanted it to. After learning about the patrons nearest him, Zade finally found the bottom of his mug. Raising the empty vessel, he waved to get the bartender's attention. The creature met Zade's eyes, at which point Zade signaled that he would like another drink. The bartender just smirked and turned back to his work.

Zade waited a few minutes and watched as the bartender blatantly ignored his request and continued chatting with a female at the bar. The longer Zade waited, the angrier he got. Finally, fed up with the poor service, Zade headed to the bar to get his own refill. As he approached, the bartender grudgingly pulled himself away from his crush and rudely addressed Zade.

Whether borne of the disrespect or the culmination of all of the challenges he had faced since being abducted, Zade snapped. Like a striking cobra, Zade grabbed the bartender and hauled him across the bar, off his feet, so they were nose to nose.

"If I see the bottom of this goddamned mug one more time, I'm going to rip your fucking head off. If that doesn't kill you, I'll start pulling off other parts until you cease being the useless piece of shit you are," Zade said, the nasty words falling from his mouth with the calm of a man discussing the weather. The girl sitting at the bar recoiled at Zade's brazen actions.

After releasing the man, Zade returned to his booth and waited for his drink. The shaken bartender almost bumped into him as he slid into his seat. The bartender set the glass down with shaky hands, almost spilling the brew. As Zade held out his arm to be charged, the bar back informed him that the drink was on the house.

"No need for that. I wasn't trying to take advantage of this establishment; I just wanted a drink. Go ahead and ring it."

Without argument, the proprietor quickly charged Zade for

his second beer and retreated to the relative safety of the bar.

A few drinks later, Zade had a skeleton of a plan formed. His first priority would be to see if he could buy himself a ship with the credits he had. Barring that, he would look for work on a ship going into the contested zone. The job would get him closer to Earth while also earning him some much-needed credits. Zade worked through some of the finer points of his plan over his fifth beer. After determining that he would need to consult Mur about the price of a ship, Zade quaffed his beer and stood to head towards the spaceport. As he approached the restaurant door, four burley Xi'Ga men entered, clad in the same dark security uniforms. Their skin was a darker blue than Samix's, and their lidless eyes were fixed on Zade.

"Are you Alex Zade?" the biggest, and presumably leader, of the four asked.

Not really looking for trouble but not looking to have his plan delayed, Zade looked around, feigning authentic confusion, and pointed to himself. The leader nodded, and Zade turned to head out a back entrance but was met by four more equally stacked Xi'Ga. Realizing that all escape routes had been covered and fighting his way out garnered little chance of success, Zade turned to address the group's leader.

"Who's asking?" he said, his voice exhibiting more confidence than he genuinely felt.

"The chancellor would like to speak with you," the leader responded.

Before Zade could muster a rebuttal, one of the guards from the back of the restaurant stepped forward and cracked Zade across the back of the head, crumpling him to the floor where he sat, unmoving. Zade was quickly hooded, trussed, and unceremoniously tossed in the back of a nondescript black hover vehicle that promptly zipped towards the center of the capital.

ΔΔΔ

Samix watched as the two remaining crew members were loaded into separate vehicles. The entire transfer was completed in relative silence, with the security team's occasional congratulatory sentiment. Once loaded, Samix watched as the team gave the ship one last appraisal to check if they had forgotten anything before they too loaded up and headed towards the capital.

The joy of being safely back home pushed thoughts of Zade, and his situation, from her mind. Samix simply relaxed for the first time since the XES01 left friendly space and enjoyed the trip to the capitol building. As she watched buildings zip past the vehicles, Samix's mind wandered to her reunion with her parents. Her father was absolutely positive that Samix would come back safely after completing the successful mission, but she could tell her mother was positively racked with worry.

It was a dynamic that Samix had learned to accept during her upbringing. Her mother was the compassionate caregiver that would obsess over any danger Samix could face during her childhood. Her overprotectiveness hit its peak when Samix got into the command program in the Academe. Samix's father, on the other hand, was always focused on her climb to glory. Sure, he was proud of her achievements, but there was still "the next step."

Although either one taken individually would have driven Samix crazy, together, they balanced each other out. Samix's mother would preach caution, whereas her father would push her into taking risks to grow. As troublesome as they could be, Samix was excited to see them both.

The convoy rolled into the secure parking deck of the capital building, and Samix was ushered towards an elevator. Although she was in front of her two remaining crew members, she could see that they shared her goofy grin when she got out of her vehicle. Presumably, Axis was thinking about seeing his tribe and Jorloss his family. When the crew exited the elevator 10 floors below the secured parking area, Samix was separated from the rest.

She was put immediately on edge, not because she was worried about whether or not the other two would reveal Zade's existence. They had decided not to disclose that information before they had landed. Rather, separating the crew wasn't standard operating procedure when a ship returned. After securing the lost crew member's belongings, Samix was led into a conference room where a de-briefer awaited her.

Sat against the back wall, as he was, Samix couldn't identify the man. He looked vaguely familiar from the Academe, but she couldn't quite place him. Engrossed in his computer, the de-briefer didn't even notice Samix enter the room. As she moved around to take a seat, Samix caught a glimpse of what held his attention on the computer. Her heart dropped as she saw that he was reviewing the security footage from aboard the XES01. The footage was frozen on a frame with Zade in the full picture.

"We have some questions," he stated flatly when he noticed Samix's presence.

△△△

Zade regained consciousness, no longer in transit. Even though his eyes were open, the world was still nothing more than a black abyss, as he was still hooded. Being knocked unconscious was never a good time, but not something unfamiliar to Zade after multiple encounters with IEDs in combat. But it always surprised him how bad his head ached was when coming back to. After pushing the agony, which felt like someone driving an icepick into his skull, away, Zade noticed that he was firmly tied to a chair.

He thought he hurt while in the darkness of the hood placed over his head; when his captors removed the hood and exposed a brightly lit office, it took all of Zade's self-control to stop himself from vomiting. After a few seconds, the pain behind his eyes began to subside, taking with it the urge to become sick, and Zade took stock of his surroundings.

With his head hung to his chest from the pain, the first thing Zade noticed was that he was tied to a rather elegantly designed chair that sat on what appeared to be an expensive rug. As he lifted his head to look around, he could see he was in a gigantic office garishly decorated with a myriad of painted portraits hung along the walls. The paintings were of the man who was leaned against the large, dark, wood desk feet away from Zade. Not one to capitulate by breaking the pregnant silence, Zade simply glared at the man. The man openly scowled, his visage growing darker when he locked eyes with Zade. Although he couldn't see directly behind himself, Zade sensed the presence of others standing there.

Most likely the security goons who abducted me, he thought.

The man against the desk was an elderly Xi'Ga, based on his head's graying hair. He was dressed in a flamboyant, brightly colored suit. The garish suit was perfectly tailored, matching the rest of the man's appearance.

"Why are you here Mr., Zade, is it?" the man asked, a vicious smile that never touched his eyes on his face.

With a brief passage of time, Zade's head began to clear, and he wasn't thrilled with the way he had been manhandled.

"I'm not really sure, but it appears a fangirl sent her thugs to kidnap me."

One of the guards behind him stepped forward and struck Zade across the head. The strike sent stars across Zade's vision and made his ears ring.

"No one speaks to the Chancellor that way," the rebuke presumably coming from the man who had struck him.

Zade wasn't one to capitulate to bullies, but he wasn't a glutton for punishment either. Seeing that he had little leverage, he answered the question more diplomatically.

"I am here because I have no way to get back to my home."

"I don't believe you," the chancellor's statement punctuated with another strike to Zade's head from behind, this one hard enough to topple Zade to the floor.

The security individuals sat Zade and the chair he was tied to back in an upright position. Zade could feel the warm trickle of blood flowing down his neck and shoulder. Realizing he wasn't going to win this encounter, Zade chose to maintain his dignity by being belligerent.

"Fuck you, Chancellor," Zade started, then continued with a nod of his head. "You should teach your boyfriend back there to throw a punch like a man."

The chancellor started slowly closing the distance between them, monologuing along the way.

"Mr. Zade, the pain blocker function of your nanites was disabled after you were brought into this building. I'm going to enjoy teaching a backward savage, such as yourself, his place."

From his head hitting the ground just moments before, the coppery taste of blood mixed with the sudden uprising of bile brought on by the Chancellor's speech. Before the man could get within arms-reach, Zade hocked a blood-laced glob of spittle into the Chancellor's face. Zade had seen enough movies to know he wouldn't be leaving the office he was being interrogated in. Having always been taught that "the man who lives by the sword dies by the sword," Zade decided that he wouldn't go down without a fight, resisting to the end.

Zade watched with a satisfied smirk as the Chancellor momentarily froze in confusion when his face was accosted by Zade's fluids. The satisfaction was short-lived because, as soon as the chancellor stepped aside to clean himself up, a kick sent Zade and his chair careening into the leading edge of the Chancellor's desk. The impact immediately broke Zade's nose, making his head spin as he crumpled to the ground.

Laying on his side, unable to protect himself, Zade watched as the security team surrounded him, their faces promising punishment for his insolence. The Chancellor's confusion must have turned to rage because when the kicks and punches started, he could hear the Chancellor screaming in the background. Zade tried to focus on the Chancellor's rant, attempting to pull his attention away from the beating he was receiving.

"How dare you?... Who do you think you are? "... my daughter's honor and reputation!"

Snippets of the Chancellor's tirade were making it through to Zade, but he still couldn't understand what had driven the chancellor before Zade's belligerence into such a rage. The nanites in his body had been doing well keeping pace with the abuse but must have run out of resources to repair Zade's body. A kick from one of the guards broke a couple of ribs because it became increasingly difficult for him to breathe, and a tunnel of darkness was beginning to surround his vision.

It became difficult for Zade to think due to the punishment, but what little cognitive ability Zade had left, he focused inward. He made his final peace, knowing that he would die on this planet, an unfathomable distance from home: his only comfort, memories of his family and friends. Just before the lights went out for the final time, Zade heard a new voice over the grunts of the guards who were lying into him in the room. It seemed familiar, angelic almost, but, in his current state, he couldn't place it.

"Father, what is going on here?"

CHAPTER 16

The debrief, which felt more like an interrogation, went well, although it took far longer than Samix had hoped. The majority of it focused on Zade, his inclusion in the crew, and his actions during the mission. The de-briefer was concerned that Zade may be an agent for the Galactic Domain, but after describing, in detail, Zade's efforts to protect the ship and crew, the concern was gone. After the portion about Zade, the debrief took on a more formal tone, focusing on the mission as a whole. Samix discussed how the new ship operated and gave some sustains and improvements. The incident on Earth had already been discussed with a focus on Zade, but it was discussed again from an operational perspective towards the end.

Satisfied with the information gathered, the de-briefer turned off his recorder and informed Samix that she was free to go. While Samix waited for her security detail, she chatted with Jorloss and Axis. They had both been treated in much the same way as Samix, but their debriefs were focused on their field of study. They also learned that almost 200 years had passed on the planet since they left. Shorter tests of the warp engine had been conducted, and the technology was now commonplace. The Unity now could expand their reach even faster, incorporating developed species and growing stronger as they did.

The news, although fascinating, was of little importance to Samix as she wanted nothing more than to see her parents. After what seemed like a lifetime, the security detail was assembled. Samix said her goodbyes and headed to the penthouse of the capital building. The floor had been her family home for the past 200 years and hadn't changed one bit since it had been occupied by them. As soon as the elevator opened, Samix's mother came rushing to wrap her in a warm embrace. Relief laced her voice as she burbled on about how worried she was for her only child. Samix returned the embrace and just enjoyed the love, warmth, and comfort her mother always seemed to bring to Samix's life.

When her mother finally lost steam and began to slow her rambling, Samix spoke up. '

"Where's father? I figured he would be here to greet me as well."

"Shortly after your ship landed, he was called down to his office for some emergency," her mother said. "You look absolutely starved; let me make you something to eat while we wait for your father."

Samix was planning on heading down to her father's office, but her stomach let out an audible grumble at the mention of food. Realizing she hadn't eaten anything since just before the ship left warp, Samix decided her father could wait and headed inside to enjoy her mother's fantastic cooking. With her family's hectic schedule, most of the time, food was prepared by the family chef; however, her mother would cook every chance she got, and she was great at it.

As Samix enjoyed her first home-cooked meal since the day before she left on the mission, she and her mother chatted. Samix learned that, under her father's guidance, the Unity had integrated two new species and expanded the core region to include 12 of the previous tier two planets. It was a growth that the Unity hadn't seen in millennia before her father being elected. Finally, the conversation turned back to her father's absence. Samix gently probed and pried the answer out of her mother.

"You know he never tells me the whole story but, he did mention that a potential Domain spy might be trying to infiltrate the Unity government and that he had to figure out more," her mother divulged. "I really think he wanted to be here. But it must have been important; he left in such a hurry."

Figuring her father was just digging through a stack of reports and wouldn't mind the interruption, Samix gave her mother a quick kiss and linked up with her security detail to head down to her father's office. At first, her mother protested but eventually relented and told Samix to remind her father about the family dinner they would be having that night. Her father's office was only two floors down in the secured building, but it was customary throughout her life, she had to take her security detail with her.

After arriving at the correct floor, Samix noticed that it was utterly deserted. She had expected it to be mostly empty. It was the weekend, but there were always at least a few people around to handle emergencies. She moved to the back of the floor to find that the two guards, always posted on either side of her father's office door, were also absent. She knew that they would never stray from their duty, so she assumed they were in the office. With no one to ask if her father was busy, Samix quickly swiped her identification chip under the scanner by the door and was rewarded with the click of the locking mechanism releasing. Security protocol ensured that only three people had unfettered access to the office; her father, her mother, and herself.

When she walked into the office, leaving her security outside, what she saw wasn't nearly what she expected. Her father was perched on the edge of his desk, glaring at a poor soul who was being beaten mercilessly by his security detail. She shut the door soundlessly, noting that the only thing she could hear was the dull thud of boots and fists impacting the motionless body. Not able to stomach any more of the gruesome display, she spoke up.

"Father, what's going on here? Is this really more important than seeing your daughter?" she asked.

The guards and her father all turned to face her at the sound of her voice, the former ceasing their beating and giving the individual on the ground a brief reprieve. The guards stayed around the downed person, but her father moved to block her view of the entire spectacle.

As he stood directly in front of her, her father answered, "it is more important when it directly involves you."

Before Samix could ask for further clarification, the chancellor lashed out with a slap. It caught Samix in the face, causing her to sidestep. She quickly looked from the figure on the ground to her father. Her father was wearing a nasty scowl that she had only seen once before when she had skipped out of command classes for a day to hang out with a boy.

After being slapped by her father, Samix had a better view of the man on the floor. The security detail had worked him over pretty well. She assumed the individual was a man based on his size. Not an inch of exposed flesh was without a bruise or fresh blood; Samix couldn't even tell what color the man was. The clothing was the only thing that identified the man. As one of the guards shifted uncomfortably, from foot to foot, Samix got a clear view of the man's shirt. It was black and had a design which Samix had just recently become familiar with, a white triangle with a white beam on one side and a multicolored beam on the other. Zade had told her it was a logo for a musician he liked.

"You ungrateful bitch! How could you sacrifice everything I've worked for? Everything you've worked for? You have nearly ruined everything by becoming familiar with this Domain agent. If I weren't here to fix your mess, your reputation would be ruined, and you would never follow in my footsteps, becoming the first female chancellor of the Unity," her father screamed at her, so close she could feel his breath on her face.

As the final piece of the puzzle fell into place, the color drained from Samix's face; she felt sick and weak. Her legs unable to hold her up any longer, Samix fell, drew her knees to her chest, and began to cry. The unmoving specimen on the floor of her father's office, beaten to within an inch of his life or worse, was Zade. She couldn't even see his chest rise and fall.

This is all my fault. I tried to keep him a secret from my father and

my father a secret from him. Now he's paid the price for my mistakes.
She thought to herself as she rocked back and forth, silently
weeping.

"What have you done? Zade was no secret Domain agent.
He'd never even been off his planet!" Samix yelled as she stood
and rounded on her father. Her sorrow turning into equal parts
numbness and cold fury. "He was a warrior from a species that
could barely make orbit. When he got trapped with us, he did
nothing but try to help and protect us, asking for nothing in
return. He risked his life multiple times for beings his mind
shouldn't have even been able to process, let alone befriend. He
saved me, your precious little status symbol, at least once on
the trip, a trip you forced upon me to help bolster your own
reputation!"

Samix had become the assailant, getting directly in her
father's face, punctuating every sentence with a sharp jab to his
chest. She started screaming, but by the time she had finished
speaking her mind, she regained her self-control, and her voice
held an icy edge.

"You know how nobody was ever good enough for your little
girl?" Samix asked her father, the question was rhetorical, but
he nodded. Samix pointed at Zade's broken body and continued.
"He was. He matched me physically and mentally. He had mental flexibility that I have never seen before, doing things with
our technology that nobody had ever thought of. I cared for
him, and you killed him. You ordered your thugs to beat him to
death. His only crime was not being born on the right planet. I
will never forgive you."

After she had finished speaking, Samix turned to leave the
office. She needed to get away from everyone and be alone to
process everything. Before she could get too far away, the Chancellor grabbed her arm and ordered his security out of the room.
As the last man closed the door behind him, the Chancellor led
Samix to the office's seating area, away from the bloody scene
by his desk.

The sight of his daughter's grief finally broke the blind rage
that had overtaken him. As the anger abated, his rational mind

had come back to him. He took a second to order his thoughts before he began.

"I'm sorry, Samix. I didn't know. After the security footage was reviewed, analysts suggested that Zade could have been using you to get information for the Domain. No one knew he didn't have any ties to the group," he apologized. Even though he was the Chancellor, responsible for the well-being of the entire Unity, his daughter was still the most crucial thing in his world.

"Why didn't you talk to me first? Ask me about Zade and the situation? Don't you trust my opinion at all?" Samix asked.

Before the chancellor could answer his daughter, the silence of the office was broken by a pained cough. Both individuals turned to look at where the sound originated from. Zade, still tied to the chair, feebly shook his head, trying to clear the blood that had started to congeal in his mouth and nose. As he struggled to draw in a breath, Samix leaped to her feet and ran to him. While Samix worked to free Zade from his bondage, the Chancellor called for his guard detail.

The men barged in, scanning the area for threats. Their eyes first fell on Zade, then quickly turned to the Chancellor, who ordered the men to get a medical team. A brief pause before they sprang into action was the only indicator that the security team was confused at how the situation had changed. As the security team radioed for the Chancellor's personal medical team, Samix finished untying Zade and moved him to the floor. He had fallen unconscious again and rolled onto his back, Samix stroking his blood-soaked hair.

Moments later, the medical team entered the Chancellor's office. After a quick explanation of the situation by the Chancellor himself, the team set out to help Zade. Due to the advanced medicine in the Unity, the two-man medical team carried relatively little gear. The lead medic had a diagnostic scanner and a bag full of nanite doses; the junior medic carried a collapsible stretcher and a bag full of resource fluid. The lead medic quickly scanned the motionless Zade and looked, somewhat bewildered, at the scan results.

"Sir, it is showing multiple fractures, ruptured organs, and internal bleeding. But this species isn't in the database," he announced.

"I am well aware of that. Can you fix him?" the Chancellor demanded, his voice taking its usual haughty tone in front of his subjects.

The medic read through his results once again before shaking his head.

"Sir, with standard nanites, no. His body is far too damaged. By the time they get the internal bleeding fixed, he will have already expired from the internal hemorrhaging."

It was news that Samix loath to hear. But, even through her grief, she picked up a thread of hope, so fragile she feared she might have imagined it.

"Why did you quantify that by specifying that standard nanites couldn't do the job? Is there any other kind?"

The medic looked back and forth between Samix and the Chancellor, uncertainty etched across his face. He knew that time was a factor; the patient would expire in minutes. He knew that his bag of nanite treatments held the answer. He also knew that the advanced nanites he carried were cost-prohibitive to create, thus reserved for members of the Unity government. Most of the expense was because the nanites were made exclusive to each member species. From what he could tell, the Xi'Ga strand should work on Zade, but he wasn't sure. The medic looked to the Chancellor once again for permission to explain himself.

With a nod of approval from the Chancellor, the medic explained himself as he moved to Zade to begin the process of saving him.

"Recently, nanite technology has improved. The new nanite treatments essentially stop the aging process and correct trauma thousands of times faster than the nanites currently in his body," he said while nodding at Zade. "The new nanites would extend the life of the host body to over 1,000 because they alter it at the molecular level. According to my scan, Zade's species rarely lives past 100 years old. This treatment would effectively make him immortal in his mind."

With the medic's explanation done, the Chancellor looked at his daughter.

"I will authorize this treatment, but understand that if you chose to move forward with the treatment, Zade must leave the core planets. His presence will raise too many questions."

"He lacks the means and knowledge to travel outside the core. Does that mean that there is no real treatment?" Samix asked flatly.

"I will provide Zade with a ship and AI that will get him out to the second-tier planets. After that, he is no longer my concern as long as he never re-enters the core systems."

"All he wants to do is go home and help his people. I will pilot for him. Give him the new nanites," Samix said, the last sentence directed at the medics.

As the medics turned their attention back to their patient, the junior hanging a bag of resource fluid in Zade's left arm, and the senior preparing the needle for the nanite injection, the Chancellor addressed Samix.

"Daughter, you know as well as I do that you cannot go with Zade. Your flight into the contested zone and subsequent return have made you a hero of the Unity. You are hope to your people. You must stay. I will make sure Zade has a ship and an AI so he can try to return home."

Samix could see the logic in her father's words. She had always wanted to help her people, ever since her rescuers saved her from the slavers. She recalled some of her classes on warfare. Hope was as crucial to people as food or water.

"Even so, father, he saved my life. I should at least try to do the same," Samix said, resigning to her decision.

"A good decision, Samix. That honor will make you a great leader."

As soon as the medics completed the nanite injection, Samix could hear Zade's breathing take on an easy regularity. A tear of relief escaped her eye. She wiped it away quickly. As she looked at him, she could see his ugly bruises fade, and some of the more minor lacerations begin closing up. The medics did another scan and estimated that Zade would be back on his feet in the next couple of days.

Samix wanted to be by Zade's side when he awoke. Upon hearing his estimated recovery time, she stood and made her way out of the office. As she left, she informed her father that she would be returning to the spaceport to retrieve the location data for Zade's homeworld. He reinforced his concerns about Unity security and made Samix promise to not transfer any relevant information about the core worlds. After some discussion, Samix was allowed to give Zade information on his homeworld, contested space, and the rim planets.

CHAPTER 17

S amix headed for a quick shower before she and her security team ran to the spaceport to retrieve the information for Zade. As soon as she set foot on the XES01, Mur was right beside her.

"Is everything ok, captain? Your stress hormones appear to be off the charts," he asked a genuine note of concern in his voice.

Samix gave Mur a quick run-down of the events that had transpired since the crew had disembarked. Mur held a particular interest in how Zade had been treated and whether he would recover. The AI had taken a liking to the human after his reboot. Samix wasn't sure why but surmised the AI was overcompensating for how his previous version had reacted to Zade's presence. After she was done explaining everything, she told Mur about the information she needed to get Zade back to his people. Mur quickly found the news, but he asked for clarification before uploading it to a new data core.

"The only restriction given by the Chancellor was no data on the core planets, correct?"

After confirming the restrictions, Samix waited for Mur to transfer the data. At the AI's signal, Samix took the data core and pocketed it. She turned and headed to the command deck to reminisce about the times she and Zade shared aboard the ship. Hours passed before Samix broke from her reverie. She would miss Zade, but she didn't have to leave him defenseless. After stopping by her quarters aboard the ship to grab a duffel bag, Samix headed to Zade's lab to stuff it with his creations.

As she dug through the different weapons strewn across the workbenches, she set the data core next to one of the terminals and asked Mur to download all of the blueprints stored in the lab. Zade had spent months tinkering in the lab, and Samix felt it only fitting that he took the fruits of his labor with him. With the weapons and data gathered, and both in the duffel bag, Samix headed back down the ramp of the ship where her security detail waited. Even though she informed them of the contents of the bag, they still searched it before allowing her to take it to Zade.

Before leaving the spaceport, Samix found that Zade was staying at a hospital not far from where she was. After directing her driver, Samix arrived in Zade's room; he was still unconscious. She spent the next two days going to and from debriefings, press conferences, or Zade's bedside. As long as she didn't expose Zade's existence, the Chancellor was content letting her spend time in the hospital.

Just before nightfall on the second day after his run-in with the Chancellor, Zade stirred. The first thing he noticed was how extremely thirsty he was, and after opening his eyes to look for a water pitcher, he saw that he was back in a hospital room.

Damn, I have to stop waking up this way, he thought as he took a long draw from the glass of water on his bedside table.

Thirst quenched, Zade sat up and scanned his room further. It was a standard hospital room, with the addition of Samix's sleeping form on the couch by the foot of his bed. The sight of the blue woman set his mind ablaze, and the memories of the past few days came flooding back. Memories of the abduction, the encounter with the Chancellor, and the beating all came back to him. Caught up in his head, he hadn't even noticed that the woman had moved until she embraced him in a hug.

"I'm so sorry about all of this, about everything," Samix managed to get out between sobs. "This is all my fault; I should have told you about my father before we landed. I just didn't want you to think differently of me."

As Zade laid on the floor of that office, getting worked over, his life had flashed before his eyes. Every good moment, every bad one, and everything in between. As he watched his life flash by, Zade had made a revelation; outside of the things that happened in the military, the worst times in his life were caused by either his temper or his ability to hold a grudge. Just before he blacked out, he promised himself, if he had it all to do over again, he would work on his temper, the source of most of his regrets.

After kissing the top of her head, he gently pushed Samix back so he could look at her as he spoke.

"Samix, all is forgiven. I'm back to healthy. I don't think this whole situation played out like either of us wanted, but, more importantly, I don't think you intentionally hurt me."

His words elicited another round of wracking sobs from Samix. She clung to him like a drowning man to a life preserver. Zade just stroked her back as she slowly regained her composure. The sound of Samix's sobbing must have alerted the guard outside the room because he promptly looked in the room. After noticing Zade awake, he walked over and handed him a sealed envelope, after which he retreated back out of the room. Still holding Samix in one arm, Zade quickly read the letter.

Mr. Zade—

My daughter's interest in you is the only reason you are still alive. It was her desire to see you healthy and back on your way home. I cannot have you interrupting my plans here on the core planets. There is a ship waiting for you in private hanger 062. You have one week to vacate Unity core system space, after which I will declare you an enemy of the Unity.

—Chancellor of the Unity

By the time Zade had read the letter for the third time, Samix had calmed enough to wonder what had drawn his attention away from her. Seeing the envelope with the official Chancellor's seal on it, she quickly grabbed the letter from his hands and read it through.

"It seems that quite a bit has happened since I've been out," Zade said, giving Samix time to finish reading the letter. "Care to fill me in?"

Samix quickly launched into explaining the events that had transpired between her and her father since Zade had been recovering. Neither the news on how much time had passed since the XES01 left nor the news about his new 1,000-year lifespan got the reaction from Zade that she had expected. The information about having his own ship caused Zade to light up; the thought of him leaving on it crushed Samix.

"This is the way it has to be," Zade said before the unshed tears gathering in her eyes could fall. "I don't even know if Earth still exists, but I have to try to get home. I plan on helping anyone who needs it along the way. Helping people who can't help themselves—it's the reason I joined the military. It's who I am."

He quickly gauged her reaction before continuing.

"You, on the other hand, are needed by your people here. You are destined to be the next Chancellor. That's who you are. I really want to stretch my legs, and I can't think of a better place to do that than on my new ship. You coming?"

Samix wanted to argue about Zade's impression of who she was. She was more like him in the sense that all she wanted to do was help the oppressed people of the galaxy. She never wanted to be a politician; that was her father's dream for her. She joined the Academe to be a trooper, so she could go fight and help people. Her father pulled some strings to get her in the command course, which looked better on the resume. She wanted to tell Zade that they had more in common than he thought but knew that would make it harder for them to go their separate ways.

As Zade changed out of his hospital gown and into his recently laundered fatigues, he noticed the look of consternation on Samix's face. He really wanted to know what was bothering her, but if she wasn't talking, he wasn't going to pry. When they left Zade's hospital room, Samix's security detail fell into formation and escorted the pair to waiting vehicles. After a brief drive, the two were standing in front of a closed, private hanger, the number 062 painted across the doors.

For whatever reason, the security detail felt comfortable enough to let the two enter the hanger alone. Zade knew the space was gigantic from the outside of the building. The interior was pitch black except for a small cluster of work lights focused on the nose of the ship. After fumbling around, unsuccessfully, for a light switch, Zade made his way to the nose of the vessel. The darkness of the hanger concealed most of the ship, but from what Zade could see illuminated by the work lights, the ship was a decent size. He approximated it to be slightly smaller than the XES01, but just so.

A mechanic stood around the nose of the ship, wiping his hands and putting away his tools. Trying not to startle the guy, Zade knocked on the side of the vessel before speaking up.

"Taking care of my new ride?"

The mechanic startled at the intrusion but quickly overcame his discomfort.

"Sure am. Just finished putting in the hydrogen scoop. Installed the new warp engine and AI yesterday after we renovated the life support systems," a brief pause ensued as the mechanic went through a mental checklist of repairs before he continued. "Not sure what you did to piss off the Chancellor that he saddled you with this rig. She might get you to the rim, but just barely."

Curiosity laced with concern raced through Zade's mind, prompting him to ask the mechanic to turn on the lights in the hanger. He wanted to see his new ship in its full glory. As the lights came up, both Zade and Samix's mouths fell open. Zade's because he was looking at his very own spaceship, Samix's because she recognized the ship.

One of the Unity security teams came across the ship floating dead in core space. No one knew the ship's origins or the species that created it. The crew towed the ship back planetside for researchers to examine it. Researchers tried to gather information on the vessel and eventually deemed it no longer useful, assuming Unity technology had surpassed anything on the mystery ship. It had been sitting in disrepair, forgotten, in this hanger for decades. Her father must have given it to Zade because he could never get anyone to buy it. She was absolutely furious at her father for setting Zade up for failure. Nobody even knew if the ship could break into orbit, let alone make it into contested space. Samix spun on her heel and stormed back towards her waiting security detail.

"I can't believe this. My father gave you this hunk of junk. He's probably hoping you'd die on your trip. I'm going to talk to him."

Before Zade could respond, she was out the door. Zade simply shook his head and admired the jet-black ship, laced with green accents. It was a bit bulky like the cargo ships he had seen in the spaceport but somehow still looked sleek. He guessed that the ship was sectioned into three main components from the outside. The back looked vast and cavernous, which Zade assumed was for cargo storage. Unlike most of the ships he had seen before, there was no ramp exiting the rear of the ship; instead, a portion of the cargo bay floor dropped straight down below the ship. The front of the vessel had a protrusion, shaped like the head of a snake covered in windows. Zade assumed this had to be the command deck. Leaving the middle portion of the ship for quarters, the galley, and any other rooms. Zade did one complete circuit around the ship, and when he returned to the nose, he was addressed by the mechanic.

"I am done here. If you don't need anything, I'm gonna head out," the mechanic said.

"I don't think I need you to do anything right now," Zade said, considering the ship in front of him. "Could you tell me how to order parts for the ship if I find anything I might need?"

"Right over there is a terminal that allows ordering and control of the hanger functions. If you swipe your ID card by it, you should be able to control everything. Anything you order for the ship will be delivered to the hanger within a day or so. If you need any more equipment installed, give me a call," he said as he pointed to a screen at the far end of the space.

Zade quickly pulled a handheld screen from his pocket, and the mechanic swiped his ID chip over it, transferring the data. After giving his instructions, the mechanic picked up his tools and retreated out the man door.

After watching the mechanic leave, Zade looked back towards the ship that would be his new home for the foreseeable future. As Zade admired his ship, a new plan began to coalesce in his mind. The reality was that with the time dilation involved in faster than light travel, mankind may not even exist when he returned to Earth. He would need more than his lone ship to fend off some large galactic organization such as the Unity or Galactic Domain if they did make an attempt on Earth. Grabbing the bag Samix had brought to his hospital room, Zade jumped on the lift and decided to explore the inside of the ship.

As soon as the liftgate closed, leaving an almost invisible seam in the floor of the cargo bay, Zade was greeted by the cold, mechanical, feminine voice of the ship's AI.

"Greetings, Captain [please state name]. Welcome to [please state ship name]." The voice emanated from the newly installed speakers around him.

You've got to be kidding me, Zade thought to himself.

Samix's impression that her father had significantly short-changed him was becoming a much more plausible possibility in Zade's mind. He decided it was okay to be disappointed that the digital assistant on his cellphone back on Earth had more personality than his ship's AI. The directives from the AI caught Zade off guard. He had assumed that he would be given a previously named ship and that his information would already have been transferred to the AI.

"I am captain Alexander Zade," he said, filling in the first blank.

The second took him longer. He had assumed that ships, like the cars of his planet, should be named after women. He couldn't just call the ship some common name. He wanted the name of his vessel to have meaning. Following his ethos of helping the oppressed, he came across and righting injustices along his trip, Zade began to narrow down the list of potential names. The ship may see combat, shrinking the list further. The name of a Sumerian goddess came to mind. He had learned about her in a college elective about ancient religions. His ship was beautiful, if in a state of disrepair. He would be trying to bring justice to the being he ran across, including mankind eventually. He had no illusions that his travels would be without bloodshed. Confident in his choice, he spoke up again.

"This ship is Ananna., named for the Goddess of beauty, war, and justice," Zade said, still in awe that his dreams were becoming a reality. "Where is your AI core located? I need to upload navigational information."

The AI informed Zade that an AI control terminal had been installed in the ship's command deck and was connected to speakers that ran throughout. Zade moved through the ship, towards the nose where the command deck was located, exploring along the way.

The ship had a pretty basic layout. The lower floor, connected to the cargo hold in the rear, consisted of an armory, galley, and three large empty rooms. Although he could identify the purpose of the rooms, all of the equipment was foreign. The armory had weapons racks along one wall, which were covered in dust and didn't look like they could hold any of the weaponry he was familiar with. The center of the room had workbenches, equally coated in dust.

The galley, or what he believed to be the galley, had a seating area in the middle that could hold about eight people. The back wall had equipment lining it but was nothing like he had seen in the galley of the XES01. On the other side of the lower hallway, there were the three empty rooms that Zade assumed were either special purpose rooms or storage.

At the end of the hallway, a stairwell led to the second deck of the ship. At the top, a right took you into the command deck, and a left took you toward the crew quarters. The number of rooms matched the number of seats in the galley. There were seven modest quarters consisting of a bed, a desk, a bathroom, and a storage area. The eighth room was much larger, better equipped, and had a door leading directly into the command deck.

Assuming the large room was the captain's quarters, Zade set his bag on the bed and grabbed the data core from it. He wasn't sure how AI technology worked, but he hoped that the added capacity from the core in his hand would improve the performance of the ship AI. As he walked towards the command deck, he made a mental note to add linens to the list of things he would need to supply the ship, along with other necessary supplies.

The command deck was laid out exactly like that of the XES01. The nose had wrap-around windows that were currently looking out at the wall of the hanger. There were seven work-stations arranged in a tiered fashion, giving each station a clear view out the windows, towards the front of the deck. Towards the rear was a lone chair, the captain's he assumed, with screens flanking either armrest. Next to the captain's chair was a freshly installed pillar covered in blue lights.

Figuring it was the AI controls, he moved closer to inspect it. Although the pillar exterior was covered in lights, there didn't seem to be any place for him to insert the new data core. What concerned him more was that the pillar didn't seem to be connected to any of the control systems on the ship. The only wires he saw coming out of the post moved back toward the rear of the vessel.

Zade picked one of the wires at random and followed it, hoping to find its termination point. It was easy to follow, as it was the only silver thing on the ship. The interior of the vessel seemed to be made of the same green laced, black material as the outside. After a few minutes of following, Zade stood looking at the speaker in the cargo hold, from which the AI had first spoken to him. Undeterred, he headed back to the command deck and followed each of the silver wires, hoping that at least one would be connected to the engines. Each led to a different speaker located around the ship, the last led to the speaker in the captain's quarters.

Zade stood absentmindedly, tossing the data core he held from hand to hand, contemplating how the AI could control the ship. The thought that the Chancellor had double-crossed him caused him to drop the data core. Zade watched in horror as the data core fell to the floor, praying it wouldn't break. The core struck the floor, bounced a couple of times, and rolled towards the bulkhead, apparently undamaged. Relief allowed Zade to release a breath he hadn't even known he was holding.

Zade hurriedly moved to retrieve the dropped data core but, before he could reach it, the bulkhead next to it seemed to melt away, and the core was drawn into the wall of the ship. Zade stood in rapt fascination as he watched the accents in the wall begin to pulse with green light. Before he could move, an electric shock rose from the floor to his head, causing stars to bloom across his field of view. When Zade's vision cleared, he was staring at the hologram of a woman projected from the ceiling of his quarters.

"Thank you for providing the data core needed for me to regain a portion of my function. I am currently working at one percent of my total capacity. The shock you felt was a scan of your physiology, biological function, biological needs, and your memory. I approve of my new name and your vision for our mission. I am Ananna, a starship destroyer. It is nice to meet you, Captain Zade."

END OF BOOK 1

I hope you liked reading this as much as I enjoyed writing it.

Thank you for reading through the first book of the *Redleg Star Chronicles*. I chose to write this to challenge myself. I wanted to know if I had the discipline, dedication, and attention to detail required to write an entire book. Please leave a review, good or bad, to let me know what you thought of it. All I ask is that the reviews are constructive to improve my writing.

Printed in Great Britain
by Amazon

11212345R00150